Banquet at Brabazan

Banquet at Brabazan

Patricia Schonstein

author of *A Time of Angels*

First published by Jacana Media (Pty) Ltd in 2010

10 Orange Street
Sunnyside
Auckland Park 2092
South Africa
+2711 628 3200
www.jacana.co.za

ISBN 978-1-77009-807-7

Set in Sabon 10.5/14pt
Printed and bound by Ultra Litho (Pty) Limited, Johannesburg
Job No. 001195

ISO 12647 compliant

See a complete list of Jacana titles at www.jacana.co.za

In memory of my brother,
Pietro Arturo Schonstein, 1949–2007

Novels by the same author

Skyline

A Time of Angels

The Apothecary's Daughter

A Quilt of Dreams

The Master's Ruse

www.patriciaschonstein.com

"Some glory in their birth, some in their skill,
Some in their wealth, some in their bodies' force,
Some in their garments, though new-fangled ill,
Some in their hawks and hounds, some in their horse;
And every humour hath his adjunct pleasure,
Wherein it finds a joy above the rest:
But these particulars are not my measure;
All these I better in one general best.
Thy love is better than high birth to me,
Richer than wealth, prouder than garments' cost,
Of more delight than hawks or horses be;
And having thee, of all men's pride I boast:
Wretched in this alone, that thou mayst take
All this away and me most wretched make.

William Shakespeare, Sonnet 91

I wonder, by my troth, what thou and I
Did, till we loved? Were we not weaned till then,
But sucked on country pleasures, childishly?
Or snorted we in the seven sleepers' den?
'Twas so; but this, all pleasures fancies be.
If ever any beauty I did see,
Which I desired, and got, 'twas but a dream of thee.

And now good morrow to our waking souls,
Which watch not one another out of fear;
For love, all love of other sights controls,
And makes one little room, an everywhere.
Let sea-discoverers to new worlds have gone,
Let maps to other, worlds on worlds have shown,
Let us possess one world, each hath one, and is one.

My face in thine eye, thine in mine appears,
And true plain hearts do in the faces rest,
Where can we find two better hemispheres
Without sharp north, without declining west?
Whatever dies, was not mixed equally;
If our two loves be one, or, thou and I
Love so alike, that none do slacken, none can die.

John Donne (1572–1631), 'The Good-Morrow'

Part One

Oberon Yoruba had been living for a week at Brabazan Bar & Lodge in Long Street, two doors down from Clarke's Bookshop, opposite Mr Pickwick's Tavern and not far from the boarded-up Da Pasquale restaurant.

He had booked into the first lodgings he'd come to and asked for a room with a view because he'd been told once, long ago, in an institution, if he remembered correctly, that a room should have a view. It didn't bother him that this one brought with it the relentless noise of traffic and the truly horrible late-night cacophony of Long Street's clubs.

He'd been feeling a little confused when he first arrived, not quite certain about who he was and where he was supposed to be going. A taxi had dropped him off and he'd walked in tentatively, carrying only a small suitcase. There was a problem with the photograph in his identity book and he didn't want to show it and risk being turned away.

Duke Ellerman, the proprietor and a perceptive witness to the loneliness of lives, was at the bar, behind the till. He was sitting heavily on a high stool, smoking, with a near-finished glass of tonic water at his side, reading *Travels with Herodotus* by Ryszard Kapuściński.

'I don't like to book people in without an ID,' he'd said, with an adagio movement of his left hand and putting the book face down to keep his place. 'Just now I find you dealing drugs and selling guns upstairs. What'd you say your name is?'

'Yoruba. Oberon Yoruba.'

'Why've you got a Nigerian name? A white man with a black name doesn't make sense.'

'I don't know.'

'You sound like the start of trouble.'

'I won't be trouble.'

'That's what they all say.'

Duke, named by his mother after the jazz virtuoso Duke Ellington, looked hard at the man in front of him and thought: 'What's it about me that always attracts the crazies?' But, sensing an unusual innocence in the fellow, he said: 'Okay, ten days and we take it from there. One grand up front, balance when you check out. No smoking in the rooms. We had a fire, once. Some fool fell asleep with a lighted stub. Could've roasted the lot of us.'

He tapped another cigarette from its packet and lit it, blowing the smoke to one side before continuing: 'Don't bring food in. If you want to eat *from* other places, then eat *at* other places. Here you've got to order from my kitchen and my bar. I've got a good kitchen.

'And no outside girls. If you want girls, you can go up to the top floor. I've got four nice Russians up there, all experienced. They used to work at Lola's. They trained in the Ukraine somewhere, so they can do the whole picture. Nice clean girls. You won't catch anything.'

'I won't have girls and I don't smoke,' said Oberon, pulling open the drawstring of a leather money pouch full of crisp, new two-hundred-rand notes for Duke to count out what he needed. With a slight frown, Duke glanced from the money to Oberon, handed him his room key and motioned with his head towards a yellow-curtained doorway that led to a brilliant-yellow stairwell, saying: 'First floor, last door on the right. Same key fits the bathroom across the passage. If you want to stay out after I've closed the bar at night, you need to let Alfonso, the guard, know to open the fire-escape door. Otherwise you won't get in. If you don't arrange with him, you have to sleep rough wherever with the *bergies*.'

'I won't stay out late.'

'And if I was you,' finished Duke, before taking the last sip from his glass and turning his attention back to Kapuściński, 'I wouldn't go showing the whole world that fat purse of yours.'

A few days before, if we stop to look, we see a man called Peter Brightstone, aged fifty-seven. He lives at the Salvation Army Home at the bottom of Buitengracht Street, right near the highway flyover, the one that was never completed and stops arrogantly in mid-air. Only a few drums prevent speeding cars from hurtling over its edge.

The man has a slight stoop caused by shyness and self-consciousness rather than any postural deformity. This causes him to lift one shoulder higher than the other. His hair is wavy and thick and beginning to grey. He is thin and his face is grooved, not by wrinkles, but by what life has drawn upon it. These lines mark an innocence that has been abused over and over by people without scruples, because they judge him a simpleton. What needs to be said is that he has never hurt a soul in his life, or wished ill on anyone, and that life should have treated him with care and love, but didn't.

An unknown benefactor pays his rent and another makes provision for a small daily allowance. He believes that his accommodation is paid for by the Jewish Benevolent Society, not because he is Jewish, but because his father was devotedly orthodox and had served the *Chevrah Kadisha* for many years. Why Peter has the notion that he is under Jewish care is not certain. A quick phone call would confirm that, having had a Catholic mother and having been baptised himself, he has no claim to Jewish charity.

Peter shares a room on the fifth floor with an older man named Gerrit Viljoen who was once comfortably wealthy, owning a butchery in Voortrekker Road in Parow and another in Kenilworth, but who gambled away every penny he had made. His house and cars were repossessed, his wife left him to live with her mother in Somerset West and he lost the respect of his two sons. They don't know where he lives or how low he has gone. Nor do they care. They feel he betrayed and abandoned them. They will be well into adulthood, faced with their own life crises, before they reflect with any compassion on their father or his addiction and fate.

Gerrit imparts tiredness to the room and is always depressed, barely managing to get up each day to dress. He spends his time sitting on the edge of the bed, staring at the floor. The only time he has ever expressed cheer was on the first day of their acquaintance, when Peter was shown in by Major Martin. 'A room must have a view,' he'd said between coughs, urging Peter to stand at the window and look out towards the harbour and Table Bay, at the ships and container vessels at anchor.

From the first day of their meeting, Gerrit leans on Peter, emotionally and for physical help. His needs grow greater and their friendship strengthens. Peter gives and cares without question or measure, asking for nothing in return.

Although Gerrit goes down to the dining room for meals, he hardly eats, shoving his food around the plate, taking a mouthful or two, but feeling pained in the stomach by it. He sips at half a cup of milky coffee and goes back upstairs. He used to tell everyone that he was at the Salvation Army for the time being; that he would soon leave; that he would be fetched by family, when various legal and monetary matters were sorted out. But now he says nothing to anyone, except Peter. And to Peter he says very little with words. His body language and his eyes express everything, so it's clear that he is grateful and that he can't do without his roommate.

If we walk from table to table, we'll hear the same story from each man – that he is here for a short spell, just through this hard patch, and that he will soon go back to his life. This story you hear on the lips of men broken by debt or drink or drugs or gambling. These are the four roads that lead here, to the Salvation Army Home, according to Major Martin.

Some men don't take their places at tables, but sit on chairs at the edge of the dining room and wait for the others to eat and leave. They don't speak to each other and appear as lonely men sketched in charcoal on Umbria paper. When the others have left the dining room, these reticent ones go to the serving hatch and accept a plateful, but with a certain distaste, knowing the food is donated by various supermarkets because it is damaged, or past the sell-by date. Not wanting to admit to their position at the butt end of charity, they poke at the food and eat with long teeth, pretending to be visitors, saying that they've come to see someone who happened to be out and that the Major asked them to stay for lunch. This is how they retain a shred of self-worth. This is how they stop themselves going up onto the edge of that unfinished highway and throwing themselves down into the traffic and a pauper's grave.

Major Martin, who has twenty-five years of service behind him, does not have to work here with his younger

Salvation Army staff, his soldiers, as they are called, among the men at the rock face of life. He can spend his day upstairs in his office, which boasts a stunning view across Cape Town, and just get on with paperwork and administration. But he has absorbed something akin to addiction. Though he has never touched drink or tobacco in his life, having been born and raised in a pious, sober home, he is pulled close to those wrecked by addiction. He can't stay apart from them, can't sit at that desk in the office, protected by his rank and years of service. He can't merely keep the ship afloat. He has to be here with them in their purgatory. He is one of them.

But we'll not linger, observing Major Martin and those in his care. We'll stay with Peter Brightstone, who is content at the Salvation Army Home, who has no problem with the food or with the compulsory prayer meetings. He doesn't believe he has reached rock bottom.

Peter leads a tidy life. He owns little and it all fits neatly alongside Gerrit's few things in the narrow built-in cupboard near the door, and in the chest of drawers between the two beds. He keeps his own and Gerrit's clothes washed and pressed and can sew on buttons and darn holes. He sweeps not only the bedroom but also the outside corridor, and even cleans the communal bathroom on their floor. His dearest possession is a blanket that his mother knitted when he was a child and which he has safeguarded through the years of his life. This is spread over his bed, above the sheet but under the duvet. He also owns a rucksack in which are stored his mother's stamp collection and an old dagger she used to carry in her handbag.

When Gerrit coughs up blood, Peter washes the pillowslip and hankies, and helps to conceal the awful fact of his friend's tuberculosis. Gerrit doesn't want to be moved to Brooklyn Chest Hospital, from where he knows he'll never return. His rheumy, tired eyes thank Peter every night before he puts out the lights. His eyes say: 'I have done so much wrong in my life. I can't go back to repair anything,' to which Peter replies: 'Sleep tight, Gerrit. Everything will be all right.'

Each morning, Peter follows a regular pattern. He helps Gerrit face the day, encouraging him to dress and go down for breakfast, even though his friend has no appetite. He himself eats heartily, packs slices of bread and a boiled egg into a Tupperware for Gerrit to eat later, then escorts him back upstairs before setting off for his daily walk into town.

Generally, he takes the same, slow route up Long Street, along its farrago of buildings, towards the 7-Eleven at the top, where he buys a Coke and a *boerewors* roll. With these he goes to sit at the Long Street Baths, where he eats and watches ladies swim lengths, or young men practise polo and underwater hockey. Sometimes the pool is full of shouting, splashing children.

From the Baths he goes across the road and lies down on a back pew of the Lutheran church. If he's lucky, the organist will be practising, filling the sanctuary with the celestial tones of hymns and, occasionally, Bach. These Peter absorbs, together with an inarticulate sense that he is turning into gold or copper.

At three o'clock, he starts heading down Loop Street and back to the Salvation Army Home. He spreads his excursion over the whole day, getting in at five.

At this hour, there might be one or two homeless men outside, holding a packet or satchel. Some stand there without anything, their hands in their pockets. They don't crowd at the door. There is no pressing rush to get inside. Generally, they stand some distance away, as though not wanting to be seen at this admission point, at this doorway that confirms their despondent position.

These are the men who are not permanent residents – those who can't give up their potions, who can't throw the clawing demon of addiction off their shoulders, who on most nights can't walk straight enough to earn a clean bed here, where the rules are few but tough.

Perhaps they're feeling ill, or the tremors are upon them, or their stomachs have gnawed holes into themselves, seeking some as yet undigested crusts of bread. But they can't be welcomed. There are too many men inside who also belong to bottled demons. Drunk and stoned people, if allowed inside, would torment the others.

Today, on this mild early-winter's morning, we see Peter change his route for some unknown reason, and not go towards Long Street. We watch him walk under the unfinished highway, where a group of Zimbabwean refugees have set up cardboard and plastic-sheeting shelters. Traffic rushes past on either side. A few small braziers are burning, giving off the acrid odour of coal. Women are boiling water or cooking *sadza* in tins.

The younger children who live here do not run around, but have been trained to sit still out of fear they will dash into the traffic. They are dulled by exhaust fumes and hunger. The older ones play their part by going out to beg. They know how to look forlorn, how to clasp their hands together and tilt their heads slightly. They know that it's best to target cars driven by women and how to say 'please' meaningfully.

Peter feels anxious here but can't turn back, so he heads

towards the traffic lights. There he crosses and walks the pavement alongside a vacant lot partially shielded by makeshift boards. The area is the size of a city block. It had been dug out for the foundation of a new building, but was abandoned following the developer's bankruptcy. Along the edge, over the embankment, is dumped all manner of rubbish which cannot be seen because it is below the level of the road. Sturdy, defiant weeds grow there and form a dense, entangled cage of thorns and spiky leaves.

As Peter walks with a hurried step, sensing he is in a dangerous twilight zone, a group of feral children suddenly appears from nowhere and surrounds him. These children don't belong to the Zimbabweans under the highway bridge. These belong to no one, nor are they answerable to anybody. They are masters of the street, the glue sniffers, the petty thieves, the rascals who know no boundaries and who, should they grow beyond these desperate years, will feed into the adult criminal class as ruthless specialists.

They circle Peter, prodding him with sticks and demanding 'Cellphone! Cellphone!' They push him about from one to the other, turning him round and round to disorient him. Then, as their small, dirty hands tear at his jacket and pockets, they shout: 'Money! Money! Give money!' When they find that his money pouch contains only twenty rand, his daily allowance, one of them strikes him a blow to the temple with a club and they push him over the embankment, throwing his purse after him. The whole encounter takes hardly a minute. The children attack so fiercely and swiftly that no passing motorist witnesses the act.

There Peter lies in the overgrown weeds, unable to lift himself, shivering and sweating in the heat and cold. He doesn't know that the tail end of a drama unfolded in this same place three nights before. Near to midnight, a car with darkened windows but no number plates had stopped. Two men in suits had leapt out, opened the boot, hauled out a corpse and thrown it, together with a suitcase, over the edge into the overgrown weeds, near where Peter now lies. The corpse was the victim of a drug deal gone wrong and the men in suits had to dispose of it fast. They planned to come back for the suitcase within a day or so, when they judged the heat from a rival gang would be off them.

At noon the next day, Peter's vitality, deprived of water, shuts down and his soul gently dislodges, like a butterfly shedding its cocoon and spreading tissue-fine wings. He is about to drift away from earthly existence, as though borne on a current of air, when he remembers Gerrit and realises that no one will tell his friend what has happened to him.

With all the will he can muster, Peter forces himself down, away from the butterfly wings and back towards his body, around which flies are already buzzing. He stirs, then rolls onto his side, heavily and in pain, with eyes smarting in the glare of the sun, and makes himself sit up. His heart pulses weakly, his mouth is parched.

Next to him lies a suitcase that he presumes to be his own, as well as his purse, which he puts into his pocket. In the dense and entangled weeds he notices a shoe. He crawls to it and sees it is the foot of a dead man whose chest is covered in congealed blood and ants, and whose wrists are bound together with rope. Peter, aware that he must get away, picks up the suitcase and drags himself up the embankment. Swooning and afraid he'll fall, he sits on the pavement and lowers his head to his knees, oblivious to the traffic which, in its turn, pays him no heed.

Later that afternoon, a clown walks past – a black dwarf clown wearing a sequined jacket that sparkles in the sun. His pants have gold braiding down the side and his tackies are painted red. He is a Zimbabwean on his way back home from the Orange Street intersection, where he spends his days begging from cars as they stop at the traffic lights. He mimics the waddle of Boswell Circus's Tickey the Clown rattling an enamel mug, inviting coins. His round, pockmarked face and crooked teeth don't detract from his cuteness; instead they add some charm. When cars transporting children stop, there is always squeaking and laughter and a sure payment. Sometimes a school lunch will be thrown out from a back window. The clown works hard in all weather, walking from car to car, pretending that life is funny, when it's not.

'What has happened, Sir?' he asks, but there's no answer. So, with gentleness, the dwarf helps the man to his feet, picks up the case and leads him back to his own dwelling, under the highway bridge near the Salvation Army Home. The clown had seen this white man walk through the cardboard settlement the day before and had wondered what he was up to, taking that route all alone.

He knows that if he leaves the man sitting here by himself he will surely be mugged again, perhaps killed this time, and that the suitcase will be taken.

The body will be discovered a week or so later, when a tourist, walking from the Holiday Inn into town, unaware that this is treacherous territory, will recognise the unmistakeable stench of decaying human flesh, having worked as a volunteer unearthing mass graves in Rwanda, and will alert the concierge of his hotel.

The dwarf walks slowly with the white man. They go past a showroom of vintage cars, gleaming and ready for hire. Just for something to say, because his protégé is silent, the dwarf points through the wide shopfront windows and names the cars as they walk by: 'Rolls Royce. Studebaker. Mercedes. Volvo. Citroën. One day, maybe, Sir will drive in one. Maybe Sir will have a chauffeur,' and he mimics a driver doffing his hat, so that his companion smiles, weakly.

Under the unfinished highway, in the early evening mezzotint light, the dwarf tells his wife to clean up the stranger. Behind one of the highway pillars, the man undresses and she sponges him down, taking water from a drum that she fills at the nearby Caltex garage each morning and for which she pays the attendants ten rand. She helps him put on a poncho, then washes his clothes and drapes them to dry near a brazier of burning coals.

Later that night, the dwarf and his wife sit with their guest around the brazier and share a tin plate of *sadza* and gravy. As soon as they've eaten, the wife dampens the bits of coal and they prepare to sleep, spreading out cardboard and unrolling a rug. They have spare cardboard for the man but no blanket, so the wife covers his shoulders with her towel to give him warmth. She touches him to still him, because he has started to cry, and gives him a small thing to hold. It is about the size of a walnut, made of kid leather and bound with cotton thread, tightly packed within which are various herbs, powdered bones, a cockerel's spur and a tiny lucky-packet crucifix. 'Hold this, Master,' she tells him. 'Hold it until the night is finished. It will cheerful you up. It is strong medicine.'

He clutches the fetish throughout the night and enters an extraordinary dream as traffic races by on both sides of the encampment, illuminating it in the vivid streaks of headlights.

The dream takes him to the reception area of an afterlife, so real that one might wonder whether Peter has somehow tumbled onto the pages of Dante Alighieri's *Divine Comedy*. It is here, upon a marble floor and in myrrh-infused air, that newly dead souls find themselves and where begins the separation of those destined for Dante's Paradiso, those expected in Purgatorio and those doomed to his Inferno, the door to which is marked by a red, downward-pointing arrow.

The walls and vaulted ceiling are painted in the most extraordinary detail of angels, musicians, winged lions, unicorns, mythical symbols and legendary, gloriously handsome Pre-Raphaelite men and women.

The place has to it the touch of Ellis Island in its heyday. Angelic clerks manage silent throngs while others make entries in leather-bound, gilt-edged ledgers, writing with plumed pens and black ink. It seems that Peter Brightstone is expected. He is given a bespoke book of regulations and directed towards a grand spiral marble ramp – a representation of which, designed by Giuseppe Momo in 1932, can be seen in the Vatican.

He begins his walk upward but, just as he feels all the burdens of life dissolve, like salt in water, he is jolted by a sense of falling and wakes up sharply. He finds himself back on the Zimbabweans' bit of cardboard, with the blaring of cars all around, but without a single memory of his name or his life or his friend Gerrit. Nor, for that matter, has he any recollection of what happened to him before arriving here. All he remembers, for some strange reason, is the name of Long Street.

This Zimbabwean couple have known the barren terrain of starvation and near-starvation in their own country. They know what it is to gather up single grains of spilt corn or rice, what it is to eat a rotting banana. They know about searching for scraps of anything at refuse sites, finding only plastic because all food has already been retrieved by others. They know about queuing for bread and getting only half a loaf, or of having the last loaf sold to the person in front of them. They know what it is to crush insects between their teeth; what it is to kill a small bird and wolf down the pitiful raw flesh, chewing the bones to release the tiniest amount of marrow.

So they'll never turn away a hungry man or a man in need, even though they live on the mere cupful of coins that a clown can procure. Furthermore, fate has been known to turn. Now, at least, they eat once a day. Providence may turn her back. They may be exposed as illegals and deported back to Zimbabwe, where President Mugabe is the incumbent Archangel of Death, come to sweep his scythe back and forth and back and forth.

The dwarf and his wife don't tell their names and are afraid to give the stranger information about themselves. In the morning, the wife takes back her amulet and puts it into a pouch hanging from her neck and tucked into her shirt. She offers her guest a cup of water, warmed on her little fire and lightly flavoured with an already twice-used tea bag. There's a domestic worker living among them who collects the used tea bags at her place of employment. She flattens and dries them and sells them for five cents each. Even after their final use, when there is no more taste or tannin to them, they will be opened out carefully. The bags will be used as kindling and the leaves stirred into gruel, to thicken it and give it the colour of meat stew.

Peter accepts a square of cold *sadza* sprinkled with a

pinch of sugar. While they eat, they're all silent, with just the noise of traffic around them. It's time for Peter to leave. He can't stay here all day. In a measure of privacy, he goes behind a highway pillar and puts on his clothes, which are dry and smell of smoke. He opens the case he believes to be his own. It has two compartments. In the first, tucked under a long, white cotton *jelaba*, is an identity book which he opens, learning that his name is Oberon Yoruba. The photo has been cut away. The second compartment is packed tight with bundles of two-hundred-rand notes. He can't remember what his profession is and why he should be such a rich man. He pulls out a wad of notes, putting some into his own money pouch and the rest into his jacket pocket.

He thanks the dwarf and his wife with five of the notes. They are speechless and slightly suspicious of this grand benevolence, so much so that they decide to move away from the area, in case the man is a criminal, in case police will come investigating. 'Where does Sir want to go?' asks the dwarf, and Oberon replies: 'Long Street.'

The dwarf stops a taxi and tells the driver: 'Long Street.' When Oberon can't say exactly where he wants to be dropped, the driver stops more or less in the middle of the top part, outside Brabazan, and accepts four hundred rand without giving change.

The dwarf doesn't put on his glittery suit today, nor does he go to the Orange Street traffic lights to beg from cars. Fearful of some follow-up, he and his wife hastily fold their cardboard and pack their meagre belongings. They walk over the highway, all the way to the edge of District Six, where they join a smaller squatter settlement of Zimbabweans.

Here, in this harsh city with its terrifyingly violent underbelly, the dwarf and his wife call themselves Sixpence and Florence. In Zimbabwe, their ancestral home, where all their forebears are buried, a country that is now nothing but razed earth, their names are Goliath and Nyaradzo (Comfort).

Brabazan Bar & Lodge was a spacious, unpretentious, popular drinking house and eatery, permanently infused with the smell of alcohol and cigarette smoke. Late at night, it carried the general despair of heavy drinkers. Four ceiling fans idly chopped the air, whatever the weather. It was said to be haunted by the benign ghost of an artist. Now and then, footsteps might be heard, sighing against the wooden floors; or the sound of a large easel being dragged down the passage might intrude on a conversation. Sometimes travellers staying in the short-let rooms upstairs mentioned to Duke that they had the sensation of a fine paintbrush moving against cheeks and lips; or of waking and catching a quick glimpse of a man, with glowing candles held in the brim of his hat, mixing pigments on a palette. Occasionally, drinkers leaning against the bar experienced him nudging them, as though he were trying to adjust their pose, to set them up as models.

On the left, as you entered Brabazan, was its impressive, seven-metre-long teak bar with carved panels and brass footrest. The bar, along with the shelving and mirrored backing on the wall behind it, had been salvaged, miraculously without damage, from the demolished Rose & Crown in District Six. Swing doors led to the kitchen. These had come from a builder's scrapyard in Ottery and been sanded down to reveal Oregon pine. They each sported, at head height, a small circular window. Beneath one, a plastic-sandwiched sign instructed 'Staff Only'.

All along the right side were tables and comfortable chairs. At the front windows, one on each side of the entrance, were deep leather sofas. These were faced by two leather armchairs and a coffee table. Near one set of seating, on a raised platform, stood an upright Otto Bach piano and stool. There was a snooker table and extra tables in a side annex, and here, late on the occasional Saturday night, certain of Long Street's prominent merchants and proprietors played poker, trying to recreate times past when they had gambled at the now closed Da Pasquale restaurant.

Each evening at nine, musicians and vocalists would arrive, sourced from Cape Town's pool of extraordinary talent. One might encounter big names like Chris Wildman, Steve Newman, Winston Mankunku, the violinist Lazar or even Vincent Kolbe, the District Six historian and raconteur extraordinaire, who always began his repertoire with Errol Garner's 'Misty'. Students from the Jazz School played, as did Congolese musicians who introduced urgent and compelling drum rhythms to Brabazan's languid atmosphere. Poets, compèred by the literary critic and editor Hugh Hodge, read their works at open microphone sessions.

Against the rear wall were positioned a 1954 Rock-Ola Comet jukebox and a 1960 Gottlieb Flipper pinball machine. Between them, behind a yellow curtain, a yellow stairway led to sixteen upstairs rooms, four on each level. Above the curtains, Cape Town station's old clock, the one lovers used to meet under, held the time at an ominous 8.15, the hour at which Hiroshima was bombed.

Duke Ellerman lived on the first floor in two rooms at the opposite end of the passage from the one Oberon now occupied. The dividing wall had been taken down, so the double-volume space allowed for bookshelves, a large television, a queen-sized bed and a comfortable lounge suite. It had a disorderly, male feel to it, with books and journals piled everywhere. Though it was serviced daily, the maid knew to leave everything in its place, as she found it.

A young British doctor, with the most ordinary name of Frederick Smith and who worked at a clinic in Gugulethu, occupied the room between Duke's and Oberon's.

The entire second floor was permanently leased by Graham Weir and the a cappella group Not The Midnight Mass, who performed at various venues around the country. Here too the dividing walls had been taken down to form a vast single area, with a kitchenette on one side and a bathroom on the other.

The rooms on the third floor were generally let to travellers on a short-term basis, but every now and then someone would stay longer. These travellers invariably found Brabazan listed in either *The Rough Guide* or *Lonely Planet* as a clean and interesting lodging house, situated in a trendy and vibey part of the city centre. The short-let rooms were compact and simply furnished with items bought at auctions or second-hand shops, so there was no overall decor theme but a pleasing melange of this and that. You'd find, for instance, a wrought-iron-framed mirror in one room and the rosewood-framed mirror of an Edwardian dresser in another. Or a *jonkmanskas* alongside a Lewis Store armchair.

The top-floor rooms were used by four Russian prostitutes who didn't sleep there but merely plied their trade. These ladies had a fashion sense anchored in the 1960s and largely inspired by Jackie Kennedy Onassis. When not busy upstairs, they sat at the bar or played pool, until someone indicated a carnal need and was led upstairs to the pleasure rooms.

Duke employed students as waitrons. His permanent staff – two cooks, one kitchen helper, an assistant barman and two cleaners – were Zimbabwean refugees. They lived at the back, in storerooms that had been converted into simple, comfortable quarters with a communal bathroom. His security guard, Alfonso, an Angolan, slept in a wooden Wendy house, also at the back. When xenophobic attacks broke out in the townships, he and the Zimbabweans were spared vicious confrontations. The violence was quelled, but hatred for foreigners did not abate. It merely simmered on and Duke's staff were grateful to be far from it.

Duke's housekeeper, Amèlia Sampaio, was a widowed Mozambican mulatto, born in Beira of a white Portuguese railway man and his black mistress. When the civil war broke out, she had been living on a mission, where her husband worked as a mechanic and general handyman.

Amèlia harboured certain inner secrets about war and loss, about barbarism, but never spoke of these, instead concealing them behind a kind and caring demeanour. Each morning she opened up Brabazan, supervised the cleaning staff, oversaw the serving of breakfast to the tenants who wanted it and generally got everything on track, although she didn't deal with the bar. Duke did that when he came down. She lived in one of Duke's apartments in nearby Overbeek Mansions, where her furnishings were simple and gave the sense that were she to leave in a hurry, she could stuff everything of importance into one bag.

Dr Smith's room was sparsely furnished, in keeping with his socialist ideals. He had asked Duke to take out the bed, cupboard, carpet and dressing table, replacing these with a compact Sony music centre, a sleeper couch, a wire-mesh miner's locker and a dress rail on wheels from which were hung a denim jacket, two shirts and his white medical coats. He also asked for the curtains to go, and in their place put up some reed blinds. These did not block the pulsing colours of neon lights in the way curtains did. Against one wall he pinned a length of bright African cloth and hung a few baskets he'd bought at Greenmarket Square.

Because he couldn't stand the idea of anyone cleaning up after him, he declined the room service that his rent included. He always came home exhausted, spent his nights surfing and blogging, and rushed off early in the mornings, so the room was dirty. Every now and then he purged it, but it remained largely a tip of chocolate papers, biscuit wrappers, juice bottles and dustballs.

He had the money to buy a car, but chose to commute by informal taxi among the working classes. In this way, he exposed himself to the same vehicular risks they were forced to take and, with them, had his ears damaged by the one-hundred-and-thirty-decibel hip-hop music that the drivers enjoyed. He and his fellow passengers put their lives on the line in overloaded, often unroadworthy vehicles, most often driven by unlicensed drivers who paid little heed to traffic laws.

Born in London to a Quaker family, he had been brought up to believe that if you had the will, it was easy to serve the poor and suffering masses of the Third World. He'd studied medicine and set off for Africa, planning to work a while in Cape Town before going to Zimbabwe, though he never got that far.

He spent the tail-end years of apartheid at the Red Cross Children's Hospital, where he administered to a quintet of poverty's signatures: malnourishment, foetal alcohol syndrome, sexual abuse, violence, and horrific burns resulting from fallen candles and Primus stoves that turned small dwellings into inescapable infernos. He imagined that once apartheid ended, so would these avoidable afflictions, but this was not to be, for poverty remained largely unaddressed by the new government.

Wanting a change from working in a big hospital, he transferred to a clinic in Gugulethu. There his patient load was huge, for his clinic served not only the immediate community, but also people from the burgeoning squatter area that surrounded it. As families abandoned the impoverished Eastern Cape and headed for the cities, shacks sprang up overnight, like a multicoloured fungus of scrap materials.

At the clinic, while permanently caffeinated on Red Bull, he continued to treat illnesses and injuries that could have been avoided. Patients presented with botched circumcisions, rabid sepsis of neglected wounds, the results of treatments administered by self-styled traditional healers and the awful injuries caused by improperly attended childbirth. He saw the haemorrhage of amateur abortions; the terminal, terrifying phases of tubercular meningitis; and the daily run-of-the-mill, endless roster of Aids and its complications. People often arrived in the last stages of their pathologies and all he could do was refer them to Groote Schuur or Tygerberg Hospital, knowing that even there treatment was not likely to be successful.

Once, a desperately ill woman was transported to the clinic in a wheelbarrow, but she died before he could call an ambulance. Another time, a dying child was brought in a supermarket trolley, but there was no chance to transfer her to intensive care. A grandmother once arrived from Philippi with a sick baby strapped to her back, having been turned away from three other clinics. When she untied the infant for Dr Smith, it was dead.

In the midst of this medical nightmare, in which he

barely kept afloat, he made friends with an old pensioner who lived next door to the clinic. This man's first name was EnkosiThixo, or ThankyouGod. He suffered from shortness of breath and arthritis and kept homing birds in his backyard. Dr Smith called him Mr Pigeons.

His were extraordinary birds in that each morning, when Mr Pigeons opened their *hoks*, they flew en masse to Long Street, to the roof of Brabazan. From there, they fluttered down twice a day to be fed crumbed sponge cake and sunflower seeds scattered on the pavement by the elderly sister of the imam of the next-door mosque. Early each evening, they flew back to the township, where Mr Pigeons, who had no money for seed, offered only cramped lodging and fresh water. Because of their diet, they were beautiful, glossy birds. They elected to live with the old man because he understood and spoke to them, almost in their own language.

He had been employed for his whole working life at the now-demolished coal-fired power station at the harbour end of Loop Street. There he was called John, as were most Africans with difficult names. On days when the wind blew in from the sea, chimney emissions would form a ball of smog and roll up into town.

Despite his weak health, he continued to smoke, tasking his grandchildren to collect *stompies* and salvage bits of tobacco for his pipe. The condition of his lungs was aggravated by his birds' guano and feathers, the damp of his poorly constructed apartheid-era house and the dust from its deteriorating asbestos roof. Most days, he walked to the clinic next door, asking for lozenges to soothe his throat and chest.

He and his dependants existed on white bread, margarine, black tea and sugar, which was all that his pension afforded. Dr Smith would have liked to give more than the lozenges. He would have liked to share his Brabazan sandwiches and offer a mug of Sip-Soup, but he didn't dare, for then a queue of ragged children and old people on sticks might form, expecting to receive these meagre comforts as well.

Instead, under the pretence of learning about pigeons, Dr Smith went next door each Friday, taking a loaf of wholewheat bread and a jar of peanut butter. These the old man would give to his unemployed daughter for his fatherless grandchildren to devour as soon as the good doctor had left.

Mr Pigeons's dream was to plant cabbages. He told Dr Smith that to grow your own big green cabbages was a good thing. As soon as his lungs were better and his grandchildren a little older, he planned to sit on a drum in his yard and there instruct them to dig, plant and water. He imagined he'd not only grow enough cabbages for his table, but he'd also have a surplus to sell.

Dr Smith absorbed this dream as gradually he began to lose touch with reality. Working shifts of fifteen hours a day, six days a week, among the dead and dying, coming home exhausted, only to frequent a digital world on his laptop and then have his sleep disturbed by a ghost that kept coming into the room, he grew pale, taut and humourless.

Duke Ellerman accommodated the Brabazan prostitutes to stop residents who wanted sex from bringing in riff-raff and hookers. He didn't want anyone involved with pimps and gangs, or under mafia control, working upstairs. There was a profitable spin-off because nonresident clients invariably had a drink at the bar, before or after, or ordered drinks and meals to be taken up to the bordello level.

His girls worked under the professional names of Anastasia, Marie, Olga and Tatiana. They mastered only a little English and Afrikaans, so they made no friends outside of their quartet. Every now and then, a Russian would come in, usually attached to a mafia or the embassy, and he'd impart some melancholy and homesickness to their day.

The girls paid Duke a percentage of their takings and he ensured that they had regular medical check-ups – not wanting to be indirectly responsible for the spread of Aids and clap. They too rented one of the apartments he owned in Overbeek Mansions. This had the overall cluttered look of a typical Soviet-era flat, with every surface and corner filled with bric-a-brac, stuffed toys, macramé items, crochet mats, ashtrays, plastic plants, découpage boxes and coasters. The walls were hung with rugs – at home, these would have given warmth to cold concrete – calendars, religious icons and various mass-market prints by Toulouse-Lautrec and Gauguin. A display unit was crammed with tea sets, glasses, vases and ornaments. A standing lamp – a *torchère*, as they called it, using its French name – cast a muted light over the room so that, viewed as a whole, it gave the sense of a cultural museum's depository.

Though they were still children when the Berlin Wall fell and the Soviet Union collapsed, they had inherited their parents' severe, thrifty natures and the habit of hoarding everything that might have further use, such as shampoo bottles and ice-cream *bakkies*. They had also taken on a visual hunger for colour, particularly yellow and orange.

Once a week, each took a turn to cook up and freeze

portions of borscht and potato-with-leek-and-dumpling stew. These imparted the comforting aroma of their familial homes.

Now and then, Duke was approached by outside girls who had lost their jobs at the strip joints on Waterkant Street. Generally, they were a little past their prime, scorched by drugs and suffering venereal burnout. He pitied them but couldn't help. They offered lap and pole dancing but he wanted none of that at Brabazan.

Even though they didn't do pole and lap dancing, the Brabazan girls offered their share of kinky. They had a few customers who were into rubberdollism, a new, fetish, body art form that had not yet hit Cape Town in any big way, but soon would.

Participants dressed in exquisite, custom-made, full-body latex suits that sported inflatable breasts and allowed for the tucking back of masculine genitalia beneath a set of fleshy labia. Full face masks and wigs completed the erotic alter egos. The suits were ordered from a man in Johannesburg known by the dollname of Spirit and who was one of South Africa's first exponents of this art.

In the privacy of its fourth upstairs room, which was furnished à la Moroccan, Brabazan offered the only group venue in town and provided a weekly dollparty that went on from dusk until early morning of the next day. Here players could enjoy a dollspace that involved cutting-edge sensuality.

Generally, this early group of dreamdolls or rubberdolls, as they were called, were sexually bored, wealthy, middle-aged and older men who took the occasional snort of cocaine. They were not necessarily sexually hung up, but simply wanted to explore eroticism in a way that they couldn't within marriage or the boundaries of regular life. They owned their own expensive suits and these were confidentially stored by the Russians in slim pine wardrobes.

Anastasia had a large, cream-coloured cat called either Pushkin or Stalin, depending on whether he was in a lyrical or vicious mood, though he grew increasingly nasty with age. She had trained him to walk on a leash and brought him with her to Brabazan. He inhaled car fumes and cigarette smoke and developed a taste for sucking at cigar butts. It was probably this toxic brew that caused his awful moods.

She also owned a green parrot named Tsarevich, whose wings were clipped so there was no need to cage him, although the cat hated him and would have killed him long ago were it not that he was overweight and lazy. Tsarevich lived permanently at Brabazan and spent most of his time on a perch at a window, where he echoed the roar and hooting of traffic with authentic replays of screaming women, smashing bottles, screeching brakes, ambulance sirens and the *bleaah-bleaah-bleaah-pah-peeh* of political motorcades. He mimicked many Russian words related to professions of the flesh. If you tapped his beak he'd humour you with '*Ek is 'n kakelaar*', which had been taught to him by an Afrikaans customer.

Very occasionally, he hopped down the stairs to sit on the bar counter or strut along it, looking like a plumed Mick Jagger. There he let off the expletives of corks popping and men belching. He could sigh deeply and, when goaded, rendered without fault Jacob Zuma's Zulu presidential campaign song: '*Umshini wami, mshini wami! Khawuleth'umshini wami!*'

He was drawn to the colour green, in its many hues and shades, perhaps because of some primal forest memory locked in his genes. He had never seen a forest, or even a tree for that matter, being a sixth-generation pet-shop-bred bird. If he spotted anyone wearing green, he'd move towards them with intent. People who didn't know him would step back, afraid he was out to peck their eyes. But he would just stare at the compelling colour of their clothes. If there were too many green garments around, he got a bit frantic, banging against legs or boots, and would have to be taken upstairs.

He never ventured from the front door. Had he taken a few steps out and turned right, he would have seen the palm tree outside the mosque. He might also have met Mr Pigeons's birds being fed cake and seed by the imam's sister.

The a cappella group Not The Midnight Mass lived at Brabazan when they did gigs in Cape Town. They rented their accommodation on a permanent basis to avoid staying in hotels and moving apparel up and down from Johannesburg.

They liked Long Street. It gave them a buzz. They enjoyed its mix of clubs, antiquarian bookstores, second-hand clothing shops and antique dealers. They were creatively stimulated by the way criminals and druglords brushed alongside purveyors of fine literature and expensive collectibles; by the way whores and boy-hookers leant up outside vegetarian, hippy, New Age places; and by the ubiquitous French of a growing Congolese population. Here and there, all sorts of unsavoury things went on between drug dealers and pimps and the varied clientele these drew. There was plenty of material for songs, and lots of food for thought, inspiration, texture and pathos in Long Street.

The troupe furnished their Brabazan space in a Churrigueresque-rococo-baroque-romantic fusion. Inside ornate antique wardrobes and carved chests were stored various costumes, all in blacks, purples, crimsons and golds in a variety of fabrics – silks, velvets, brocades, lamé and linens – new and antique, sequined, beaded, embroidered and plain.

When the performers were in residence at Brabazan, their room had the combined atmosphere of a medieval-churchy-theatrical changing room and a stage upon which a production was about to begin. It also gave the sense of possible entrapment, with the feeling that should an unwary soul enter, doors might disappear and exits might never be found again. One also felt that trapdoors might open into dark basements and walls slide apart to reveal passageways twisting into other worlds.

When the singers weren't there, it felt like a storeroom of antiquities and gave the sense of a vacant playhouse, a feel of after-the-show, when the cast and audience have gone and the furnishings reveal themselves for what they really are – mere theatrical scaffolding.

The windows, which faced Long Street, had fringed and tasselled lambrequins draped across their pelmets. They were curtained in much-too-long, heavy crimson velvet that bunched in heaps on the Persian-carpeted parquet floor. All but one of the windows wore block-out blinds; thus little natural lighting entered and this added a sense of mystery. In addition to sleeper couches, there were deep sofas and ottomans with many cushions. Ten people could have slept there, and often did, without feeling crowded. If anyone wanted privacy, they had merely to open out one of a number of restored World War One hospital screens.

In the centre of the room was a long oak banquet table upon which stood two brass candelabra that had once graced the chapel altar of St Aidan's College in Grahamstown. The walls were covered with posters of various gigs as well as mirrors, Venetian masks and tapestries. Cast-iron crucifixes hung alongside silver Ethiopian crosses of various sizes.

In the far corner of the room, at the window without block-out blinds and where the curtain was never drawn, was positioned, to gaze out over Long Street, a life-size statue of the Virgin Mary. This was not the usual run-of-the-mill statue of the Catholic world, but was heavy with aura. It did not always live in the Brabazan room, but was merely on loan. Every so often her owner, Pasquale Benvenuto, who lived a few doors up, above his now boarded-up restaurant, would fetch her and keep her with him until he became exhausted by her and sent her back.

The statue first came to Brabazan after Graham Weir had found her outside on the pavement during one of the worst rainstorms Cape Town had ever experienced. Pasquale had put her out because her presence had become too demanding, too emotionally heavy.

Graham had arrived for the start of a new season, ahead of the other singers. His taxi dropped him in Long Street and he saw the statue standing forlornly in the rain. At first thinking her an apparition that might suddenly disappear, he stood staring in disbelief, then made his way tentatively towards her. How could he walk past her, beautiful Mother of God, in this deluge? Her eyes looked back at him benignly. When he realised she was a statue, he looked around for who might have put her there, but saw no one. Not wanting to leave her and risk her being taken by someone else, but unable to manage her and his luggage, Graham put down his suitcases, picked her up and made his way to Brabazan, watched first by Pasquale from his upstairs window and then by Duke's housekeeper,

Amèlia, as she came through the swing doors from the kitchen. When she saw the statue, she was momentarily transfixed by panic, as memory pulled her back toward the church of the mission where she had once lived. There, a statue of the Virgin Mary, quite as beautiful and no doubt as sacred as this one, had received the prayers of many people, over many years. But she had failed to succour, in their final hour, a group of villagers and nuns who had sought refuge in the church, believing themselves safe there, when crazed soldiers attacked the mission and torched their sanctuary.

Amèlia, her feet now leaden, forced herself into the present by recrafting the obvious: She was here. At Brabazan. Working for a kind man. There was no war in Cape Town. The recent xenophobic attacks had not affected her. This was just another Catholic statue. It had nothing to do with Mozambique's civil war. It had nothing to do with anyone she had lost. She lifted each heavy foot and placed it one in front of the other, walking out into the alley, where she began to cry.

Graham Weir carried the statue through the yellow curtains and up the yellow stairwell. In his room, he wiped her dry, taking care, for she had fine lines all over, showing evidence of terrible damage and then the most skilful repair. He ran a finger over her face, over the lines of the injury, wondering what had happened. A cold shiver ran through him and he realised he was soaking wet. Remembering his luggage, he ran down for it. But, of course, it was gone.

Pasquale was standing there waiting for him, under an umbrella. Before Graham could ask whether he'd seen who had taken the cases, Pasquale said: 'Look after her. Just for now when I can't. But don't love her too deeply. She'll break your heart. I'll fetch her back one of these days. But without hurry.' He closed and latched the door and went upstairs, where he lay on his bed, listening to the rain.

Graham went back to Brabazan and took a hot bath. It would rain for two weeks and lightning would strike the steeple of the Lutheran church – something that had not happened before.

From then on, the statue would move between Brabazan and Pasquale's room, depending on her owner's mood and need and whether Not The Midnight Mass was in residence. When Pasquale's statue of the Virgin Mary was with him, in his times of delusion, he spoke to her, slept with her in his bed, draped her with his old army jacket if the weather was bitter, fanned her if it was hot. She tormented him by remaining dead still when he faced her, but moving as soon as he turned away. From the corner of his eye, he would see her take a step, with such grace as to make him weep. She would look across at him and smile or lift a hand or bow her head, but as soon as he looked at her, she would freeze, holding that benign smile to torture him.

The room assigned to Oberon Yoruba was small, without an en suite, but with a private cubicle bathroom across the passage. It was furnished with a bed; a narrow free-standing wardrobe; two red mock-leather poufs; and a dressing table upon which stood an orange crocheted doily and a vase of yellow sunflowers. These were in full, gorgeous bloom, and had been placed by the previous tenant. There lingered the smell of the perfume of yesterday's occupant, and this had a hint of Indian patchouli.

The overhead bulb had a long tubular shade which, when switched on, dropped a small pool of light onto the wooden floor. Two cheaply framed pictures, *Dreaming of Immortality in a Thatched Cottage* by T'ang Yin and Vladimir Tretchikoff's *Lost Orchid*, hung on either side of a small, plastic glow-in-the-dark crucifix above the bed.

Tretchikoff's original oil painting, once dismissed by connoisseurs as kitsch art, would be bought by a certain Anton Taljaardt as Lot 49 at the 2009 auction of disgraced mining magnate Brett Kebble's art collection, for 2.9 million rand.

Later there would be ongoing critical discussion as to whether it really was the original. The Afrikaans newspaper *Die Beeld* reported differences between the Kebble painting and a reproduction of *Lost Orchid* in a book of Tretchikoff's work, published by Howard Timmins in 1969. The Timmins's reproduction and the Brabazan print both depicted a spent matchstick on the step above the orchid. This detail was missing in the Kebble work.

Tretchikoff's granddaughter, Natasha Mercorio, denied that the painting sold on auction was an original and stated categorically that the signature it bore was not her grandfather's. Whatever the outcome would be, the print hanging in the room assigned to Oberon Yoruba imparted its own aura of forgotten and neglected beauty.

A French door opened to a wrought-iron lovers' balcony that looked over Long Street. This and a side sash window were curtained in sun-filter fabric of faded beige. With not particularly keen observation, one could discern, beneath the room's old paint, the embossed design of a William Morris wallpaper, the whimsical Willow Bough.

A corner vanity basin without a plug and patterned in web-fine cracks, with taps that trickled warm and gushed cold water, was shielded by a folding, intricately carved, Indian cedarwood screen. This had once been inlaid with tiny ivory carvings of flowers, leaves and vines, but was now stripped of those lovely bone pieces.

The screen had been crafted in Kashmir. Perhaps, during the time of the British Raj, it had been used on one of the houseboats on Dal Lake to shield the washstand and basin in a lady's room. Perhaps, when that lady returned to England, for whatever reason, she had taken the screen with her, to remind herself of the cedar forests, the surrounding mountains and the mists that graced them. It could be that, in her old age, she gave the screen to a favourite niece, heading for South Africa with a newly posted military-officer husband.

Whatever its beginnings, the screen found itself at Fraser's Camp trading store in the Eastern Cape. Travellers could stop to take tea or a light meal in the dining room at the rear. Fraser's Camp, which served as a postal agency, and where still stands a military watchtower built in 1835, earned a reputation for its excellent freshly squeezed pineapple juice and pineapple jam tarts. Generous Sunday lunches attracted people from nearby farms and from Grahamstown.

During the late 1970s, when the Ciskei was declared a Bantustan by the apartheid government, nearby Peddie was rezoned a 'black' town. White commercial travellers, making the long journey between Cape Town and East London, no longer stopped overnight at the Peddie Hotel. The owners of Fraser's Camp built a set of simple rooms to accommodate these itinerant salesmen and added a good breakfast to their menu.

The Indian screen stood in the dining room and it was there that the spoiling began, with diners picking out bits of the inlay as souvenirs, until it was completely denuded. It was then thought to be worthless and sent to Grahamstown for auction. A certain Miss Katzen bought it to use as a divider in the shared room of her university residence. At the end of her first year, she brought it to Cape Town, putting it up for sale in her father's second-hand furniture shop, which is where Duke bought it.

So, although his room was a mishmash in decor terms, Oberon Yoruba was content with it. He liked the sunflowers and the painted orchid. The screen gave off a wistful feeling. Everything served his immediate, modest needs, for it hadn't occurred to him that he might deserve better. The trait which most marked him was humility and he was lacking in conceit or arrogance.

The only belongings he now had with him, all neatly placed in the cupboard, were a pair of denim jeans and two golf shirts, underwear, a jersey, socks and sheepskin slippers. All these he'd bought on his first afternoon at Brabazan from Zip Zap Clothing across the road. At night he slept in the white, ankle-length, Indian-cotton shirt he had found in the suitcase. The case, with all its money, he kept on top of the cupboard.

Despite the residents and the steady flow of drinkers and diners at Brabazan, Oberon, its newest guest, had spent his first three days feeling rather lonely up there above the traffic, not having made a single friend since booking in. He'd settled into the routine of rising early, eating breakfast and heading off for a walk, only getting home after five. He ate his evening meals alone at the far corner table, from where he watched people loading the jukebox and playing pinball. He was too shy to strike up conversations.

It just happened that he never encountered Dr Smith, nor any of the Russian girls and their clients, in the corridors or downstairs when he ate. He didn't cross paths with members of Not The Midnight Mass either, though they were in residence. They were performing at Theatre on the Bay, so they only got in late each night. They slept till lunchtime and practised in their room every afternoon.

On each of his first days, after breakfast, Oberon walked the length and breadth of Long Street, all the way from the Baths to the docks and back again, eating lunch at the vegetarian Porto Bello, taking care not to stray off this main artery, for he knew he'd never find his way back to Brabazan. Although he had the déjà vu certainty that he'd walked this city before, and had many times observed its details, he had no proper memories of having done so.

On his fourth day, he found Porto Bello inexplicably closed, so he came back to Brabazan. It was full of businessmen, secretaries and legal people from the nearby Supreme Court – all power-dressed and super-slick. This was the usual lunchtime crowd enjoying light meals, wine and mineral water.

After he'd eaten, he decided to take an afternoon nap. Not wanting to lie down in his clothes, he changed into his nightshirt. He'd just dozed off when he was woken by beautiful a cappella voices. His unlatched door creaked ajar and there now drifted in the sounds of heaven and the smells of frankincense and myrrh. He opened his eyes, taking a moment to orient himself, not immediately recognising where he was. He got up slowly, put on slippers and, still in his nightshirt, made his way up to the second floor, towards the sweet, strident singing.

He tapped on the door from where the sounds came, but there was no answer, so he opened it. There before him stood the figures of two men and three women, singing in exquisite harmony, rehearsing. He crept in and sat on a sofa, closing his eyes.

'By Jupiter, an angel!' exclaimed Graham Weir when he saw Oberon. 'Or if not, then an earthly paragon! Why, he must be a seraph newly tumbled out of heaven.'

Oberon stayed through the afternoon. The singers merely took the presence of this man dressed in a celestial robe as natural. He seemed so in place among their religious iconography.

Duke Ellerman's own world had narrowed in on him. He never took a holiday, because he wouldn't have known what to do outside of his routine. When he wanted a break, he merely rose early and took a half-day off, getting back by two-thirty at the latest.

He woke at nine each morning, when Amèlia brought him a tray of rooibos and rusks. He took his time in the shower. She came back at ten with a full breakfast of fried eggs, tomato, sausage, bacon, baked beans, mushrooms, toast with marmalade and coffee. This kept his cholesterol levels at peak and saw him through to early evening when he usually had steak and chips. He ate his breakfast slowly, read both the *Cape Times* and *Die Burger*, watched the BBC and CNN news, and then went downstairs to begin his day.

Of late, Duke was mulling over two problems. He'd constantly been harassed by gangsters wanting protection money, but had managed to avoid entering that cesspool of exchange. Since the end of apartheid and the influx into the country of foreign crime syndicates, mafia groupings had strengthened while policing and the judiciary had weakened. The tone of protection rackets had changed. In the apartheid days some *skollie* or other would come in and make an offer or a threat or a demand. Duke would just tell them to get fucked and that would be the end of the story. But nowadays, it would be a man wearing a suit and a brass knuckleduster. He'd lean up close and smell of rich perfume and ask whether you liked your bar and business and, if so, what was it worth to you. He might be fingering worry beads or flicking his brushed-chrome Zippo lighter on and off. His breath would be heavy with mint mouthwash. There could be a diamond inset into a tooth.

Duke had already experienced two such visits. He knew that, by the third, he would have to agree to pay, or suffer a shootout on the pavement or the trashing of his premises. He could, of course, just sell up. But then how would be spend his time?

His second preoccupation concerned street children. There were many, and his guard, Alfonso, had his share of trouble with them. But Duke had noticed that, recently, these children were being picked off Long Street by someone.

In the old days, the street children who lived in the city centre were reasonably disciplined. They were brought in from the country areas by a guy who lived up in the Bo-Kaap, owned delivery vans and took on the subcontracts to deliver daily newspapers. The children were taken from their rural homes on the pretext that they would be educated. Their parents were promised some pitiful wage and the children then tasked to sell newspapers at the traffic lights. They sold them all – the *Cape Times*, the *Argus*, *Die Burger* and *Die Beeld* – and earned themselves the name of Argie Boys. They were so much a part of the cityscape that no one batted an eye at seeing an eight- or ten-year-old barefoot child selling the news. They were fed and housed by their 'employer' and kept under a measure of control. It was said that some of the children slept in chicken cages in his backyard and that others slept in garbage bins in the city. Those children didn't sniff glue or run amok. Only when they grew older and stopped selling papers did they enter the streets on their own devices. They rarely returned home to their impoverished farm-worker parents.

An investigative journalist, Roland Stanbridge, did his best to expose how the entire media industry rested on what amounted to child slave labour. Initially, his editor was keen for him to examine this, until it was clear that these children were delivering his company's own newspapers. Stanbridge was ordered to drop the story, which he discreetly handed on to the editor of the *Herald*, the coloured community's newspaper. That editor, as the only person who could order the presses to be stopped, 'went fishing' on the day of publishing and so the story was told. For his courage, he was dismissed.

One night, a group of these youngsters, locked inside a delivery van, burnt to death when it caught alight. After that, whether because of or in addition to Stanbridge's story, the use of Argie Boys came to an end, so nowadays you didn't see them. What you were confronted with were feral children, mostly orphans, all unwanted, who sniffed glue, did petty crime and weren't harnessed by anyone in the Bo-Kaap.

Six months ago, Duke could have counted up to two dozen children living rough on Long Street between Wale and the Buitensingel intersection, but now there were half that number. Alfonso, too, had commented on the decline. Duke knew that neither the government nor the city council had schemes for street children. There were no social workers gathering them up and placing them into care. St John's Hostel, up at the top of Kloof

Street, had once housed white orphans and social-work cases, but the property had been sold and developed into high-income apartments. He also knew that shelters like Ons Plek and The Haven, which were run by non-governmental agencies, were all voluntary. Children had to take themselves to the door.

Once, outside Brabazan, he'd witnessed one of the parking guards grasp a boy by the wrist and take him across the road to two men in black suits waiting in a double-parked car. The guard shoved the boy in the back and the men drove off. This unsettled Duke but there was nothing he could do about it. The child wasn't his to report as missing. He didn't even know the urchin's name.

But now, there was a new worry to ruminate. He'd just received a letter from Billy-Jean Jones, a one-night stand whom he'd picked up years before at an infamous Long Street party, and whom he'd not thought about again beyond that isolated sexual encounter. The letter informed him that her thirteen-year-old son was his and that she was sending the boy back to him, the father he'd never known. The contents of the letter caused Duke's mental focus to shift disturbingly from the predictability of his day-to-day life and towards his heart.

Shortly after dawn of the seventh day of Oberon's sojourn at Brabazan, unconnected and unknown to him, a certain Miss Pearlie Theron stood on the balcony of her apartment, number four Maynard Court in Vredehoek, just a half-hour walk from Long Street. She looked across the city, allowing her gaze to wander over Devil's Peak.

Eight months previously, almost to the day, her

wonderful, ebullient, colourful, mischievous and completely clandestine affair with her long-time employer, Mr Thespian Winter, the importer, had come to an abrupt end. She had spent the past months as though under the spell of a Grimm's wicked witch, imprisoned in a castle overgrown with tangled, impenetrable briar.

'How has it come to this,' she asked, addressing her old, fat black cat as he rubbed against her legs, 'that I should end up facing the rest of my days without Thespi? Shall I abide in this dull world, which in his absence is no better than a sty?

'How must I manage? What beauty will there be? How will I ever again enjoy a little feast, or a glass of wine? There can be no living, none, without him.'

Such questions unfolded each morning, like a sad, arhythmic poem, for she always woke with a heavy heart and then went to stand on the balcony to take in the view, looking for solace but finding none, though the cat tried his best to soothe her, empathising with her despair.

Previously, she would have begun each day with eloquent notes from one of the works that had fuelled her romance: *The Barber of Seville*, perhaps, or *Rigoletto* or *Bolero*. But all music had been silenced and dancing steps halted. Her drama was over, extinguished like a candle flame by a gust of wind, even though it had once unfolded like a performance at the Globe Theatre or on Broadway. Her life had been reduced to a low-budget, poorly costumed movie in which she wandered aimlessly, looking for her script, feeling she had forgotten her role, not knowing how to reclaim it. Of what use now were the lines of a Viola or a Helena or a Sappho?

In the eight months since her married lover had been institutionalised at Deerpark Retirement Home with sudden-onset amnesia (a death of sorts), she hadn't had a single visitor nor ventured out except to buy a few groceries. She felt she'd lost touch with reality and feared that, if anyone spoke to her, she'd reply with something absurd, something abysmally stupid. Perhaps she'd become invisible in these past months. Perhaps her life had been a dream, from which she'd just awoken, discovering that she had no life at all.

Her affair with Thespian Winter had been altogether too self-contained, too secret. She had made no proper friends, only acquaintances, outside of their relationship. There had been no need to bring anyone into the bubble of their lives, which were adequately full of the characters from the plays and operas that enriched their passion. Of those *real* people with whom she interacted – mostly the tellers at Spar or the bank, or the Chinese cook and waitrons at the Lotus Tavern on the docks – none knew the complexities of her private life. So no one had come to mourn her loss or to comfort her or to help her look for light in her now unpredictable future. Because Thespian's business had closed so abruptly, not even his clients had had the chance to show Pearlie, his long-time secretary, any sympathy.

Yet, someone in the apartment block had noticed that she was alone. One day, there was a knock at the door. When Pearlie opened, she found, on the doormat, inside a cardboard box, wrapped in a towel, an enamel bowl of chicken and peanut stew on rice. There was also a pot-bread and a jar of mild, sweet, home-brewed ginger beer. She looked down the passage, but saw no one. There was no accompanying note, only a small carved Nigerian figurine.

To add to all Pearlie's sorrows and preoccupations, some fool, in a diabolical act, had started a fire near Rhodes Memorial some two months before, in March, during the last hot days of summer. The arsonist had set the whole mountain aflame, relying on the southeast wind to drive it all the way round the front of Table Mountain, engulfing Devil's Peak.

Pearlie had watched the flames through the night, mesmerised by the titanic movement of scarlet and orange as it ran across the slopes, devouring everything, until it was heroically halted by firefighters just before the line of properties at the edge of her suburb.

For weeks, ash covered everything, blown by the wind in protracted lamentation. Black crows circled like undertakers and hired mourners, cawing in feigned sympathy, dragging claws against Pearlie's sore heart. All this added to her sense of loss, compounding the sad fact that she was forbidden to visit Thespian.

His son-in-law, that awful Radison man, had phoned to tell her that only Mr Winter's immediate family had visiting rights. He said that a restraining order would soon be served, preventing Pearlie from going anywhere near Deerpark Home. He, the son-in-law, would lay a charge of harassment if she 'tried anything funny', as he put it.

A restraining order? Harassment? What was he talking about? Pearlie had no intention of harassing anyone. She just wanted to see Thespian, her best friend, her only friend – her husband, actually. Why should she be intimidated? This was a free country. She had every right to call on Thespian, to walk around the grounds of the home with him, to take him something nice to eat, some nougat or a slice of cake. And she would have done so, except that the son-in-law added something sinister.

He told Pearlie that if she so much as put a foot on the driveway of Deerpark Home he, personally, would punish Thespian. 'I'll hurt him,' he had told her in a schoolyardish way. 'He's just a vegetable now. With no mind. He had no mind before, choosing your sexual favours, but he definitely has no mind now. I'll punish him. Like a bad child. I'll pinch him and stick pins into him and burn him with my cigarette. I'll make him cry like he deserves to cry.'

That threat alone was enough to keep her away, for she realised that here was a croaking raven, bellowing for revenge. It caused Pearlie to worry, for perhaps Thespian was being mistreated anyway, whether she called on him or not. Was that ghastly son-in-law already sticking pins into him? Was he withholding food and drink? Was he bathing her man in ice-cold water and putting him out into a draft to give him pneumonia, as a villain might do in a Brontë novel? She had no way of knowing and imagined the worst.

She mustered the courage at least to drive around Deerpark Home, which took up a whole city block. It was a tall, bleak 1960s building with verandas that were fenced in like chicken coops. In front, there was a pergola surrounded by a pretty indigenous garden, planted through a bequest in memory of a loved parent. Messages on stones read: *A garden is a lovesome thing* and *One is nearer to God in a garden, than anywhere else on earth*. But there were never old people enjoying the fresh air. Everyone was kept indoors. Only staff sat under the pergola, smoking and chatting during their breaks. In any event, the designer had omitted to install a wheelchair ramp, so access to the garden was only for the able-bodied.

The months unfolded slowly and, apart from the changing seasons, there was nothing different to each day. But now, as she stood on the balcony, Pearlie resolved to break out of the entrapment by doing something she'd never done before. She decided, after lunch, to take a walk down to Long Street and have a drink.

The next day, the eighth of Oberon's stay at Brabazan, an explosion of xenophobic hatred raced across the country, leaving Stygian darkness in its wake. It had started some days before in Alexandra township, near Johannesburg. There a young Mozambican man was burnt to death on a pile of his own blankets and meagre belongings as he tried to flee a mob bent on ridding the country of foreigners. Archbishop Emeritus Desmond Tutu, prompted by the horror, proclaimed something to the effect that South Africa's Rainbow Nation was now nothing but a bloody, torn *bandiera*.

In an unconnected incident, across town in her shack in a squatter camp bordering the Black River, Thandi Koliti, a night nurse at Deerpark Retirement Home, came face to face with the ugly side of *muti* harvesting.

She'd woken early, lit a paraffin lamp, stoked up a Primus stove and put an enamel kettle on to boil. She pulled on gumboots, picked up a packet of garbage and made her way through oiled puddles to toss it behind the row of latrines that lined the edge of the river. She looked neither at the walls of the tightly packed shacks, nor up at the majestic back of Table Mountain, touched as it was in morning's umber light. Her gaze was on the muddy track between the zinc-walled dwellings.

As she hurled the bag onto the makeshift dump, which was laden with the tart smell of decay, her vision caught the colour rather than the shape of something buoyant in the dirty, barely flowing river. Screwing up her eyes, she made out that it was a child's body, face down in the brown water and trapped by floating rubbish.

In fact, though she had no way of knowing this, it was a torso, clothed in a bright T-shirt, its head, arms and legs hacked off cleanly as if by a butcher's saw. That it was limbless was not obvious at first glance, because the shirt covered the amputation sites. It seemed that the arms and legs were dangling down in the water. An accumulation of plastic bottles and a wedge of polystyrene had settled where the head should have been.

Thandi pressed a hand to her mouth as a spasm seized her stomach. She hurried back to her shack and got on with the business of dressing her boy and girl for school, making sandwiches and a pot of tea for them and her mother. She held back an inner rage. If she had let herself go with it, she would have started screaming. No matter how much she tried, or how much she saved, or how much she bribed the staff at the council's housing office, she could not get away from this ghetto.

By ten that morning, metro workers had retrieved the torso and placed it on a stretcher, covered with an emergency blanket, while they waited for Dr Smith, who had been called from the nearby clinic.

After he had confirmed that it was human, it was dispatched to the city mortuary in Salt River. There it would be recorded in a register, numbered, tagged and prepared for autopsy by Chester April, an assistant who had held down his gruesome job for the past twenty years.

City council cleaners assisted police divers in searching for the missing body parts. A crowd of onlookers gathered, mostly children, and they hampered the work. Dr Smith stood among them for a while, feeling dizzy, his stethoscope hanging round his neck like the albatross of the Ancient Mariner. He couldn't face going back to the clinic and instead went home to Brabazan, where he got into bed, curled up, and began to hum softly.

Even though the river's surface was raked of all floating muck, and its foul depths dredged, it failed to offer up more than the rusted chassis of a Morris Minor, a truck tyre, tins, bottles, numerous car batteries, broken glass, lots more plastic and an awful amount of E. coli bacteria which would affect the health of those working in the water that day.

It was accepted – simply to give parameters to the case – that the head and limbs had been discarded elsewhere or, more likely, taken by dogs.

Thandi Koliti decided not to go to work that evening and sent an SMS to the matron at Deerpark, saying she needed compassionate leave for the night and that she would explain everything when she came in the next day. She then switched off her cellphone, knowing this was taking a chance, for she'd already abused the system of sick and compassionate leave. But she couldn't leave her children alone with the ghost of that floating body still hovering, as she knew the phantoms of the murdered did.

Though her mother would be in the shack with the children, the old lady was frail and of no use in chasing spirits. The matron would just have to understand that Thandi was a single mother living in a dump, trying to protect her family from the stink and pestilence it contained.

The law required an autopsy to be performed whenever death was ascribed to non-natural causes. Thus, in the microcosm of the Salt River mortuary, which served a vast section of Cape Town's metropolitan area, Chester April processed Sisyphean volumes of those who met their end violently.

He normally greeted each corpse delivered to his care. He acknowledged them, not just for the sake of common courtesy, but because sometimes someone would be brought in who had been pronounced dead at the scene of the crime or accident, but was actually only comatose.

Very occasionally, just as the body was about to be placed into airless, impersonal cold storage, it might yawn or groan or move a finger. If a mirror was held to its nose, evidence of breath would be seen, and then a slight pulse detected. Chester never wanted to be caught out by such an eventuality, which is why he greeted loudly. If he was in any doubt as to the state of things, he would give a prod with an autopsy hook.

You had to keep your wits about you when working in a mortuary, where possession was a real hazard. A soul detached from its body might hover, afraid to move on. Chester had developed quite a measure of skill at sensing the presence of such hesitant spirits. Generally, he spoke with gentle, coercing words, sending them on their way. But sometimes he had to shoo them out, as one might evict a pesky dog: 'Go now! See, you're dead. It's over for you. You can't hang around.'

There were those who ignored his directives and hid behind doors or inside drawers. They might make their way to the staff tea room and wait for someone to doze off, intent on seizing that body for themselves and trampling the sleeping soul within it.

Over the years he'd developed a certain level of spirituality, a hard stomach and a detached, clinical attitude. Being exposed to so many newly dead folk, the questions concerning the when and how and why of the soul's departure were all too present. This was especially so each Monday morning, when he was faced with the bodies of numerous young men killed over the weekend in drug- and drink-fuelled gang violence. They were generally covered in disfiguring, poorly executed tattoos and were seldom claimed.

He had absorbed the attitude of the specialists and medical students he worked with, coming to admire anatomical structure rather than focusing on the damage done to it. Like them, he was able to detach from the violence that brought each body to his workbench, and to get on with the job. Clad in surgical gown, plastic apron and rubber boots, his eyes protected by goggles, his hands by the three layers of latex, chain-mail and rubber gloves, he'd cut a corpse open for the pathologist. He'd begin at the rear of the right ear, cutting towards the notch of the sternum and then down to the umbilicus, before swinging right and down to the top of the leg. Opening the abdominal cavity, he'd relieve the person of any residual decorum, revealing vital organs and the secrets they held. Peeling down the scalp and facial skin and opening the skull ensured that the final bastion of dignity was down and the individual was now no more than a carcass.

But, despite his experience and ability to detach, Chester nearly threw up when the child's torso was brought in. It prompted him to conclude that some people were driven by devils. It was the worst death he'd seen – a mere youngster, not only murdered but also mutilated and then dumped into a poisoned river to bloat and further disfigure, taking on the appearance of an oversized, crinkly worm. The torso had the strangest-looking white skin and, though Chester recognised it as albino, he wondered whether there had been some bleaching pollutant in the water.

He stared down at this part-body and decided to go home. This one was not for him. One of his colleagues would have to prepare it. Outside, he breathed deeply of the autumn air, though it was laden with the smell of burning rubber, wafting over from Ndabeni Industria, and the stench from the abattoir, from where a bull had recently escaped.

Chester took the train to Cape Town station. Instead of heading home, knowing his wife would not be back from work, he decided to walk around among the living and set off up Strand Street, turning into Long. He stopped at Debonair, which was having a closing-down sale. In the window, an elegantly posed mannequin wore a white suit and red trilby. It was labelled with the knock-down price of ninety-nine rand.

Debonair had been all but cleared of its stock, with just a few jackets left hanging on rails. A short, scrawny, bow-legged elderly woman with big dangly earrings and hair frazzled by a home perm stood at a glass counter, smoking. Little lines radiated out from her lips, cut there by years of pulling hard on cigarettes, and into these lines the red of her over-applied lipstick bled. Her cheeks and brow, ruined by equally long years of sun, were plastered with foundation and powder that filled the cracks and wrinkles, highlighting them somewhat. Because colour had not been applied to the neck, the face, completed by turquoise lids and black-defined brows, was a true mask, its line ending just below the jaw.

'There's nothing left,' the woman pronounced, walking across the shop in high-heeled sandals that clapped at the floor. 'The sale's been on all month. You left it a bit late, sonny.'

'I'll take the suit in the window,' replied Chester.

'Brommer!' she shouted, and a man in his forties, clearly her son, emerged from the partitioned back room. 'Take the suit out,' she instructed.

He too was smoking and was as ravaged by lifestyle as she was. His greased, combed-back hair reflected the shop's neon light in an oleaginous sheen. He wore tight denims, baseball sneakers and a sleeveless vest. Each ear lobe was burdened with silver rings and he had a stud below his lower lip. His arms and neck were covered in tattoos that had lost their definition so that, from a distance, they looked like bruises. Each knuckle was inscribed with a letter, spelling HATE on one hand and LOVE on the other.

Chester and the woman watched Brommer flick the cherry off his cigarette, which he then tucked behind an ear to smoke later. He ambled to the shop window and took the suit off the dummy with a gentleness that did not match his looks. You might have expected him to undress a young girl with those delicate movements, not a lifeless form. And if you saw him undress anyone in that manner, you might have been worried about her.

He draped the jacket and pants over the counter and went back to whatever he was doing at the rear of the shop.

'You want to try it?' the woman asked Chester. 'Looks like your size. But you can try it if you have to.' She pointed with her chin to a cubicle.

'No, I can see it's my size,' he replied.

'That's what I said. You want it?'

'Yes, please, I'll take it.'

'Dirt-cheap too. You won't have this luck again,' she said and, in the same breath, called out: 'Brommer! Mister Brommer Crawe!'

Her son ambled in again and she told him: 'Wrap it for this sonny. Give him the hat too.'

Brommer took the suit and disappeared. He was gone an inordinately long time during which the woman took Chester's money, smoked a Camel and hacked a dry cough. 'I hope you don't want a receipt,' she said. 'The shop's closed already. I'm just selling off these last things.'

Eventually, her son came out with a meticulously

wrapped parcel. It was packaged in the way that would have been recognised, nostalgically, by anyone who'd ever bought clothing from Stuttafords in Adderley Street, long ago, in the sixties or seventies.

He handed it to Chester with the slightest bow and without a word, then clasped his hands behind his back and went to stand in the sun on the pavement.

Chester continued up Long Street and entered Brabazan, drawn there for no particular reason. He sat at the far end of the bar and, in eloquent, fairly studied English, with the clipped South African accent of a person whose home is bilingual, ordered a beer. Duke noticed that he seemed troubled.

This was, without doubt, a *muti* murder. The youngster was a victim of superstition and ignorance, killed so body parts could be harvested for the ingredients of magic charms. During the past few years, Chester had observed, among the usual stabbings and gunshot killings, a steady rise in such murders. There were an extraordinary number of child victims among them and this bothered him. In common with young gangsters, their bodies were seldom identified and so never claimed.

Cape Town was full of urchins who belonged to nobody and who slept in the streets. At night, along Buitengracht Street, one of the city's old perimeters that still bore its Dutch name, you'd find children huddled together, sleeping on the pavement. You could entice one into your car simply by offering a piece of Kentucky Fried Chicken or a packet of chips. You often didn't actually have to give anything, you just had to *say* you were going to: 'Come with me. I'll buy you a Colonel Burger.' In fact, you could just pick up a sleeping body and put it into the boot of your car and then traffic or do whatever with it. If any of the other children protested, you could just give them a *klap*, because they would be high on thinners. You were sure in the knowledge that if they went to the police to report the abduction of one of their friends, nobody would pay the slightest attention.

Most *muti* harvests took a piece or two from the victim. This was the first time Chester had seen a body with the whole *catastrophe*, as he saw it, taken off. And there was something else. Whoever had abducted the boy had not simply seized someone opportunistically. He had gone out looking for an albino, because people without pigmentation, who looked like phantoms, who were known as nobodies and ghosts, whose red-rimmed eyes reminded one of night wolves, were said to make extremely potent *muti*. And if they were children, then the medicine was known to be doubly powerful.

It would be days before a forensic detective came to have a look. All he said, when he saw the remains of the body, was: 'Oh, fuck!' He set to work without engaging with anyone. He recorded that the torso, which he judged to have belonged to a boy of about twelve, sported a line of neat, cicatrised, ritual markings just above the breast line. He recognised that the scars were neither Xhosa nor Zulu. The practice of scarification among those groups was not seen nowadays on young bodies. This was, without doubt, a boy of Central or West African origin, and the scars were well enough established to have been incised in young childhood.

Acknowledging the autopsy report, he noted that the amputations were surgically exact. This was no hack job. A murder docket was opened and the Missing Persons Unit notified. The detective went straight from the mortuary to the Castle Bar for a drink.

The next day, Chester, for the first time in his career, couldn't bring himself to go to work. His attendance record, a source of pride, was near-immaculate and punctured only by the odd bout of flu or gastroenteritis, and always substantiated by a doctor's certificate.

The nature of his job had never driven him away, even during apartheid, when all sorts of police-inflicted and unnecessary deaths passed before him. He had grown accustomed to the smell and pallor of death, the cold corpses and the complete absence of creative energy in the workplace.

Now, he sat at the kitchen table, still in pyjamas, feeling strangely broken. He pushed away the breakfast his wife had prepared, saying: 'I'm sick to my stomach. It's time for me to quit. I can't look at another dead body. I'm just going to phone in for compassionate leave and then walk around town.'

At home, he never spoke about his work. His wife knew not to ask. Right from the start he'd made it clear that from five o'clock, when he left the mortuary, what was inside of it and what was outside were to remain distinct. But now he couldn't keep his off-duty thoughts away from the job. He would struggle with that torso. It would pop up randomly, like a jack-in-the-box.

Chester watched his wife leave, then spent the morning feeling morose. She kept phoning, unsettled by his uncharacteristic behaviour. Eventually, he told her to leave him in peace, took the receiver off the hook and switched off his mobile. When the noonday gun sounded, he put on his new white suit with a black shirt, not bothering with a tie but leaving the first few shirt buttons undone. He set the red trilby at an angle and headed for Long Street and Brabazan, looking altogether suave. He was not a habitual drinker. Actually, he hardly drank at all, but he had found the atmosphere at Brabazan to be soothing and companionable when he'd gone in the day before, and the beers had made him feel better.

Chester April and his wife, Connie, were practising Anglicans and regularly attended St Paul's in Bree Street. Their priest, Father Bart, had been a staunch opponent of apartheid and his main focus, as a shepherd of souls, was on brotherhood. To this end, long before democracy, he began preparing his congregation for the inevitable. White folk traditionally sat in the front pews and coloureds at the back. He began slowly to integrate them, first one row white, then one row brown. As soon as everyone felt comfortable with this, he asked that the various families intermingle. He lost some of his flock, but urged the others on with sermons focused on Christ's love. Eventually, the view from his pulpit was nicely homogeneous.

By the time apartheid ended, Father Bart's parish was ready for closer contact and he suggested a picnic at De Waal Park. There, one Saturday, his congregants shared the contents of their food hampers. It was so convivial that Father Bart decided to make it a biannual event.

Soon after one of those picnics, a work colleague of Connie's, a South African called Billy-Jean Jones, recently returned from a long exile in Hong Kong, invited the Aprils to her brother's wine and guest farm in Robertson for a lunchtime braai. Her brother, Kleinboet de Jongh, and his wife, Susanna, were entertaining a party of family and tourists. The twenty people were seated for luncheon at a long table under four spreading oaks. Just beyond, some metres away, stood a fifth oak. All were over a hundred years old and heavily branched.

The ambience was altogether delightful, what with the whitewashed Cape Dutch homestead, its well-tended flower beds and the vineyards that spread out across slightly undulating land. In the distance loomed the majestic Hottentots Holland mountains. There was not a cloud in the borage-blue sky.

Kleinboet and Billy-Jean were of mixed Afrikaans and English ancestry going back to Jan van Riebeeck's Dutch settlement in the 1650s on the one side and the British 1820 Settlers on the other. Susanna's great-great-grandmother was a Miss Fick of Ficksburg, so she too came from a long lineage. Both sides of the family had slave and Bushman blood in their veins, but this had been diluted enough not to compromise them during apartheid.

All week, Kleinboet dealt with agronomy, viticulture and the financial and staffing matters of his farm, but at weekends he turned to his true passion – cooking and baking. He explored different culinary paths and traditions and was comfortable making both paella and goulash. The farm pantry was filled with preserves, jams, pickles, cured meats, biltong, sun-dried fruits, breads, biscuits and rusks. His collection of recipe books included Hildagonda Duckitt's famous contribution to South African cuisine, *Hilda's Diary of a Cape Housekeeper*, Hilda Gerber's *Traditional Cookery of the Cape Malays,* and various compilations of *You* and *Huisgenoot* recipes.

Earlier in the day, he'd prepared chicken and apricot *potjiekos*. This was delicately spiced with his own masala blend. It had been simmering for a few hours and was succulent, the meat falling from the bone. Closer to lunch, he'd braaied lamb chops and *boerewors*, along with *roosterkoek*.

Beers, Cokes, ciders and white wines were kept cold in a tin basin of ice in the shade. His own Merlots and Cinsauts were uncorked to breathe. There were jugs of freshly pressed watermelon juice and pitchers of water fragranced with slices of lemon and sprigs of lemon grass.

When the meats were done, the kitchen maids brought out *stywe pap*, *borrie geelrys*, potato and beetroot salads, *sousboontjies* and mango atjar. People ate slowly and enjoyed many helpings. They were on dessert – *melktert*, *malva poeding*, *poffertjies*, fruit salad and thick cream – when Kleinboet began talking about his new borehole.

One of his farm workers, an old Bushman, he explained, was a water diviner and rainmaker. He was too old to labour on the lands, but his skills with water were widely known.

'You know,' said Kleinboet, 'Riempie was born here on my land. He found all my borehole water. And now he's located this new water source, a strong underground river quite near the winery over there. We're pumping out nine thousand litres an hour. But the availability is twelve thousand, if I want that much. It seems to be a new river. Or one that has changed course, because in the past it was not apparent to him. Sometimes they do change their course, the underground rivers. I don't know why. It happens. Maybe there's a shift. Some movement.

'But not only can he divine where there's water, he can also make it rain. In the dry years, when I tell him I need rain, he calls it. The problem is just that no one has bothered to learn from this old boy. He's the last one. When he dies, it will all go with him. Then we'll be buggered. None of the youngsters want to learn. They only want cellphones. You can't make rain with cellphones!'

Kleinboet burst out laughing and reached for two bottles to top up glasses.

'Anyway, maybe you're interested in this. He can also make lightning strike. From a clear sky, from out of nowhere. From a sky just like this one today, he'll pull in clouds and damn well suck up lightning.'

'No. Surely you're teasing about the lightning,' said one of the guests. 'I mean, I can go with the rainmaking. And finding underground water. We've got diviners back home. But lightning? No. You're having us on, surely?'

'As true as God. I promise you. But, okay, let me demonstrate,' said Kleinboet and he told one of the maids to call Riempie from the compound.

Billy-Jean and Susanna exchanged knowing glances, aware they were in for a performance, for Kleinboet enjoyed provoking foreigners.

It was some time before a wizened old man presented himself. His face was etched by sun and the history of his ruined kinfolk. He had on his church clothes and shoes and walked slowly towards the homestead, leaning on his daughter's arm, and followed by a bunch of children, curious to know why the *Baas* had called him on a Sunday. Now, hat in hand, he and the children stood a little way off from the table. Kleinboet beckoned him and the children followed, glancing furtively at the table and its platters.'I want you to show these people, Mister Riempie, how you can make lightning. They are from England. And that *Baas* there is from America. They don't believe what goes on here.'

Then he turned to his guests and said: 'But first, if you really think he can't make lightning, then one of you must go stand under that tree over there. I'll ask him to strike it. If you think I'm fooling, have the courage of your disbelief.'

Silence fell around the table, followed by nervous laughter. No one stood up to test the diviner's skill or to challenge the farmer's claim.

'Okay then. Let me put the children under the tree,' said Kleinboet and he called out: '*Haai! Julle kinders! Staan onder daardie boom!*'

A hubbub ensued among the guests: 'No, please don't do that.'

'No. It's not necessary.'

'Are you mad?'

'For Pete's sake! Leave it be!'

Kleinboet laughed and said: 'You see! You people! You know he can make lightning, my little Riempie. You know that these leftover Bushmen have power, these few who still know what the old ones got up to.'

He took a bottle of beer out of the ice and tossed it to Riempie, saying: 'Off you go, man.'

Korrel, waatlemoen and fig *konfyt* were brought out and placed on the table with brie and camemberts, crackers, *soetkoekies* and the last of the *roosterkoek*.

'Would you have stood under the tree?' asked Connie, slicing into a cheese.

'Not on your *blerrie* life!' answered Kleinboet.

This was the first time Chester had eaten the bread and drunk wine at the table of people who'd kept apartheid vital in its time. He didn't feel uncomfortable with this, for apartheid was over, and his church picnics had prepared him, somewhat. 'How like us,' he'd thought. 'They eat the same kind of food that my mother and wife cook.' Then he judged the thought simplistic. Though he ate with pleasure and enjoyed the day, he was too reserved to enter into conversation, so he kept quiet and left it to

Connie. He felt particularly ill at ease with the discussion on lightning and the power of the rainmaker.

That night a massive bank of black clouds gathered and rolled in, like a line of gunners. A single lightning bolt struck the top branches of the fifth oak and it burst into flame. The clouds opened up and it began to pour. The unseasonal front moved to Cape Town and steady, unrelenting rain fell for two weeks. It was during this rainstorm that Graham Weir found the statue of the Virgin Mary outside the boarded-up Da Pasquale restaurant.

Part Two

Pearlie Theron had lived in Maynard Court from the second year of her employment and at the start of her eighteen-year-long affair with Thespian Winter. He owned the gracious two-storey Art Deco apartment block and she'd never had to pay rent.

Not until recently, that is. Not until that awful day, eight months before, when she'd arrived at work not knowing that her 'Camilla', as Mr Winter playfully called himself during certain of their love games, had been committed to Deerpark Retirement Home. She'd found the office lock secured and a letter, addressed to her, taped to the door.

It was from the attorneys Weinberg, Sonenburg & Sisulu, in Adderley Street, signed flamboyantly by Sisulu. It advised in blunt, uncaring legal jargon that Mr Winter had taken ill; that African-Sino Trading would be closed with immediate effect and its affairs wound up in due course; that her employment was at an end; that she would be paid a severance package to the value of six months' gross salary; that the credit cards in her name, but linked to Mr Winter's accounts, would be cancelled; that the company's contributions towards her medical aid and pension would no longer be paid; that she was never to make contact with the family of Mr Thespian Winter; and that her occupancy of number four Maynard Court would henceforth require rental. She was to call at the letting agent's office to pay a deposit and sign a lease agreement, just like any other tenant.

With handbag over her arm and key in hand, Pearlie

stood on the tiled landing of the fourth floor of Union Castle Building in St George's Street, at the door of the office she'd worked in for so many years, not knowing what to do.

Thespian had not visited her in the past three days because of Rosh Hashana and was only due to come to the office in two days' time. How odd, she'd thought to herself, standing there, that she had not sensed anything, that she hadn't had the least inkling that something was wrong. And how strange that he'd taken so unexpectedly and seriously ill, he who, at sixty years of age and despite a polio-weakened leg, could still make love like any old *bok* – albeit with a dose of Viagra.

Feeling numbed and feeble, she took the lift down and called a taxi on her cellphone. The wind came up and blew around her in a caress of sorts, as if to say it was not party to her new-found sorrow.

Back at the flat, she took off her office clothes and packed them away with a certain sense of resignation. Usually, after work she'd put on a gown or kaftan. Now, she just slipped her feet into heeled slippers and stood at the bedroom window, naked, not knowing how to dress for her new life. She looked out over the city, across the panorama within which the day unfolded towards noon and late afternoon. By nightfall, she was still there at the window, waiting for what she knew not. Only when she noticed the moon in the sky did she begin to cry. Her face relinquished its composure and the tears fell, soaking through the insufficient hanky with which she tried to mop them. She lay on the bed, still clutching the lawyer's letter, imagining that the Japanese poet Izumi Shikibu had, centuries before, written lines for this very moment:

My black hair tangled
as my own tangled thoughts.
I lie here alone
dreaming of one who has gone,
who stroked my hair till it shone.

Thespian Winter was the first South African importer to understand and make use of emerging Chinese export markets. Originally, he had imported fabrics, fine furnishings and chandeliers from London, New York, Rome, Paris, Prague and Berlin. Trading as African International, he had secured a name for himself in quality and unique design. In the early 1990s, while most importers, merchants and consumers still equated 'Made in China' with junk, he learnt of the Chinese drive to export to the West and seize world markets.

He took a few trips to China and, with the help of its government's competent trade mission, investigated a variety of manufacturing processes and shipment procedures. He found himself pleasantly surprised at the range and quality of products and decided to shift away from European brand names. He hired an excellent agent with offices in Beijing and Hong Kong. Changing his company name to African-Sino Trading, he began importing mock-plush of such high quality that it easily competed with what he had previously sold.

The Chinese merchants with whom he met and did business were courteous in an Old World sort of way, imparting an air of honesty and integrity to every transaction. Once they knew him, the need for signed contracts and irrevocable letters of credit fell away. His word was as good as a bank-guaranteed cheque. The merchants dispatched consignments promptly and he paid when the container was loaded on board ship. They were gentlemen, through and through. In all his years of dealing with China, not a single shipment was delayed, damaged or lost on the high seas, which is extraordinary given that about eighty thousand containers a year are said to fall off ships and float like icebergs.

These days, Thespian sold mock-everything to retailers at such good prices that even poor households could boast glassware, crockery and scatter cushions as fine as any designer goods and furnishings imported from Europe. On the Cape Flats, in shacks along the N1 highway and in the most overcrowded council flat in Plumstead could be found Melton, Wedgwood and Royal Doulton lookalikes.

He was a conscientious businessman, taking full responsibility for an order from when it was placed until it was delivered, unpacked and checked into his warehouse before removal to his clients' premises. The retailers he supplied could safely count on him and they respected him for this. At Christmas time, they sent him bottles of Scotch, boxes of chocolates, diaries and even complimentary stays at holiday resorts.

His wife didn't like this shift to the Chinese, declaring the goods cheap and embarrassing, so nothing from Thespian's various catalogues entered his family home. Pearlie, on the other hand, loved it in its entirety and liked nothing better than to watch the unpacking and processing of new samples as they arrived.

Pearlie had worked as Thespian Winter's personal assistant since 1988 and been his mistress since 1990, the year President FW de Klerk released Nelson Mandela from prison and set South Africa on an unambiguous road towards democracy.

The advertising and shortlisting for the job had been conducted by Live-Wire Employment Agency. The final interviewing of their three recommended candidates was done by Mrs Winter. Two of the girls were in their mid-twenties, well spoken, confident, capable and too pretty. By comparison, the third applicant, Pearlie Theron, aged thirty, though also competent and skilled, seemed unfashionable in the extreme. She arrived for her interview wearing a two-piece floral suit, a length of beads and a fifties-style hat with a raked-back brim. She held a clutch bag in one hand and an umbrella in the other, though there was no sign of rain. The suit made no attempt to conceal the weight her midriff carried; rather, it enhanced it. Her stockings were lamé and her heels too high, considering the fat legs, according to Mrs Winter's judgement, who later asked Ms Trudi Butler of the recruiting agency: 'Is she for real? Which ark has she stepped off?'

And yet, in the same breath, she realised that the interviewee's attire was perfectly in order, for it implied a non-threatening person. Non-threatening in the sense that Mr Winter couldn't possibly find her attractive.

Mrs Winter well knew the danger a secretary poses and how easy it can be for a little affair to develop, there in the tight proximity of desk and filing cabinet. In her opinion, a secretary shouldn't be pretty and lively, nor too interesting, nor exotic, nor coquettish, nor vivacious. Her salary shouldn't allow her to keep abreast with fashion, nor to have beauty treatments. She should be an automated cardboard cut-out with no personality whatsoever, one that switched on in the morning and off at night. Or the nearest human equivalent to this. This was why Mrs Winter always insisted on conducting the interviews for her husband's secretaries.

At the time of her job interview, Pearlie had been living in Cape Town for about three years, during which she'd held two secretarial jobs, the first with a medical doctor who'd moved his practice to Blouberg, to where she didn't want to commute. The second was with a manufacturer of duvets and pillows, where she developed an allergy to the fine, airborne particles of fibre filling. Both employers gave good references.

She had a letter from her *dominee* back in her hometown of Port Nolloth, advising that he'd known her since childhood and could vouch for her good, gentle nature. Her school certificates showed reasonable marks. She had a secretarial and office management diploma, which included bookkeeping, from a private business academy in Springbok. Her computer skills were said to be excellent, her integrity sound.

When Mrs Winter asked what her parents did, Pearlie replied that they were both 'late', that is, deceased. She was the youngest of six, a *laatlammetjie* who, because her parents were well on in years when she was born, had ended up being orphaned young and subsequently brought up by her oldest brother, Wolfie, and his wife, Madge. They were rather resentful and therefore hard on Pearlie, but not unloving.

Wolfie Theron had served in 32 Battalion. He'd seen and done some nasty things up in Namibia and Angola during South Africa's border war, where he'd become fluent in Portuguese, fighting with his fellow Defence Force Recces, alongside FNLA defectors and French and British mercenaries. Three-Two, as his battalion was operationally known, earned itself the name *Os Terríveis* – The Terrible Ones. At home, when Wolfie had too much to drink, if ever challenged over the most minor thing, he would rage and smash bottles and remind everyone that he could throttle a man with one hand. Locked in his gun cabinet, along with his regular weaponry, was an AK-47 and various items taken from dead enemy bodies, including a fetish made from human hair and bone. In the cabinet was also Wolfie's captured FNLA uniform and boots, his camouflage of those war days, the costume he occasionally longed to put on again and go blast away at black people.

Madge ran a gun shop. She was a strong woman who weathered all the nonsense that life and Wolfie dished up, and who could bottle jam or kill a pig with equal dexterity. Her hands and arms were scarred by kitchen burns and cuts, her face dried out through lack of care and her sense of femininity long shelved.

Wolfie and Pearlie's other brothers were in the 'diamond business'. This could have meant that they bought and sold gems illegally, but was supposed to mean that they were employed as divers by De Beers, the concession holder, to vacuum the seabed of its diamondiferous gravel.

Wolfie got himself into some illicit deal and was killed, shot dead and dumped at the side of the road just outside Port Nolloth, unable to defend himself against the mafia mobsters who wanted him out the way. The other brothers continued with the work, anchoring their boat in view of the shore and diving into the cold Atlantic water, clad in wetsuits and goggles and breathing through air pipes. The gravel they vacuumed up was sorted on board into large and small, bagged and taken ashore. There, in a secure shed, the gravel, which effectively belonged to De Beers, was further sorted for its diamond yield.

Theirs was a hard, dangerous life for which payment was erratic. They were supposed to receive half the value of the retrieved diamonds, but were certain that they were being cheated. They, in their turn, would spirit away whatever precious rock they could and then sell it on the black market. The dream of finding a huge gem that would allow them to hang up the pipes drove them hard. Mostly, they'd all be sucked up, much like that gravel, and spat out when De Beers suspended their search for diamonds along that stretch of coast. When that happened, the Theron brothers' livelihood was cut, for they were skilled at nothing else.

Pearlie disclosed none of these details of her background to Mrs Winter.

Even so, her full name, Elsie Geertruida Theron, had, in Mrs Winter's judgement, the resonance of a poor white.

The instructions she gave the new secretary, if summed up, were to devote herself to the job and to oversee Mr Winter's office meals.

'I want you to order his lunch every day from Maxi's. They'll deliver,' she told Pearlie. 'They do healthy lunches. He'll ask you for all sorts of unhealthy things. But you must just get him soup and a wholewheat roll. Or a pita with filling. If he wants, you can get him grilled chicken or fish from Café Bon Bon. But no red meat. He has enough of that at home. And he needs to cut down on coffee, so give him decaf. I don't know what to do about his cigarettes. Oh, and every morning make him a cup of green tea. And there must be a jug of filter water on his desk. And also cut down on his chocolates. He'll send you out for chocolates.'

She rattled off this list like the fabric-care instructions on a garment label, ending with: 'I don't want to come into the office. I'm too busy. I really have too much to do. I'm leaving it all up to you and hope you do better than the last stupid girl. I don't want him stressed. See? He has a problem with angina and there's a history of heart trouble in his family, if you need to know. He must take it easy.'

Once Pearlie and Thespian became lovers, Mrs Winter's instructions fell by the wayside. Pearlie then ordered lunch takeaways from Mesopotamia, Butcher's Grill and Bella Napoli. The office kitchenette was well stocked with treats.

Their affair began without intention or design, developing slowly and with caution. In fact, it almost never happened, because Pearlie had started looking for another job, recognising that there was no prospect for growth where she was. It was lonely in the office, just her, the boss and the warehouse boys. Days would go by when he hardly spoke beyond dictating letters.

At home, Mrs Winter had been going on and on for days about some trivia. When Thespian got back from work each evening, he'd be met by her near-hysterical carryings-on. She'd been decorating the house and arguing endlessly with the painter and the people retiling the pool. Then she'd had a minor car scrape with her 4x4 while manoeuvring into a parking bay. She'd got into a fearful dispute with the other driver, whom she blamed, though the fault was hers. The new au pair was proving to be unreliable and, to add to this, a waiter had phished her credit card. Before she noticed, thirty thousand rands' worth of computer equipment had been bought with it.

The tensions escalated and she kept throwing them at Mr Winter as though everything was his fault. One night he shouted that he'd had enough, that he couldn't cope with this domestic frenzy on top of his business pressures. He wanted to leave then and there, to go to a hotel, just for some silence. He picked up the car keys and was about to storm out, but felt a pain in his heart and went to lie down.

The next week, standing next to Pearlie at her desk and looking at a pricing sheet, Thespian had brushed against her. Her soft curls touched the back of his hand and his arm sensed her skin under the blouse. Like a match striking flame, something very small and warm ignited. Something pressed him against her soft, generous breasts. Something brought her arms around him and held him. Something drew their lips together. He had thought: 'What am I doing?' and the same question had come to her mind.

If ever they were to be asked 'How did it begin?' neither would be able to say. Except he might offer: 'I needed comfort. That was all. In the beginning. I felt alone. Even though married, I was lonely. I wanted to be held. My wife never holds me. She's not interested in what I do. I smell of cigarettes. I suffer from gout and angina. I have haemorrhoids. See this gammy leg? I'm not much fun, you know. And nothing to look at.'

The affair developed despite the safety nets Mrs Winter believed were in place. Thespian was a little uneasy with the infidelity, for he'd taken his marriage vows with sincerity. He thought it best to lay down certain terms. These were the fairly amateurish provisos of a simple, platonic, no-strings-attached sexual liaison that had no long-term future to it. He and Pearlie wouldn't go out in public, obviously. They would meet at her apartment in Claremont once or twice a week and he would have his wife believe he was working late. There were to be no demands for commitment and Pearlie should not initiate contact with his family. If any of his family phoned or came to the office, she was to deal with them in a purely professional manner and not become familiar.

In return for Miss Theron's sexual favours, he would give her an additional cash allowance, not reflected on her salary slip and therefore not taxable. He would also give her a credit card for any reasonable little extras she might need.

Pearlie slipped into the stereotypical role of mistress and her social life diminished. She drifted away from her circle of girlfriends and stopped going to her book club. Alone, she went to the fortnightly Sunday markets at Kirstenbosch and the various springtime church bazaars. It could safely be said that she had no real friends, if a friend is one in whom you confide and who knows that you are living an unfulfilled life, waiting for your lover to divorce and commit to you. She was no different from other mistresses in believing that, in the end, she would get the goods, that she would get her man. So she'd fantasise about strolling the promenade together, sitting somewhere for a coffee and croissant, greeting his friends, occasionally stopping to talk, being introduced as his life partner.

Sitting in her *salottino*, in the dim of an early evening, she might play a game of patience, waiting for her lover's phone call. On her table might be a basket laden with seductive fruit – a *cesto di frutta* – grapes and bananas and apples and watermelon slices, plucked at dawn in a garden near Eden, voluptuously placed, in pastel colours, symbolic of so much tenderness.

It crossed her mind that Thespian might simply be using her, as previous men had done, for she seemed to attract only married ones who had no long-term vision where she was concerned. She imagined that his lack of commitment was a religious matter and that it might be easier if she herself were Jewish. Perhaps then the status quo would change and fortune smile upon her.

One day, when opening and sorting the office mail, she read about the Claremont Congregation's Jewish

Emphasis Week and the start of a new term in Hebrew lessons. She phoned and enrolled for evening classes in Beginner Hebrew Intensive – four lessons a week, for four weeks.

The teacher was a young student rabbi who was working a short stint as a kosher slaughterer and giving private lessons to supplement his income. He was a rather arrogant Israeli, born in Tel Aviv of South African Jewish parents who had emigrated there in the early 1970s. He'd avoided compulsory conscription into the Israeli army by taking the rabbinical route. Pearlie had never seen an orthodox Jew and was intrigued by his ringlets and by the fact that he made it clear, as he introduced himself, that she was not to touch him.

At the first class, one on one, Pearlie learnt with shock that Hebrew had its own dedicated alphabet that ran, along with its pages, from right to left. For some reason, she'd imagined Hebrew to be similar to Afrikaans. It took only two lessons for her to realise that the language was beyond her capabilities. She told her teacher this, forfeiting that month's tuition, which she'd paid in advance.

He mentioned that she might find things easier among the Reform Jews, where converts tended to go. At least the services weren't conducted exclusively in Hebrew, but had a measure of English to them. She went along to the Green Point Temple Israel, but there felt awkward and unwelcome. No one had stepped forward and taken her by the hand, into the bosom of the religion, as they do at charismatic Christian churches. She never went again.

Perhaps it would be sufficient to make her apartment Jewish, she thought. From Beinkinstadt, the Jewish shop on the edge of District Six, and on the advice of its kindly coloured shop assistant, who seemed depressed but who knew an awful lot about Judaism, she bought a *mezuzah* for the front door, a set of Shabbat candles, a platter for Passover and a menorah. She also bought the books *Shabbat for Beginners*, *Judaism for Dummies* and *The Kosher Home in Ten Easy Steps*.

But these practical titles were of little use as they also required understanding of that terrifying, backward-moving alphabet. So she just placed them on her sideboard with the other Hebraic artefacts, as a display of good intention.

In those early days of the affair she tried hard to get things right for Shabbat. She'd drive to Goldie's in Sea Point and buy fresh challah, chopped herring and gefilte fish, as well as two portions of lamb with vegetables. But Thespian seldom stayed for this carefully presented kosher meal. They hadn't yet learnt how to refine the details of their time together. He'd see the table set for two, with the food on the warmer tray, and feel bad. Later she'd eat alone and finish off the wine as she watched a soapie, while the Shabbat candles burned down forlornly.

Though Thespian didn't want to lose her as his secretary, he thought it best to undo the sexual liaison and began so by saying: 'No. Yours doesn't need to be a Jewish home. I'll put up the *mezuzah*, but there's no need, really. Don't struggle with all this.'

He planned to come less often and finally not at all. But it was like giving up cigarettes: the only way to do it is just to stop, and he couldn't. The comfort of Miss Theron's thighs, her non-demanding nature, the way she allowed his lovemaking to proceed a little further than he was used to at home – all these he couldn't end.

In truth, Pearlie was not entirely Gentile. There was a drop of Jewish blood in her veins, but this had not reached her through a matrilineal route, as was required to be of any use in orthodox terms.

Somewhere in her ancestry, there had been a Jewish *smous* who drove a wagon from Port Elizabeth into the hinterland beyond the British frontier. He had traded pots and pans, copper thread, beads and even powder and bullets with the amaXhosa, bringing back exotic skins and ivory which he sold for high prices, for their value far exceeded what he'd paid for them. For a while, his forays into the native territories of Kaffraria and British Kaffraria were stopped by trade fairs instituted by the British, in an attempt to control all trade. But these lasted only a few years and he was soon back to his long, lonely trips.

Instead of marrying a good Jewish woman, for there was none to be found, he had chosen a Dutch *jongedochter*, Anna Hilletje van der Heiden, and so broke the matrilineal line through which Jewish heritage would have reached his descendants.

Their eldest daughter, Adriana, had also wed into a Dutch family, the Van den Boschs. From there, the marriage lines went through the Cloetes, Botmas and De Wets until they reached the Therons in Port Nolloth, where Elsie Geertruida was born. She was named after her great-grandmother but was affectionately called Pearlie because, as a baby, her little face was round and white – 'just like a pearl', her brother Wolfie had told her.

About a year and a half into the relationship, just as Thespian made his decision to end the affair, Pearlie was given notice to vacate her flat in Blythewood, and an apartment in one of the blocks Thespian owned, Maynard

Court, became vacant. This was a top-floor, three bedroomed, generously proportioned place with a lounge–dining room and a balcony. It came with a lock-up garage and storeroom.

Thespian offered it to Pearlie, and from this point the affair changed from perfunctory to wondrous, from banal to cinematographic. The palimpsest of their original story was effaced to make room for the new.

Thespian allowed Pearlie time off to move while he was on an extended business trip. It would be some months before he called on her in her new home, and only when everything was in place. He gave her a generous amount of money to pay for the flat's redecoration and to stay at a nearby bed-and-breakfast during renovations. She'd never known the pleasure of fixing up a place without concern for money. But, whereas Mrs Winter, who lived in such ease, never put limits on her own spending, Pearlie didn't take advantage of Thespian's generosity. She shopped around, looked for bargains, drew from African-Sino's warehouse and was not too proud to buy second-hand.

She liked the Art Deco look of the apartment, with its brass taps and deep porcelain kitchen sink, so she did not modernise as such. The wallpaper was stripped, the bathtub re-enamelled and missing tiles replaced. The floors of both kitchen and bathroom were resurfaced and patterned with mosaics of coloured glass and mirror. She chose lime green, pink, purple, crimson, turquoise and orange for the walls of the various rooms.

The *bont* 1960s carpeting was lifted and the parquet flooring sanded and waxed. The window lintels and door frames were stripped of layers of paint and the wood sealed in matt varnish so its lines and knots were exposed. She had a Michaelis art student paint a trompe l'œil in the kitchen. The balcony was partially enclosed and a wall fountain in the shape of a conch installed. Overhead beams were secured from which hung a plastic grape vine, heavy with realistic bunches. A few fake birds and butterflies were strategically positioned and a line of Caltex oil cans, planted with aloes, were placed along the balcony wall.

Despite having been brought up in the Dutch Reformed faith with its stark Calvinism, Pearlie delighted in Catholic iconography. She bought three cast-iron crosses at the Dorp Store in Roeland Street, framed pictures of the Madonna from the Catholic Bookshop and some wooden rosaries from a Zimbabwean outside Spar. In the bathroom, alongside a group of mirrors, she hung a photo of the Voortrekker monument and a watercolour of a trek-wagon pulled by a span of oxen across a hot plain, with a violent-red aloe adding heat to the day.

Number four Maynard Court was transformed into a melange of Art Nouveau, Art Deco, retro and chic. The atmosphere consolidated around all things Latinate – Catholic, Mexican, Italian, Portuguese and Spanish – setting the stage for a life of such temperaments. The table would be bare wood, as in a trattoria, the meals rich with béchamel, seafoods, ragout and pasta. Flowers would be plonked into an empty olive-oil tin, not purposefully arranged. A glass bowl would be filled with chillies just for the scarlet and green of them, or with sweet potatoes alongside pineapples for their mix of purple and yellow. The Jewish handbooks were put away and forgotten.

On Thespian's first visit, he had the distinct feeling of entering the bold colouration of a new world, one not quite real. It prompted thoughts of sailing ships driven by trade winds, of hot ocean currents and maps that had been long lost. Thereafter, the more often he visited, the more he uncovered sides within himself that had been concealed, as though the maps were guides to forgotten aspects of his own personality. The colours Pearlie had chosen, the way she placed things and her eclectic collection of this and that gave him an artistic confidence he hadn't experienced before. The domestic ambience overflowed with precisely the bounty that his own home, under his wife's curatorship, did not display.

He reflected that, as a child, he'd played the violin. 'I want to play again,' he told Pearlie. 'I want to play the fiddle. Not those awful scales, but gypsy. I want to play gypsy and Irish.'

In those days, Max Peyer still had a string instrument workshop not far from the flat. One Saturday morning, Pearlie bought a violin and some sheet music. Thespian started to play, not too well at first, but certainly able to express melancholy and vivacity.

He found that touching and sorting Pearlie's clothes and underwear gave him pleasure, so he took over the task of keeping her cupboards and drawers in order, calling himself the 'wardrobe mistress'. One day, after making love, he put on Pearlie's kaftan. It smelt of her and made him feel strangely beautiful, though to an outsider he would have looked perfectly ridiculous, what with his moustache, the thin line of his beard, and his hairy arms. The silk of the garment against his body stirred long-lost childhood sensualities. He'd been his mother's last child, a fifth boy. She hadn't cut his hair until he was seven, tying it back with ribbons. She'd dressed him in frilled shirts and velvet breeches. The feel of those fabrics, of lace against his face, of tumbling, heavy curls and of perfume were synonymous with his mother's love. But they were all put aside when his hair was cut short and his clothes changed for his first day of school and his entrance into the real, harsh, masculine world of his father.

Now, in number four Maynard Court, where happiness and sexual pleasure would bloom like algae in a warm pond, his penchant for wearing women's clothes revealed itself. He filled a wardrobe with girly things – nightgowns, frilly dresses, camisoles, petticoats, stockings, garters and a purse full of his own cosmetics.

Often, when Thespian visited Pearlie, he'd slip on a frock and little bobby socks with Turkish slippers, a length of beads, earrings and lace gloves. She called him Camilla and he sometimes called her Frida, after Frida Kahlo, the Mexican artist, because of the colours Pearlie loved and her strong eyebrows.

He had a perfume blended by Jean Southey of Bishopscourt, a specialist importer of essential oils. This heavenly mix of geranium, rose and bergamot became his and Pearlie's signature fragrance. Because they both smelt the same, he never brought home, on his collar, the fragrance of another woman, and so their affair was never detected through olfactory exposure.

When Mrs Winter remarked on his shift away from his regular brands, he explained that because these fragrances had been synthesised, and were now sold cheaply at the Parade, every second man on the street smelt of Calvin Klein or Dolce & Gabbana.

While Thespian expressed a creative side through wearing feminine clothing and playing the violin, Pearlie allowed her passion for hats to develop. She'd always worn them and her early ones were cheap copies of those that the wives of apartheid-era politicians flamboyantly donned. Archival photographs testify to the extravagant millinery creations worn to the openings of Parliament and other grand occasions by, for example, former president PW Botha's wife, Elize.

The media ridiculed them, describing them variously as cupcakes, pork-pies, meringue peaks, watermelon halves and other such derisive names.

In later years, Winnie Mandela's hats and turbans would also be mocked, and cartoonists had a field day with them. Not one of those journalists and magazine columnists saw the art in the millinery pieces. But art forms they definitely were.

In the early 2000s Pearlie came across the website of the famed Spanish hat-maker extraordinaire Cristina de Prada. From that point her hats stepped up from mere copies of ostentatious pieces to valuable collectors' items.

Once a quarter, Pearlie ordered something new, emailing Cristina certain key words that would find life fashioned from a variety of materials. The key words had to do with what was current in Pearlie's life at the time. When she and Thespian were reading Oscar Wilde's *Lady Windermere's Fan*, this inspired a hat created around a peacock's spread tail. Vivaldi's *Four Seasons* led to a mini top hat decorated with fruit; *Out of Africa* to a zebra-skin-patterned fedora with a band of beads; *Summer in Baden-Baden* to a broad-brimmed explosion of ostrich feathers; and *The Great Gatsby* to an elegant cloche graced with a scarlet flying bird.

Cristina de Prada's creations were unique. On completion, they were wrapped in tissue, placed in a dedicated box, insured and dispatched by courier from Barcelona. Thespian had a special cupboard made for them.

One day, Thespian presented Pearlie with a book of Shakespeare's sonnets and these they began reading to each other, their favourite being the Ninety-first, which they came to know by heart, in common with so many of the world's lovers. He introduced her to *Twelfth Night* and *Measure for Measure* and from then on Shakespeare filled their lives. Henrietta Dax at Clarke's Bookshop sourced antiquarian editions for Thespian, all leather bound and gilt edged, and he built up a considerable collection.

He ordered DVDs of all the BBC productions of and about Shakespeare and installed a large plasma screen in the bedroom. They'd watch these over and over again, coming to know whole tracts by heart, able to recite alongside Sir Laurence Olivier and Dame Judi Dench, peppering their own everyday speech with Shakespearean expression. They also began gathering volumes of love poetry and would recite words translated from Japanese, Indian, Chinese, Latin and ancient Greek masters of erotic description.

Within Maynard Court's warm embrace, their world was directed by everything theatrical and life was celebrated with exuberance. Sealed away, their love and intimacy deepened. Beyond the walls, they behaved with decorum. Should ever they have walked past each other in the street, he would have raised his hat and she would have nodded back. He might have enquired after her well-being as a caring boss would of his secretary. At the office they behaved as a sedate working team. He was Mr Winter, the proprietor, and she was Miss Theron, his secretary and personal assistant.

Sometimes he was gruff, sometimes he ignored her and now and then he shouted. Occasionally, he used the same tone towards her as he used with the warehouse packers. But that was all work mode and they were comfortable with it. It was entirely professional at African-Sino Trading, as it should be.

Thespian was inspired to propose to Pearlie in their second year together, after they'd watched *Gone with the Wind*.

From Atkinson's Antiques, next door to Clarke's Bookshop, he bought four items: a 1940s-era diamond engagement ring, its jewel held in a high, claw setting, with a matching wedding band; an Edwardian diamond pendant with chain; and a bracelet.

The linked chain bracelet, also an Edwardian piece, was fashioned in red gold. It was as light as air because each link was hollow, as were the clasp and two gold lucky beans attached to it. Created in India by the jewellers Hamilton & Co. of Calcutta, the bracelet lay in its original velvet-lined blue box.

That evening, he had come to the flat after his supper at home. He opened Pearlie's door just a bit and extended an arm so that all she saw was an arrangement of chrysanthemums and carnations. This he held there for a moment before following it in with a 'Tra-la-la!'

She was sitting on the couch, barefoot, having just eaten a mozzarella, pesto and tomato sandwich, and now drinking a glass of rosé, listening to Michael Bolton singing various operatic arias. Thespian went down on one knee. He took her drink and put it aside, saying: 'Drink to me only with thine eyes, and I will pledge with mine. Or leave a kiss but in the cup, and I'll not look for wine.'

With a shy smile, he continued: 'If ever any beauty I did see, which I desired, and got, it was but a dream of thee,

Pearlie. Will you marry me? In the only way we can do it? In our own privacy? In this little Mexican world of ours? Will you be my beloved wife, to have and to hold until death do us part?' And here he slipped the diamond ring onto her finger, while Bolton's voice, with Donizetti's '*Una furtiva lagrima*,' confirmed '*si può morir d'amore*' – one can die of love.

She started to cry, for here were the goods, here was her man, asking for her hand. She was not destined to be an ordinary mistress after all. He took her in his arms and wiped her tears, then kissed a cheek, quoting: 'I can express no greater sign of love than this kind kiss.'

He instructed her to sort out a wedding dress and for this she went to Second Time Around, where she bought four antique wedding gowns, one Italian, three made in London. They were all a medium size.

'Are you a collector?' asked the owner, Brenda Scarratt, recognising that her customer was too large to fit any of them. And for what would she want four dresses, otherwise?

'No,' replied Pearlie. 'I'm getting married, I want to get these all undone and then sewn up into one dress. I like the old material and lace. I want a big dress with a huge skirt because my wedding will be very small.'

'Oh, really?'

'Yes. It will just be me and my groom.'

'No friends or anyone?'

'No.'

'Are you from out of town?'

'No. We live here. I used to be from out of town. From Port Nolloth. Past Springbok. But not any more.'

'So, why no guests?'

'Just because,' said Pearlie, examining a pair of elbow-length gloves.

A little confused but not wanting to probe, Brenda wrapped each dress in tissue and placed it in a dedicated box, saying: 'I know just the person to do this for you, the fashion designer Jessica Aronson. Her studio's in the Dean Street Arcade, in Newlands. I always send people to her who buy antique garments that need alteration or reworking. She understands how to treat old fabric and is amazingly creative.'

Jessica was delighted by the challenge. She set two apprentices to unpick the four dresses and painstakingly salvage each bead and button, each piece of lace, each hand-embroidered panel, each scalloped segment, until eventually two work tables had laid upon them the exquisite components of the bridal gowns, all slightly hued by time and so no longer pure white. These the apprentices washed by hand in lukewarm water. Jessica had learnt from Brenda Scarratt that the best way to wash antique material was to build up a lather with a bar of Sunlight soap, and to gently squeeze this through the cloth, before rinsing and drying, allowing for a short time in the sun to whiten it.

From these pieces Jessica fashioned a wedding gown with a beaded, drop-sleeve bodice and a generously layered skirt. She advised Pearlie to buy a marcasite headband and to have her hairdresser create a coiffure of loose curls, instead of wearing a veil. She made Pearlie two sets of silk underwear, reminiscing that as a young student designer she had started out making these: 'I've a friend called Romaney. She runs Romana Florist in Long Street. She was my first real customer. I used to sew up the sweetest undies for her and that's when I got to love lace. It developed into a passion for antique fabric.'

On Jessica's recommendation, Pearlie bought silver stilettos and silk stockings. As a gift, Jessica made her a bridal purse from a piece of Kashmiri embroidery.

By chance, Jessica was one of the designers Mrs Winter frequented. Some days after Pearlie had collected her dress, Mrs Winter came in for a fitting.

'It's the strangest thing, Mrs Winter,' Jessica told her client. 'I've got this new customer. A dear, sweet lady. I've just made her wedding dress. She's overweight and not conventionally attractive. But really nice. You know, you'd like her to be your auntie, that sort of person. Anyway, she brought me such an exciting project. She had four antique wedding dresses, which she wanted made up into one. I thought she was going to have a huge wedding, she was spending so much on the dress – we took hours unpicking them, even before I started on the design. But she told me there would be no guests. It would be just her and her groom. That's what she called him. My groom. So old-fashioned.

'Well, she told me he's already married and they're going to have a private ceremony, giving rings and saying promises. And then have a little banquet. Isn't that different?'

'Not really,' said Mrs Winter, not at all interested, glancing at her image in the mirrors – front and side.

'She has an awful lot of money,' continued Jessica, turning to her sketch pad, rethinking her interpretation for Mrs Winter's svelte figure. 'Of course, I don't ask people about their private lives. But it just comes up in conversation. You know how it is? People chat away. She said she's her lover's secretary. He gives her everything she wants. He's some rich Jewish importer. She has no limit on the credit cards. Fancy that.'

'Yes, fancy,' replied Mrs Winter, changing the subject back to her own interests. 'Actually, can you rather give cuffs to the sleeves? Deep ones. With three buttons covered in the same fabric. I think that will look showy.'

Weeks later, Jessica pinned, above her work table, a photo of Pearlie in her dress, at her last fitting. She felt it was the most beautiful garment she'd ever designed. But though Mrs Winter glanced at it, she didn't recognise the face, for her image of Pearlie remained one of plainness.

Thespian had a new tuxedo made, not by his regular tailor, but by a Muslim in Wynberg, a man who had been in the trade all his life, as had his father and grandfather before him. In these days of off-the-peg, ready-to-wear suits, specialist tailors struggled to make a living. There were always politicians and mining and crime magnates. But this particular tailor had not secured such high-flying clientele. He kept bread on his family's table by making brightly coloured satin suits for the Cape Minstrels' end-of-year parade, so he was overjoyed to be making a suit for Mr Winter.

Pearlie and Thespian had to wait some months before they could marry. For her birthday, Thespian gave Mrs Winter a week away at The Hydro in Stellenbosch and told her he would take a business trip at the same time. Their children would be under the care of au pairs and nannies.

Two days before the wedding, on the Wednesday, a personal decorator serviced and prepared the flat. She set the table – in keeping with the décor – with a royal-blue tablecloth, yellow crockery, crystal and silverware. On the Thursday, two generous creations, ordered by Thespian, were delivered by Romana Florist – white lilies, white agapanthus, white daisies, white chincherinchee and crimson roses, as well as a small bridal bouquet for Pearlie of forget-me-not and baby's breath.

Pearlie spent all of Friday morning at House of Hair & Beauty just down the road, where everyone knew about her special moment but not the name of her lover. They knew he was married and rich and Jewish, but that was all. Over the years she had never once let slip any further information, though they teased and prodded and cajoled and tried to guess.

Her beautician, Abigail, had waxed and creamed her, and her hairdresser, Tiara, a biker in her leisure time, had forfeited the first day of the Buffalo Rally just to be there for Pearlie.

'Don't worry!' she'd reassured her favourite client. 'I'll catch them up. They're staying two nights in Knysna. As soon as I've done your hair, I'll set off. All my kit's packed.'

Tiara created a fanciful mop of curls, as suggested by Jessica, and sprinkled these with a little glitter. Abigail did her make-up. While she was giving the last touch of colour, an old man arrived at the door with a rucksack full of plaster of Paris ornaments – angels, moons, stars and suns. Tiara bought two angels and later explained that he was a pensioner and big-time boozer, struggling to make ends meet. Somewhere in their design history the angels had been copied from a Botticelli, but they reflected none of that artist's delicate touch.

'Okay, darling. You enjoy your wedding,' said Tiara, handing over the angels and a ribboned parcel. 'This is from all of us.'

It was a small musical box. When its lid was lifted, a

ballerina twirled round and round to a tinny rendition of Johann Strauss's *Blue Danube*.

Pearlie got home in time for the delivery, by Lindy Levy Caterers, of the wedding meal, the menu for which was not quite classic, but drawn up by Pearlie according to the things she and Thespian particularly enjoyed. The platters were placed in the kitchen and would just need heating, later that evening. The small, two-tiered iced cake had arrived by courier from Johannesburg the week before. This had been baked by Carol Bosch, a friend of Madge, Pearlie's sister-in-law, who made cakes for every Theron wedding. Madge believed that Charlize Theron, the movie star, was distantly related to them, and was certain Carol would one day bake a wedding cake for her too.

Pearlie had ordered her cake 'on behalf of a work colleague'. It was the real thing, rich with dried fruit, nuts and cherries, poured over with brandy and covered with a layer of marzipan. Over each tier was spread a tablecloth of white royal icing, decorated with tiny, delicate roses, violets and lily of the valley, all made of sugar. Carol had sourced a 1920s porcelain model of a bride and groom, and this was wrapped in tissue, waiting to be placed on top.

At four-thirty, Little Dove, one of the Chinese waitresses from the Lotus Tavern, came to help Pearlie dress. Little Dove did up the small buttons running down the back of the gown, secured the marcasite headband in Pearlie's curls and put the silver stilettos on her feet. When the bride was ready, Little Dove went back to the docks. She would return later by taxi to serve the wedding feast.

Perfumed and beautiful, Pearlie sat on her sofa, waiting for her betrothed, who arrived at six o'clock on the dot, in his tuxedo, with a boutonnière on the lapel. He wore boots of Spanish leather, with a slight heel, inspired by one of Bob Dylan's songs. He'd taken a room for the day at the stamping ground of his bachelor days, the Mount Nelson Hotel. There he'd showered, shaved and changed. A hired limousine with tinted windows delivered him to his wedding.

He tapped three times to announce his arrival and then let himself in, locking the door and the outside world behind him. When he saw Pearlie sitting there, utterly beautiful, his heart gave a tweak of pain and he had to take a deep breath.

Some of her critics of later years, had they seen Pearlie on her wedding night, might have said, cruelly, that she looked like a cream puff or a pile of candy floss. In fact, she looked amazing, with her cheeks aglow, her bosom heaving, her eyes sparkling like all the stars of heaven, the fabulous fabrics of her bridal skirt hugely layered about her. If anything, she could be likened to a giant, highly perfumed, erotic jungle blossom.

Her husband-to-be, in sartorial elegance, walked straight up to her and bowed, in imitation of Crown Prince Rudolf, played by Charles Boyer in *Mayerling*, as he addressed Baroness Marie Vetsera. Stretching out his hand, he helped Pearlie to her feet. The centre of the room had been cleared of its coffee table and, in this space, they made their marriage promises. Before leaving, Little Dove had lit incense and candles – tall, white, cathedral types – and these imparted an authentic, Catholic touch.

They'd both learnt by heart their simple lines, composed by Pearlie, with a little help from *Marriage Vows for the Non-Conventional*. These they now recited for the first time, though they'd say them each night thereafter (Thespian into his pillow, when in Mrs Winter's bed) before falling asleep.

'I, Thespian *Camilla* Winter ...'
'And I, Pearlie *Frida* Theron ...'

Here each smiled broadly, before continuing in tandem:

'Do promise
To love and cherish
You, my Beloved
My Sun
My Moon
My Star
My everything
From this day forward
Forever and a day.'

Pearlie recited three lines from *Romeo and Juliet*: 'My bounty is boundless as the sea, my love as deep. The more I give to Thee, the more I have, for both are infinite.' Thespian replied with the full Sonnet 18, 'Shall I compare thee to a summer's day? Thou art more lovely and more temperate', before taking from his pocket the jewellery he'd bought at Atkinson's Antiques.

He placed the wedding band upon her finger, above the engagement ring, saying: 'So smile the heavens upon this holy act.' Then he clasped the bracelet onto her wrist and, finding his way through her curls, placed the chain with diamond pendant about her neck.

Pearlie gave Thespian a ring fashioned by Mike Cope. This held an amethyst in a fleur-de-lis setting. Inside the band was engraved *Forever Yours, Pearlie* and the date. With reverence, Thespian said: 'I now pronounce us man and wife: Mr and Mrs Pearlie Theron, of Vredehoek, in Cape Town.'

From that night, whenever he visited, he would take off

the ring of his legal wedding and put on that of his true love. There was a porcelain bowl in the entrance hall that they called the Situational Bowl and in this one or other of the rings was kept.

Little Dove returned from the Lotus Tavern, dressed in black with a white apron, to serve the wedding feast. The bride and groom sat at table and she began, first uncorking various wines and then bringing through the entrée of shrimps with cashew nut sauce. This was followed by butternut soup with a blob each of basil pesto and sour cream. The fish course was grilled hake and calamari with lime and ginger served beside crisp potato wedges. Then came veal piquant with fragrant basmati rice, accompanied by a tomato, rocket and chive salad sprinkled with roasted seeds and dressed in olive oil and balsamic reduction. The palates were sweetened and the meal concluded with Lindy Levy's special cheesecake. This cheesecake, most often described as sublime, had found its way from fifteenth-century Spain to Eastern Europe and then to Africa on the wings of the Jewish Diaspora, its recipe handed from mother to daughter and never disclosed outside of the family. Rumour has it that gold bullion was once offered for its alchemical formula but not accepted, such was the gustatory value of the recipe. The term 'to die for', though now a cliché, first surfaced at the Sedgefield Market, where Lindy sold slices to connoisseurs who thought that death by this cheesecake far surpassed that by chocolate.

The marriage feast went on until midnight, without haste. The portions were moderate, so there was no gluttony. Even so, Pearlie and Thespian ate and drank until they almost burst. Then they retired to the couch for wedding cake and coffee. In the background, completing the ambience, not too loud and on repeat, a CD of

Celedonio Romero and his son Celin played exquisite classical guitar.

Pearlie's gift to Thespian was a ceremonial Mogul dagger. Its ram's-head-shaped hilt and scabbard were studded with semi-precious stones. It was with this that he cut the cake, slicing through the icing with its razor-sharp blade and allowing Pearlie to make her secret wish.

Later, the figurine of bride and groom, together with the precious dagger, musical box and plaster angels, would take centre place in a ball-and-claw display cabinet. This Thespian had bought from his father-in-law's second-hand furniture store, having it stripped of varnish to reveal the fine oak wood beneath.

Throughout the night, Little Dove had served silently and almost invisibly, moving between the dining table and the kitchen, loading the dishwasher as she went along, and wrapping leftovers so the kitchen remained orderly.

To ensure confidentiality, Thespian had left for her, propped among the tea caddies, an overly generous envelope of two thousand rand. This she tucked in her pocket, then closed the kitchen, gave a sweet smile and little wave, and went out to her taxi. All Thespian would have to do next day, shooing Pearlie out of the kitchen, was switch on the dishwasher and later pack everything away.

'I cannot bear for you to take off this dress, Pearlie,' said Thespian, following her through to the bedroom, undoing his tie, hanging up his jacket. 'You look so very beautiful. I could leave you like that till the end of my days. It would be sufficient to gaze upon you and no one else.'

'No. We must work a plan, my darling,' she said, lifting the voluminous skirt, somehow flicking off her silk undies and stockings without falling over, and manoeuvring herself onto the bed.

He found the silk garter at the top of her thigh and, in keeping with wedding lore, took it in his teeth and gently pulled it down her leg and over her soft foot.

They made love with him on top, the skirt hoisted up just enough for contact and penetration. To an onlooker, the skirt might have seemed like a cloud borne on her tummy and upon which he floated.

They fell asleep like that. Sometime in the early hours he got up to fetch a shawl and to gaze at her lovely face under the moonlight streaming in through the open window.

Thus, Thespian had made the easy move from adulterer to bigamist.

Next morning, he prepared tea and brought it through with slices of wedding cake and cheesecake. They each took a headache powder and he chewed an antacid tablet. He handed her a leather folio containing gold and platinum share certificates and an endowment policy and said: 'I never want you to feel dependent on or beholden to me.'

Then he undid the many buttons and they made love again, naked this time, like two smooth, sweating whales, before he ran the bath, adding lavender and vitamin E oil. Sitting on a leather stool, barely containing his happiness while his bride soaked in the hot water, Thespian reflected on his pleasant fortune. Her eye make-up was smudged and her hair tangled, but this did not detract from the beauty he saw.

They spent two days in the flat, listening to music and finishing off what was left of the food. Thespian had bought a volume of love poems, which they worked their way through. They elected Byron's 'She Walks in Beauty' to be their nuptial poem, with Ovid's 'Elegy to His Mistress' a close second.

On the third day they drove out to Fynbos Estate, near Malmesbury, and stayed in a quaint cottage on the hill, overlooking a vineyard and grove of olive trees, away from the farmhouse. There they enjoyed the tranquillity of the countryside, having their meals brought to them so they didn't have to bother with cooking. They drank bottles of the estate's choice wines – Jack's Red and Cosmos Rosé – pronouncing these the best they'd ever had. The farmer, Johan, was the son of the Communist Party members and trade-union activists Jack Simons and Ray Alexander. He'd spent his youth in Zambia, in exile with them, and only returned when apartheid reached its end. Jack's Red was named after his dad.

As Thespian and Pearlie were leaving, the farmer's wife, Diana, asked whether they'd like a cat and handed them a black kitten, which Thespian named Tarquinus Superbus, after the Roman king, and which Pearlie changed to Sparkey. He would be fed pink salmon trickled with olive oil and finely chopped parsley for the rest of his life, cultivating a burnished and beautiful coat, and far exceeding the nine lives generally allotted to cats.

Thereafter, on each anniversary, Pearlie and Thespian recommitted to their marriage vows. Pearlie would wear her bridal gown and Thespian his tuxedo. Her weight stayed miraculously constant at two bars over the recommended body mass index. He broadened a bit and eventually, when he could barely do up the pants and jacket, had the tailor let them out.

They would celebrate with not quite the same grand menu, but would have a replica of the wedding cake made, always by Carol Bosch, and on this would stand their good-marriage figurine. Thespian would bring out the Mogul dagger for its annual task of cake slicing. The Romero CD would evoke the magic of their marriage night. Thespian would order, from Fynbos Estate, a box of their honeymoon wines. They didn't dare go there again, however, because it had become famous for wine tasting and wine-making workshops and there was a risk of bumping into someone who might know Thespian.

He couldn't spend a week in the flat, as was their desire, but only one night, leaving Mrs Winter to think that he was away on business. As his health wobbled a bit around weight, blood pressure and blood sugar levels, the stamina of their lovemaking declined. But it never lost its sense of fun and playfulness, and always included Thespian lying upon that cloud of bridal lace.

Each year he chose a piece of jewellery from Atkinson's for his second wife. Even though Mrs Atkinson remembered him from year to year, she asked nothing but knew, as do all dealers in fine jewellery, that this special piece was for a secret sweetheart. In her experience, husbands seldom took much time or care when selecting for their spouse. Indeed, they often made the purchase over the phone and asked for it to be gift-wrapped and ready, so they only had to collect and pay.

Through all the years of their affair, Thespian and Pearlie uttered not a bad word about Mrs Winter, nor ever longed for anything to be different. Their make-believe, covert world was more than sufficient. That which existed outside of the relationship was mundane and they didn't do mundane. Their love involved Cupid and arrows, Shakespeare and Ovid, the goddess Aphrodite-Venus and all things gastronomic and bacchanalian. It devoured such catchwords as ecstasy, joy, eternity, orgy, revelry and bliss.

It trapped songbirds to its bosom, transcending everything to do with ordinary carnal contact and sucking love poetry dry of every romantic notion.

Pearlie had an intrinsic happiness that allowed her to find joy in the simplest things. She wasn't pretentious or greedy. She was a simple, honest-to-goodness homegirl and this added vivacity to the relationship.

The thing about Mrs Winter, if we were to compare her with Miss Theron, is that she had no idea of how to play. She had no sense of fun or the ridiculous. She was too preoccupied with her appearance and therefore unable to let go in any hedonistic or comedic way. She couldn't risk looking absurd. Heaven help anyone who took the mickey out of her or made her the centre of a tease.

Imagine Mr Winter arriving home with the costumes of Mr Frog and Miss Mousie and a recording of that old traditional song 'Froggie went a-courtin'. Then picture the two of them in their pared-back lounge, white arums strategically placed in slender vases – him with a sword and pistol at his side, she in a Dolly Parton country-and-western dress with frilled petticoat, the two of them quickstepping, slapping the air, stamping their heeled boots across the imported beechwood floor.

No, it couldn't happen. It simply wouldn't work. Only Pearlie could be a Miss Mousie, with her gorgeous, big breasts bursting out over the laced bolero, her locks tumbled, her armpits sweating and staining her sleeves, a line of perspiration above her paprika-bright lips. Only in her lounge could there be a singalong with a pulsing, compelling, banjo-strummed tambour beat:

Mr Froggie went a-courtin' and he did ride aha...
He went down to Missus Mousie's hall aha...
Where he'd often been before aha...
He took Miss Mouse upon his knee aha...
Sez 'Miss Mouse, will ya marry me?' aha

with each line punctuated with kisses and demonstrations. No, Mrs Winter couldn't participate in such tomfoolery, nor would she eat cornbread and drink whisky, alongside such wedding guests as a flying moth, a bug, a weevil and a big black snake, as did the characters of that lively swamp-song.

It should not be imagined, however, that Thespian didn't love his wife. He did, in a platonic, habitual, predictable way. They were a couple who were bringing up three daughters, who had created a firm, domestic base together and who belonged to a close community of family and friends.

The marriage had no depth to it, definitely no passion, and no escape route, for it was well charted through and hinged upon all the landmarks of anniversaries, birthdays, religious festivals and the highlights of their girls' lives. You couldn't walk out of such a marriage without leaving behind unimaginable scandal and a dreadful mess over the division of spoils and property.

Thespian was a benevolent, generous and kind husband who avoided arguments, simply listening to his wife lambaste, complain and *gaan* on about things without responding. This gave the impression that he was weak. But he just wanted tranquillity in the home. He thought parental arguments weren't good for children and didn't want his girls ever to witness a fight between their mother and father.

He gave his wife unlimited spending and spoilt his

daughters, so none developed any true sense of value, instead placing undue worth on material things and not understanding moderation. They developed no compassion for the poor, but became arrogant with their wealth and lifestyle.

Nannies, maids and au pairs came and went, often leaving under unpleasant clouds. These domestic assistants gave Mrs Winter freedom and leisure time. She routinely redecorated, renovated, refurbished and redesigned the house. Once, she redid the entire kitchen, dividing it in two so as to be competently kosher, with *milchig* on the one side and *fleishig* on the other, with separate sinks, fridges, stoves, utensils, pantries, entire dinner services and silverware keeping meat and dairy apart.

Another time she enclosed a portion of the back stoep to create a new family room. Then she built an apartment atop the garages, for guests. One year she decided on a lavender garden and everything was dug up and replanted in all the hybrids – English lavender, sweet, Italian, Spanish, white and hairy. After two years, when the flower beds were established and had already given glorious seasons of beauty and fragrance, Mrs Winter decided to install a Japanese garden, with camellias, ornamental peach and plum trees, and ponds of carp and goldfish. There was even a raked sand garden. This was, in time, replaced too, for she read in a magazine that the way to go was waterwise and indigenous. So the whole lot was dug up and a botanist brought in from Kirstenbosch Gardens to advise on fynbos, silver trees and proteas.

Thespian went along with everything his wife wanted to do. He accepted all things at home as they were. His two worlds were like ships afloat on a tranquil, glass-flat sea, all puffed along in a mild breeze, heading in the same direction, never colliding.

Mrs Winter rather fancied her eye for the tasteful and was proud of her ability to combine choice pieces, modern and antique, to create a stunning whole. Her furnishing was chic and expensive, with the overall line being Swedish and minimalist. Coffee tables were studiously burdened with *Harper's* and *Vogue* and exclusive design magazines.

She positioned herself at the absolute cutting edge of home and landscape design and fashion, and was a trendsetter par excellence. She was the first in her group of friends to convert a Louis XIV armoire into a drinks cabinet, the first to drape Nguni cowhides over her sofas and across her floors, the first to build a loggia in the garden for wine-tasting soirées.

She had two motor vehicles, a restored Karmann Ghia convertible for small whip-around trips and a more impressive, black, M-series Mercedes 4x4, which she drove round town, double-parking, mounting pavements and looking altogether like a movie star.

Once, in a spurt of creative energy, she decided to open an upmarket coffee shop and, for this, Mr Winter bought premises in Upper Orange Street. She set up a lovely place, modelled on Parisian equivalents, called Chez Moi. The interior was covered in exquisite wallpaper designed by Lorenzo Nassimbeni. Their patterns were carried through to specially printed upholstery material, setting a tasteful ambience.

Mrs Winter employed a super-efficient gay manager (headhunted from Melissa's) and a clutch of well-trained waitrons. Only the best organic coffees and loose-leaf teas were served alongside petits fours, profiteroles, custard curls and other sweet and savoury dainties. You could order a platter of bite-sized quiches: feta and spinach, ricotta and sweet basil, tomato and anchovy, for instance.

In hot weather Chez Moi offered spoonfuls of homemade ice cream in delicate glass bowls, created by Italian consultants, in such delicious combinations as mint with mixed berries, or fig with cinnamon and honey. And yet you could order a simple vanilla or chocolate, the pure taste of which couldn't be matched anywhere in town.

Chez Moi was an instant hit and soon became one of those intimate places where the well-to-do came, especially wives, for bagels and salmon, or for hot chocolate and orange cake, after a morning jog or session at the gym, certain that they wouldn't be sitting next to anyone below their social standing, because the prices were high.

But Mrs Winter soon tired of her project and it saw barely eighteen months of life. She didn't want to sell Chez Moi, knowing that its class and atmosphere would never be sustained, and she didn't want to be associated with it once it became 'ordinary'. (Thespian had subsidised it heavily.) So one day she simply closed shop, after the last customer of that afternoon.

She was an attractive woman with a good figure. A permanent-make-up artist had lightly tattooed a cerise-pink outline around her lips, with brown-black close to her eyelashes and in definition of her eyebrows, so she had a soft 'made-up' look to her even without maquillage. She visited her beautician and hairdresser once a week, cultivating a 'tousled' and sun-streaked touch. All this gave the impression that she stepped out of bed already gorgeous.

An itinerant manicurist called weekly to do nails and feet. She had massages and therapies and alternated between Pilates and yoga. The city's most prominent plastic surgeon tucked her tummy, revised her Caesarean scars and augmented her breasts, so they could be showed off in the neatest of tops, without a bra. He also administered Botox at regular intervals, so her face bore no frown or crease. At home, she had her own sunbed in an annex to the bathroom and here maintained a soft, all-over tan without risking burnt or peeling skin. Altogether, when studying Mrs Winter, one saw a pleasing sight – eye candy, to use a trendy term. As a woman, you might long to look like her, particularly if you were her age, for ten years of her life certainly showed no sign of having passed.

However, her good looks and figure did nothing for the Winters' sex life, which was straightforward, quick and devoid of meaning. There may have been some residual shyness, left from when they first broke his virginal barrier – hers was already down – expecting something like what happened in films, but finding only clumsiness and premature, messy ejaculation on his part. They dutifully had sex once a week, every Sunday night, and showered straight afterwards because she didn't like the smell. Each Monday morning the linen was changed. If one questioned her closely, Mrs Winter might admit that she hated sex.

The things Thespian and Pearlie did for each other never found expression in the Winters' marriage bed – not even simple gestures, like him sucking Pearlie's lovely plump toes, or their straddling each other in various positions. When he ejaculated early, well, that was just part of the fun.

Mrs Winter kept a kosher home, following the blueprint of her mother's kitchen, with its combined Ashkenazi and Sephardic contributions from both sides of the family. Mr Winter had also grown up in a kosher home, but didn't feel too strongly about it. The cooking was done by a caterer who came in regularly to stock the freezer.

The Winters ate out a few times a week at one or other of their favourite restaurants – the Five Flies in Keerom Street, Beluga in Oranjezicht, Willoughby's at the Waterfront, or Bukhara when they felt like a curry.

Once a year, they took a holiday somewhere exotic, like the Seychelles, Madagascar or Mauritius, where there was endless sun, spa treatments and seafood. They travelled to Italy and France and took two cruises, one up the east coast as far as Maputo and another along the west coast to Walvis Bay.

They owned timeshare properties at Plettenberg Bay and the Drakensberg but didn't use these, because there were no servants and Mrs Winter didn't do domestic routine. Thespian had bought them without consulting her and kept them on as an investment and for his girls to use when they were old enough.

When the Winters vacationed, Pearlie went home to Port Nolloth, to her brothers and their wives. This would not be a holiday as such, but it got her out of a Cape Town joyless without Thespian. And it was quite nice to be with her family again, even though they kept urging her to marry. Sparkey would spend the time at Pamperona, a cattery in Constantia.

At each visit, her sisters-in-law would press for information about her love life and try to set her up with men they deemed suitable. They eventually figured she must be lesbian, agreeing with Madge, who announced, after seeing Pearlie off at Springbok airport: 'I guess she's just one of those beefy-Bovril, chunky-dyke types. And you know, it's probably Uncle Frikkie's fault. Remember that time he messed with her when she was a little girl? When Tannie Retha died? That weekend? Well, maybe he just scared her off men well and good. That old bastard. I hope he's dead and rotten somewhere.'

The truth was, Uncle Frikkie hadn't molested Pearlie. He'd taken her out to show her the little *Fenestraria* plants, with their sturdy leaves and delicate flowers, growing in the quartzite ground just outside town. 'By the time you're grown up,' he had told her, 'these will all be gone and extinct. They only grow here in this square mile of a place. When the estate agents come, we can kiss these *blommetjies* goodbye.'

She had come home quiet and upset, causing everyone to presume something had happened.

Nor was Uncle Frikkie dead. He was in Pretoria Central, an awaiting-trial prisoner on a pyramid-scheme charge, now in his tenth year there, while magistrates postponed his case time and again, until it was eventually thrown out.

Thespian was born into big money and had known only comfort in his life. His great-grandfather had been an ostrich baron in Oudtshoorn, smart enough to anticipate the eventual crash in the feather market and to invest his fortune in property. Thespian had been well educated at SACS and the University of Cape Town, where he honed his inherent entrepreneurial skills. He grew his business into the success it was because he never ran on overdraft and gave credit only where credit was due. He read the financial papers, monitored his own stocks and shares, and knew where every rand had gone. His properties were managed by an efficient letting agency.

Thespian dressed well in tailor-made suits and shirts

from Pierre-Michel. Twice a month, he drove the short distance from his office to Antonio Papa's Etna Salon in Thibault Square, where the smells were masculine and the talk political, sportive or financial. There, he sat in one of four comfortable, old-fashioned barber chairs. Antonio would wrap him in a white shroud, bringing out combs, cutters and brushes, and then proceed to shave, trim, tidy and colour as though he were preparing an artist's model.

Papa, who'd arrived from Italy in the 1960s, was himself the son of a barber. He'd named his salon after Mount Etna, the active stratovolcano on the east coast of Sicily, his homeland, and had been cutting gentlemen's hair for over fifty years. Many a time Thespian found himself sitting alongside someone of importance, for Papa was responsible for the good coifs of a number of politicians, including Colin Eglin, the one-time leader of the opposition. He had clipped the nose and ear hairs of some well-known Nationalists and could have dispatched a number of apartheid's scoundrels with the slightest slip of his cut-throat razor, had he been so inclined. But never a drop of blood stained a collar at the Etna Salon.

He tackled what still grew on the head of the present finance minister Trevor Manuel, who, on the occasions that he walked out of Etna Salon as Thespian walked in, was gracious enough to nod a response to the other's greeting. Thespian, always well informed about those in government, knew that Trevor came from humble origins, having grown up in Kensington, a poor coloured area in Cape Town.

'Who could ever have imagined this one-time revolutionary sitting pretty in a fancy barber's chair, had they known him during the struggle?' Thespian once commented to business associates he was lunching with.

'Who could've guessed,' he continued, 'how obligingly

he'd take to being pampered and groomed, if they'd seen him in those anti-apartheid days, when he championed for the oppressed at UDF rallies, his clenched fist raised, his little child straddled on his hip?'

Thespian, with gentle probing, asked of his colleagues who of them would have believed that, upon appointment as Jacob Zuma's minister in the presidency, Trevor would succumb to the all-pervasive, self-aggrandisement of African politicians by accepting a BMW 750i with all its accessories, and costing the country well over a million rand? Trevor had been a sort of Che Guevara of the Cape Flats, and it would be said of him that he was not white enough during apartheid and not black enough after democracy. Even so, Thespian's wry eye observed him manage the divide and dress the slick, well-groomed part of politician without difficulty. Trevor's mother, humble and unpretentious despite her son's success, preferred to remain in her home in Kensington, among the neighbours who knew her, and with whom she'd faced her own struggle through hard times.

It was at the Etna that Thespian could safely have shared the facts of his dual life, for the barber repeated nothing he was told. If ever a politician had divulged lascivious information about romances and affairs and prostitutes, or deals and arms procurement and tender-rigging, Antonio Papa breathed not a word of it. He must have known, long before the media got wind of it, about Trevor Manuel's romance and forthcoming marriage to Maria Ramos, one-time director-general of the National Treasury of South Africa, but not even that sweet fact escaped from the bowels of Etna.

During apartheid, Thespian had voted for the Nationalist Party because he couldn't buy into the one-man-one-vote sing-song of the liberation movements in the rest of Africa, which the Progressives were entertaining. He'd believed apartheid's rhetoric, that Africans running important ministries and public services would just drive these into the ground. He felt vindicated now, in post-apartheid South Africa, when someone at Eskom had failed to keep the coal stocks up, resulting in massive nationwide blackouts; or when the once fully functioning Khayalami hospital was closed in 1997 for no discernible reason, and all its expensive equipment seemingly abandoned.

As an astute businessman, he'd be blunt, even if he sounded racist, and say: 'Look at the hospitals. Look at the railways. When last did you go near the station? Did you feel safe walking there on the station roof with all the criminals? When last did you see a traffic cop pull over an unlicensed, unroadworthy, overloaded taxi and then keep it off the road? The only place you'll find a traffic cop nowadays is safely behind a speed camera in the affluent suburbs.

'Look at the education system. Would you put your child into a government school? I can safely bet that St Cyprian's and Bishops are full of the children of ministers. And not only our own. They are educating the children of Angolan, Mozambican, Congolese and Zimbabwean government officials and elite. Schools have been run down in Africa. And ours are on the way. Please. Don't talk to me about this so-called democracy.'

If he could have looked ahead to January 2010, when the education department disbanded its failed outcomes-based system, replacing it with no more than the promise of a plan, he would have felt vindicated in his harsh judgment, pointing out that educators had been forced to wander through an opaque wilderness.

The one thing he repeatedly said about Afrikaners, on the other hand, was that they made good roads and ran a railway service better than any in Africa. If Cecil Rhodes's dream had been put into Afrikaner hands, reasoned Thespian, the vision of railway tracks running from Cape to Cairo would now be reality. There would be trade and movement of people. All the countries through which the railway ran would have wealth and promise, instead of being basket cases dependent on foreign aid which their leaders squandered on palaces and Mercedes Benzes. Thespian saw himself as a realist, maintaining that trade cannot work without transport. 'If you can't get your market produce from A to B,' he'd argue, 'and if the potholes are so deep that you can't drive the road, then your economy, and therefore your country, is over. It's a simple equation.'

He'd point out that rolling stock now stood in a train graveyard near the docks. Darling station had been sold to the satirist Pieter-Dirk Uys and his alter ego Evita Bezuidenhout. Stations in Port Alfred and Grahamstown had also been sold. 'What kind of government sells off the means of its railway transportation system?' Thespian repeatedly asked. But no one could answer him without also sounding racist, though they would heed his words when S'bu Ndebele, the minister of transport, advised Parliament in October 2009 that South Africa's road maintenance had so fallen behind that it would require in excess of thirty-eight billion rand to restore the country's crumbling road network.

Despite his wealth, Thespian was not insensitive to the needs of others and conducted, unbeknown to anyone, a regular *mitzvah*. This good deed involved the tithing each month of a tenth of his entire income to the Salvation Army. Once, coming out of his office late at night, he'd seen a man, unshaven and suffering alcoholic withdrawal, propped up against the steps. The sight of this broken man was haunting. We, who look in from the wings, recognise him as Gerrit Viljoen, Peter Brightstone's roommate.

The next day, aware that 'there but for the grace of God go I', Thespian phoned the Salvation Army, took their bank details and made provision for his donation. He made only one condition: each inmate was to be given a daily allowance, enough for a packet of cigarettes, or a croissant and tea, or a sandwich, or a ticket to the movies. He did this to afford these destitute men some sense of independence and to restore a smidgen of dignity.

Though she would have preferred otherwise, Mrs Winter's origins were not top drawer. She was the only child of a used-furniture dealer who had a shop in Lansdowne Road, Katzen's Second-Hand.

The family had lived in a rented semi-detached in Wynberg, just off Main Road and opposite Atlas, the grain dealers. That's where Mrs Winter grew up, a short walk from St Michael's Children's Home and a stone's throw from the Wynberg Hotel, where the author Olive Schreiner spent her last days. The house had a patch of garden at the front and a yard at the back with a corrugated-iron fence and washing lines. Everything in the house had once belonged to someone else.

Most second-hand furniture dealers could make a fairly good living in the Cape Town area. Even if one had to offer lay-by or give some form of credit to customers, there was a sure and reliable market among the cash-strapped lower classes. And it wasn't too complicated a route from trading in used furniture to dealing in antiques. With a bit of study into the various periods, one could do well.

Although Mr Katzen was honest and hard-working, he wasn't a good businessman. In contrast to Thespian, he didn't keep his records in order and his pockets were stuffed with scraps of paper, receipts, cheques and even crumpled banknotes that would eventually end up in the wash. If asked, at any moment, how much money was in his account, or who his debtors were and what they owed him, he wouldn't be able to say with any confidence. He both over- and underestimated the value of items and then had no luck. So he might sit with an oak wardrobe with bevelled mirrors for months, only to let a student have it for a song the day before someone came in looking for just such an item. He sold many tables and sideboards, believing them to be pine. Had he taken the trouble to scrape away a bit of dark varnish or green paint, he might have discovered valuable stinkwood or yellowwood.

His wife worked in the shoe department of the old Garlicks Store, in the city. Those were the days of high customer care, and Mrs Katzen would measure a person's feet and bring out from the back shoes that were individually wrapped in tissue and packed in boxes. Her own shoes were well worn and not fashionable, her feet sore from long hours of standing. She developed bunions, corns and varicosities, but never complained.

The Katzens' combined incomes barely covered rental

and household expenses. In bad months, they would rely entirely on what Mrs Katzen earned. They never managed to buy their own property and drove around in a Ford pick-up. For a while Mr Katzen tried his hand at selling encyclopaedias, in the days when these were sold door to door, long before the Internet and Wikipedia. He also had a go at selling insurance policies, but he was too honest for this, always frightening off potential clients by underscoring the small print.

In 1990, he made his first big business decision. He chose to move his shop from Lansdowne Road to the Werdmuller Centre on Claremont's busy Main Road. He was prompted by various adverts he'd read in the property pages of the *Cape Times* and by the confident encouragement given him by the letting agent.

'I can assure you,' the agent told him, 'you'll be exposed to a denser commuting and purchasing crowd. This will up your sales considerably. The Werdmuller is close to Claremont station and you'll be guaranteed a passing trade of people going to Main Road. They *have* to walk past the centre, whether on one side or the other.

'And that sweeping walkway was designed *precisely* to drive customers up and into the building, right into your shop. And don't just consider the passing trade. I took the liberty of measuring your present shop space. You'll have *four times* the area. You'll be able to display properly instead of stacking things on top of each other.'

When Mr Katzen hesitated over the higher rental, the agent patted him on the back, saying: 'But your income is going to rocket. You'll have to go to more auctions to pick up stock, Mr Katzen. You'll have to trade in that clapped-out truck and buy a decent one. You'll clear the floor in no time. Believe me. Stay with me. I know the retail world like the back of my hand.'

Mr Katzen learnt too late that when a salesman saponaceously says 'Believe me', it has the same truth to it as a politician saying 'Trust me'.

The Werdmuller Centre, designed by Roelof Uytenbogaardt and completed in 1976, was a fine example of modernist architecture. Its iconic status was underlined by its inclusion in Mark Irving's *1001 Buildings You Must See Before You Die*. But even as an internationally admired building, it failed hopelessly as a shopping mall.

There seemed to be something jinxed about the building. Its flow just didn't work. Passers-by didn't feel compelled to enter its cavernous, raw-cement interior to browse. No provision had been made for a large 'anchor' retailer like OK Bazaars or Checkers, so small shops had to go it alone in attracting clientele. It seemed vacuous and rather scary and it echoed. A woman there alone might feel fearful.

If an *igqirha* had been consulted, he would have walked through and around and up to the roof and down to the parking basement and then stated the obvious: The Werdmuller Centre had been built over a San burial ground. Bones had been disturbed, broken and thrown out with all the rubble of excavation. He would have indicated that there remained, on site, a single piece of skull bone, a shard of patterned ostrich eggshell and a few beads. These had to be retrieved, if possible, and afforded a dignified burial. Alternatively, a cleansing ceremony should be performed to restore a sense of homage and dignity. Until this happened, the building would remain 'wrong'.

Because such a diagnosis couldn't credibly be delivered to the proprietors, Old Mutual Properties, and because the desecration of the site was not made good, the building fell into disrepair and remained mostly vacant.

Only when he was installed, with all items of furniture placed and dusted, and he standing at his door, waiting for the rush of sales, did Mr Katzen realise that he should have spent time outside the building watching the movement of shoppers, particularly on a Friday and Saturday and at month-end, when people got paid.

He would have learnt early, instead of now when the five-year lease agreement bore his witnessed signature that, yes, there was greater pedestrian traffic, but only on the pavements, outside, where there was hectic informal trading going on. Commuters hurriedly purchased, from vendors displaying under gazebos, all sorts of cheap Chinese products, as well as every type of vitamin and over-the-counter medication that had passed its sell-by date. Alongside these gazebos, big mamas cooked curried chicken wings and sausages that gave off delicious smells as they sizzled on *skottel braais*. Commuters could snatch up a hot roll with *chakalaka* and eat on the way to work.

The crowds moved back and forth, sometimes thick, sometimes thin, sometimes slowly, sometimes in a quickened, urgent step, between the station and Main Road. The crowd imparted a sense of Africa that one didn't feel further up at Cavendish Square. But there was no en-masse venturing into the Werdmuller Centre, into Mr Katzen's shop, to clear his floor and fill his purse. Thus he didn't earn enough to buy a delivery truck nor find himself at auctions replenishing stock. Worse, he'd forfeited his reputation, built up over many years, among the locals of Lansdowne Road. No one knew him here.

Thespian found out about his father-in-law's

predicament quite by chance. He had cautioned him about making the move in the first place, but Mr Katzen was brimming with confidence, so Thespian did not interfere. He happened to be in Claremont one day and decided to drop off a carton of samples of a finished line of vases and tea sets. He found the shop closed with a 'To Let' sign on the door. He learnt from the watchman that the furniture shop had closed some two months previously.

Thespian stepped in decisively. He arranged for a monthly stop order and offered the Katzens one of his apartments. Though they accepted the money with gratitude, they chose to stay in their Wynberg home, which was comfortable and sufficient. They used his money sparingly and never failed to thank him. When they died, their estate returned a sizeable amount saved from Thespian's allowance.

The Werdmuller Centre was eventually marked for demolition and the site for redevelopment. A group of concerned architects tried to have it preserved, placing it within a pantheon of iconic buildings, and showing how new uses and conservation methods had been found for a host of other modernist structures.

Haunting pictures were taken by the architectural photographer Gaelen Pinnock, in black and white, to record the building's complex and important design. But all this was to no avail. Down it would eventually come and the building erected in its place would suffer the same fate. It too would fail as a commercial centre, for those last San remains were never removed, but further crushed in the new excavation.

The Katzens' daughter, the future Mrs Winter, initially attended Wynberg Primary, but was later granted a full bursary, based on her parents' financial situation and not her scholastic aptitude, to attend Herzlia, the Jewish day school. It was there, among the children of some of Cape Town's wealthiest, that she came to understand her family's poverty and to be embarrassed by it. Her newly critical eye noticed for the first time that her mother wore the same clothes over and again; that her father had had his suit forever; that his tatty toupee sometimes swivelled; that their car belonged on a scrap heap.

It was at Herzlia that she vowed, by hook or by crook, to marry rich and haul herself as far as possible from their semi. She never brought friends home, instead fabricating a story about herself.

Mr Katzen took out a loan for her to do a BA in English and drama at Rhodes University in Grahamstown, where she found that the studious life was not for her. Even so, her single year on campus was a transformative one, for she took from the drama class the ability to 'act rich', to walk wealthy and stand as though she were blue-blooded. She rid herself, under the tutelage of the excellent Jane Osborne, of her flat, South African Jewish accent and took up the more suitable, upper-class colonial, Afro-British diction. This was so authentic that she could easily have been employed by the British Council. But she had more ambition than that and proceeded to hunt for a rich man.

In her first week back in Cape Town, she met Thespian Winter at the home of her friend Talia Ginsburg, who had purchased a crystal chandelier from him and whom she had invited over just to see how good it looked in her drawing room.

Talia, knowing that her friend was trawling for a husband with substance, had called her over as a tease, first briefing her about his wealth, independence and availability, but failing to mention that he wasn't at all good-looking. He was heavy of frame, with a big nose and close-set, slightly squinting eyes. As a child he'd contracted polio and this had left him with a withered left leg and a limp.

Even so, the key to Miss Katzen's dream life stood before her. Yes, he was ugly and way too interested in Shakespeare. But, outside in the driveway, was his Jaguar Mark 10 and, according to Talia, he lived in a suite at the Mount Nelson Hotel.

She lost no time in seducing Mr Winter. It was easy because he failed to see her intentions and it's not as though there were other women beating a path to his bed. He was flattered by her advances. She got herself pregnant within the first month of their barely developed relationship.

He met her parents only a fortnight before their wedding, at the Mount Nelson, where he was indeed living, and to where he invited the family for a meal. Mr and Mrs Katzen had bought new clothes, on account at Edgars, for this occasion and for their daughter's forthcoming marriage.

Mr Winter wanted a low-key wedding, but his bride-to-be needed extravagance. She chose the wine farm L'Ormarins in Franschhoek and elected to honeymoon in Paris. He bought a house on a double plot in Bridle Road, in Oranjezicht. There Mrs Winter adapted to rich living with ease and learnt to entertain lavishly.

She prided herself on her Passover and Rosh Hashana tables. On each of these festivals, for first night, she invited her choice friends. On second night, her parents came over. She remained ashamed of them, ever fearful that they might divulge something of her impoverished past. They remained humble and good folk. And though they knew they embarrassed her, they never tried to make the grade.

They were who they were – Mr and Mrs Issy Katzen, the second-hand furniture people, still living in their semi in Wynberg, with their same lounge suite and bed linen and with absolutely no pretensions.

Pearlie and Thespian did not confine their relationship to the flat. They went out quite often. Some of their outings were above board and had the approval of Mrs Winter. Actually, it had been her idea in the first place, that he take his secretary out to dinner now and then. This was inspired by something she'd read in *Oprah* magazine, about giving secretaries little perks to make them feel valued.

'Just don't take her anywhere we go,' she'd instructed.

So Mr Winter took his secretary out for a meal once a fortnight, to Artscape at Christmas time and, on Secretary's Day, to the Maynardville open-air theatre in Wynberg to watch live Shakespeare plays. He'd asked his wife whether she wanted to accompany them on any of these outings and she replied: 'Are you *crazy*?'

Pearlie and Thespian loved the intimacy of Maynardville, enclosed as it was by trees and shrubbery, and where they could look up at the grandeur of the night sky. He once commented: 'Is it not a marvellous coincidence that both our theatres, this one under the stars and our own at Maynard Court, share the same name?'

Some paths crossed – Cape Town is not such a big city – but two were carefully engineered. Most Saturdays, just after eleven, Mr and Mrs Winter went to the organic food market at the Old Biscuit Mill in Salt River, and so did Pearlie. The place was always crowded and busy, being very popular, especially among richer citizens, who went there for the expensive home-cured meats, pies and designer wines and cheeses. The Winters would set off clockwise around the food stalls and Pearlie would follow at a discreet distance, shielded by others. She and the Winters would fill their baskets with breads and slices of delicious things. The couple would then sit at one of the long communal tables, joined by friends and sometimes their daughters and an au pair. Pearlie would not be too far away, eating on her own, demurely looking out from under the low brim of her hat.

Mrs Winter only once noticed her in the crowd and urged her husband in the other direction with: 'Oh God, there's your awful secretary. Please don't stop to talk if she spots us. I'll walk away if you do.'

Another place they all frequented was the Potters' Market in Rondebosch. There, twice a year, Pearlie bought platters from Marinella Garuti to add to her growing collection. Medieval Portuguese, Italian and Spanish design influenced and informed this potter, so her ceramics, redolent with olives and grapes, quails and lilies, all fitted well into the atmosphere of number four Maynard Court. Marinella bottled olives, pepperoni and *melanzane sott' olio* and Pearlie kept her pantry well stocked with these.

Mrs Winter steered towards the more modern, starker works as well as to wood-fired, Japanese-influenced bowls and plates. So she and Pearlie never hovered at the same stall and were spared the horror of wanting to buy the same item. Again, the Winters moved clockwise around the park, with Pearlie a safe distance behind, stopping at tables and inspecting the wide range of lovely things on display, while peeping at her beloved from under her brim. It was nice to know that there, in the crowd, was someone who loved her. 'You're playing with fire, my Pearlie,' Thespian would gently caution her when next together.

On the rare occasion that his wife was away on a Saturday night, Thespian took Pearlie *langarm* dancing in Athlone, where there was always a live band and where people wore formal attire. He invited her onto the dance floor with: 'Come now, what masques, what dances shall we have? Sound music! Come, my Queen, take hands with me!'

Here, the patrons were people of colour. It was unlikely that a white couple would turn up and there was certainly no chance that anyone from the Jewish community would waltz or foxtrot across the floor. Even so, they didn't draw attention to themselves and always, between dances, sat in a corner with their bottles of wine and plates of snacks, never interacting with others.

The Lotus Tavern, on the floor above the Chinese Seamen's Institute, on the docks, was an unpretentious place. This was where Thespian took Pearlie on their fortnightly eat-outs.

The tablecloths were wipe-down plastic; the bowls and plates were melamine; the windows grubby on the outside from dockside and sea air, and grubby on the inside from stir- and deep-fry vapours. But the food was authentic, generous and delicious. The owner had no idea about wines so these were generally 'plonk'. Thespian brought his own bottles, a white and a red, but wasn't charged corkage. These he and Pearlie would polish off and then call for a glass each of 'house'. The waitresses would laugh and say: 'You see! You like! You like!' and bring out two fortune cookies as well.

At the other tables sat Chinese sailors and the odd adventurous diner. Now and then a celebrity, not wanting to be spotted by anyone, might frequent this out-of-the-limelight place. The Lotus Tavern would be 'discovered' one day by trendsetters and become so busy that diners would have to book weeks in advance. But, in their time, it remained a private, special place for Thespian and Pearlie and there was never a risk of bumping into magazine editors and gossip columnists such as Jane Raphaely or Gwen Gill. Not even Lin Sampson partook of tofu and prawns there, though one would have expected her to know about the Lotus Tavern, for she was always trawling the underbelly of the city for stories.

The cook was a burly man, probably of Mongolian descent. He towered above his waitresses, all brought in from a village in China's Anhui province and never given the chance to assimilate into Cape Town. During lulls in the kitchen, he sat in the dining room, smoking or playing cards with his assistant. He wore baggy cotton shorts, Crocs, a vest and a stained apron. His arms were strong and hard and spoke of forced, heavy labour, not the gentle movements of fine chopping and stir-fry tossing. His legs too were firm. They told of Mao Tse-tung's legendary Long March of the 1930s, though he was too young to have participated. Perhaps his limbs merely expressed what his ancestors had suffered.

He knew only rudimentary English and had no intention of expanding his skill in the language, believing it to be the tongue of ghosts, with their corpse-like hue, pale, lifeless eyes and occasional flaming-ginger hair.

In his spare time he read poetry – the same poems over and again, from two well-worn anthologies. He had copied one out on the restaurant wall, in large, elegant calligraphy, using black and red paint. Once, Thespian asked their waitress for a translation. Rising onto her tiptoes, wringing a corner of her apron in concentration, she read with a tentative voice:

A lonely man is sitting under the moon.
He is holding a bowl of rice-wine.
The moon is reflected in the wine.
Now he is not alone.
Now there are three figures.
Now there is the man himself and the moon and the reflection of the moon.

The waitress gave a self-conscious laugh and said she was sorry not to have translated it properly, for it was a difficult poem.

Thespian became a bit glum, saying: 'It's a sad poem.'

Pearlie smiled at him across the table, over bowls of crispy duck and black bean curd. 'Maybe the waitress got it wrong,' he continued. 'Maybe it means something else. It sounds like a sentence is missing.'

'Maybe,' she replied and lined her bowl with noodles, her toes curling up pleasurably in their sandals as she anticipated the next mouthful. 'But it sounds quite complete to me. It's not sad.'

Though they were certain never to meet any of the Winters' friends at the Lotus Tavern, there was always the possibility of bumping into someone at Artscape or Maynardville.

For such encounters they were prepared. They never held hands or sat too close, instead feigning an old-fashioned formality, calling each other Mr Winter and Miss Theron. If they did happen upon anyone who knew the Winters, Thespian would introduce Pearlie matter-of-factly with: 'Hello, Hymie and Mona, you might have met my secretary, Miss Theron, telephonically. I'm treating her to a show for Secretary's Day.'

Turning to Pearlie, he'd say: 'Miss Theron, this is Mr Meyer from Meyer Brothers Distribution, and his wife, Mrs Mona Meyer.'

And here he would light a cigarette, offering one to Hymie, while Miss Theron stood a little removed, clutching her handbag and gloves, looking not the least interested.

Later, Mona Meyer would comment to her husband: 'What a strangely old-fashioned girl his secretary is. I haven't seen anyone wear a fox stole in years. And did you see, she was eating an apple? Why would anyone bring an apple to the theatre?'

Pearlie and Thespian had only once had the opportunity to go out and brazenly mingle in a crowd. This was at the famed Long Street masked party, which Pearlie had heard advertised on the radio.

By chance, Mrs Winter had planned, months before, to go to St Francis Spa in Port Alfred, so she was away that weekend. The daughters were in Plettenberg Bay with their au pairs and various boyfriends. Thespian took the wonderful gap and moved into number four Maynard Court.

Pearlie decided they would go as a matador and flamenco dancer and for this went to Laura & Hutch Dress-Up in Plein Street, just down from Parliament. This was not the usual run-of-the-mill costume hire. Laura Hutchinson, the owner, had studied drama, but decided to specialise in wardrobe rather than take to the stage, though every now and then, especially after a good feast with friends, she was known to enact some excellent impersonations. Her most hilarious was the gin-bemused, gun-toting, anti-terrorist, sunburnt, racist, ex-Kenyan, Rhodesian, white 'madam' sitting on her veranda overlooking her dahlias and supervising a garden boy in his uniform of khaki shorts and shirt. Under normal circumstances, Laura would have been the perfect friend for 'Mr and Mrs Theron', what with all their interest in Shakespeare and melodrama.

Laura attired Pearlie in a flamenco dress of deep russet with the tremendous flare of two godets and polka-dot ruffles. The dress came with a black Manila shawl and embroidered shoulder bag. Laura sold her three red silk flowers, the traditional *peinetas*, or decorative combs, to clip into her hair, red stockings, loop earrings and a set of glass bracelets. Pearlie could have hired shoes and castanets but, following Laura's advice, ordered, via the Internet, a pair of Gallardo flamenco dance shoes and a set of Filigrana castanets.

For Thespian, Laura brought out a matador's outfit with skin-tight pink pants, a white shirt, red tie and an embroidered silk jacket. This was an authentic costume, a real *traje de luces*, a dress of lights, covered in little chips of mirror which would have glittered magically in the sun to disorient and madden a bull. The costume was completed by a yellow cape, a bicorner hat known as a *montera* and a dangerously sharp sword, an *estoque*.

Laura didn't routinely rent out the matador costume. It was too valuable. Only real connoisseurs of dress-up and drama were permitted to wear it. She took a large deposit and Pearlie had to sign her name to accept the prohibitions and instructions regarding its use.

It was a tight fit for Thespian and he barely managed to get into it. Had it not been sewn so well with fortified seams, stitches would have burst. When he dug into a pocket, he found the desiccated ear of some poor bull killed in a Spanish arena after being weakened by a picador's lance and blood loss.

After the event, Pearlie found herself unable to return the costumes and asked Laura whether she could buy them. Laura was happy to part with the flamenco dress, which was easily replaceable, but the matador costume was another matter. Pearlie became intransigent and a tug of words ensued. Things got ugly. Laura's lawyer delivered a letter demanding the return of the costumes, failing which a charge of theft would be laid.

Pearlie, in a moment of madness, dug in her stiletto heels. She wanted those costumes more than anything. She wanted her and Thespian to be able to dress Spanish again, any time, to recreate that party and its freedom which had allowed them, in their black half-face masks, to confidently hold hands, walk arm in arm and touch lips in a crowd.

The lawyer's letter threw Thespian into a spin. This was the very story the *Sunday Times* would seize. He wanted no scandal and tried to reason with Pearlie, but she clenched her fists and shouted that she wanted those costumes and, by God, she would have them.

Thespian had never seen this behaviour in his beloved and demanded that she see reason, that she snap out of her capricious insistence and pull herself together. While she stood crying, watching in disbelief, he folded the costumes and slipped them into their bags. He promised to take her to Spain. Surely there were hundreds of matador outfits all over the Iberian Peninsula? They would buy all the Spanish costumes Pearlie wanted.

Thespian drove the costumes back to the hire shop, not trusting anyone else with the task, apologising to Ms Hutchinson and dropping a sizeable tip onto the counter. After that, Laura never dared rent out the matador outfit. She bought a Victorian-era museum cabinet from Katzen

Second-Hand and in this the costume was permanently displayed.

Few could have known the true value of that matador outfit, the price beyond money, the intrinsic, folkloric value of it. It had once been worn by none other than El Cordobés, the most famous bullfighter of his generation, perhaps the most famous of all time, who had survived a near-fatal goring by a massive bull named Impulsivo.

The whole time of the affair, Pearlie lived only for herself and Thespian and their fantasy. She never attempted charity work and the only kind deed she did with regularity was to make tea for Seymour, the caretaker of Maynard Court. His responsibilities extended to Florida Heights, another of Thespian's apartment blocks. Seymour's was a 'live-in' position. His remuneration included a single room at the back, too small to share with his family, who lived in a shack at Marconi Beam informal settlement. The room was furnished with unwanted items given him by tenants or salvaged from what he found outside the surrounding apartment blocks on garbage days. His dream was to own a car and to be able to motor into Marconi Beam, looking like a moneyed gentleman. Like his boss, Mr Winter.

Seymour's job was fairly straightforward. He cleaned up the needles that the wind shed from the tall pine trees growing in almost every Vredehoek garden. He cut the grass, trimmed the *spekboom* hedge and dealt with the wheelie bins on garbage days. He also swept the stairwells and kept the gutters and drains clear. Tenants regularly asked him to change high light bulbs or polish brassware.

Once, after the fire on Table Mountain, he was called to catch a field mouse in a ground-floor flat.

Every Saturday, he washed Pearlie's car and once a month he did her windows. On those days, she gave him tea with a meat pie for lunch, serving them in an enamel mug and plate that she kept under the sink. He'd sit outside on the low back wall, eating the snack and rolling a cigarette. Then he'd rinse everything at the outside tap before coming up for his money.

Recently, had she been wanting to do extensive good deeds, Pearlie could have responded to the many calls to help victims of xenophobia who were housed in tented camps at Bluewater, near Muizenberg, and at Ysterplaat. But, even if she had wanted to, Thespian wouldn't have let her get involved. Appeals had reached him from various Jewish charities and he'd given a cash donation. The assaults on foreigners, whose own countries had imploded economically through dictatorship and kleptocracy, were unfortunate, yes. And the recent spectacle of a Mozambican man burning to death, shown on television and in all the newspapers, with everyone just standing around, even the policemen, was truly terrible. Even so, any activity that required going into the townships, or these new camps, was dangerous and pointless, in his opinion.

At the time of Thespian's sudden removal from active life, Pearlie was the only white person living in Maynard Court. Not because the tone of Vredehoek had gone down, but because, after apartheid ended, Thespian thought it safer to have persons of colour in the block. Even though their affair had gone undetected for so long, fate might deal an ugly hand. Someone visiting a friend might recognise him on the stairwell, or a tenant might take note of his regular comings and goings and then see him elsewhere with his wife. In these days of cellphone cameras and YouTube exposures, you just couldn't be too careful with your secrets. Imagine the gossip circuits! It was too awful to contemplate.

His black tenants, all handled by his agent, were carefully vetted and were charged high deposits and rental. There was never trouble with defaulters or the threat of the building being hijacked, as was now prevalent in Johannesburg.

Pearlie had no problem with her black neighbours, though she did not interact with any of them. Before she'd met Thespian, she had briefly belonged to the Black Sash. She'd been invited to join by a work colleague but, though she went to meetings, she was never really interested in the politics of it all and was rather afraid to actively oppose apartheid.

Once, in the height of winter, she'd gone out with her Black Sash group to Crossroads, where illegally built shacks were being demolished in an attempt to stop black people moving into the Western Cape. These were the days when only black men could enter the region, and then only with a pass. They were forbidden to bring their families, who had to stay behind in the rural areas of Transkei and Ciskei. If their wives and children joined them, they risked arrest.

It was a cold, wet day and Pearlie came home emotionally shaken and wishing she hadn't borne witness. A special follow-up meeting was called, where it was suggested that, as an act of compassion and contrition – a sort of 'washing of the feet' – each member should take home a mother and her children, to allow them to have a warm bath and enjoy a hot meal. It was thought that such a deed would give a sense of the fraternity and goodwill that apartheid concealed. This would symbolise the wish to end racial segregation, from the most humble level upwards.

The following Saturday, hired buses transported a contingent of women and children to Mowbray terminal. There the various Black Sash members collected their charges. They had been instructed to find out the Xhosa names of their visitors and their meanings. Pearlie's guests, who smelt of cooking fire and damp, were Nonkululeko (Freedom) and her children Vuyo (Joy) and Zolile (Tranquillity). Her tongue struggled with these, so she kept to their second, English names – Winifred, Sidwell and Bosman.

In those days, Pearlie still lived in Claremont, in Blythewood on Protea Road. Blythewood comprised two double-storey apartment blocks that faced each other across a manicured garden. Pearlie's backyard, in which stood a potted lemon tree and the washing lines, opened onto Corwen Road, where she parked, leading her guests through the kitchen door. Ideally, she would have opened the front and let the children play on the grass. But then her neighbours would have known that she was entertaining outside of the colour bar and might have called the police. She kept the Venetian blinds down.

First, she led the family to the bathroom, giving them towels, facecloths and soap. She could hear that they didn't get into the bath, but merely filled it a little way up and used it as a large basin, leaning over it to wash.

She served a meal of rice, beef stew and pumpkin, with jelly and custard for dessert. All this she'd prepared the night before. To finish off, she made tea and buttered some currant buns.

Her guests were shy and self-conscious. There was no conversation. The woman could barely speak English and had absolutely no idea how to engage with her hostess. She wouldn't have come, except that she knew there would be a meal.

So Pearlie didn't learn that Winifred had come from Port St Johns to be with her husband, knowing that, if she left him to himself, he would find himself a young woman at the shebeens. He would then stop sending money home, and eventually stop coming home at all. She had seen this pattern among other families and knew of the ease with which cities swallowed rural men.

Pearlie would never know about the trading stations, where wives would gather once a month for a letter and remittance from their husbands. From these remittances, the trader would deduct money owed for groceries bought on credit, leaving only a few rand in cash. She had no idea that most of these people were illiterate and that they relied on others to write their letters.

She didn't know how it was when a remittance just stopped coming, how a wife would ask: 'But *Baas*, are you certain? Please, look again.' Or how sometimes word would come of a death in an iGoli mine shaft, to be followed some years later by what was left of a small pension, after it had been trimmed by of the fees charged by intermediaries and lawyers.

She didn't know how a man, having left his village strong and strapping, might return with a debilitating miner's lung disease, or a missing limb, and how he would sit outside his hut feeling useless, depressed and angry. And how if, by God's grace, he managed to get hold of a quart of brandy, he'd drink the lot, straight from the bottle, letting the golden liquid gurgle down his throat as though into a drain, and how he'd fall over and have to be covered with a rug, as he lay there.

She had no idea that there were times when there was

absolutely no food in a hut, out there in the way beyond; when a mother would scrape together dry cow dung and light a little fire of it, then put some river water on to boil, telling the children: 'The food is coming. I am cooking.' She might throw in some wild herbs, so that there was the aroma of a meal, while her children kept asking: 'When will we eat, mother?' and she would repeat: 'The food is coming. I am cooking it. Wait my children.' And she would sit stirring the pot, until the children fell asleep, their stomachs gnawed smaller by hunger.

And in the morning, she'd say: 'But you ate, my little ones. You ate last night. Have you forgotten? Now it is all finished. Look at the pot. You licked it clean. You ate everything. There was nothing for the dogs. See how lean they are. See their ribs.

'But wait until tonight. Tonight I will cook for you. I am tired now. Meanwhile run out and search for something wild to chew. And if you see someone's goat standing, and no one looking, then suck from its teats. Suck that warm milk, my children, take turns with it. Chase the kid away and suck in its place.'

None of this was made known to Pearlie, and it would probably have been useless knowledge, for what could she have done with it? How could she have made a mental picture from something so foreign as hunger?

She let her guests have the towels and soap, and gave them packets of meal, jam, peanut butter, sugar and various tins. She dropped them back at Mowbray terminal. For a long time afterwards, the children would ask their mother to take them back to *uMlungazi*, the White Lady. And their mother would tell them that the White Lady had gone to England.

Pearlie had cleaned the bathroom and toilet and poured boiling water over the cups and plates. She couldn't stop herself doing this. It was almost instinctive. This was the legacy apartheid had encoded into her from way, way back, when her Dutch ancestors had captured *Boschjesman* children and reared them as little tame animals to work in their homesteads, feeding them morsels from the table as they sat meekly on the floor. Pearlie's ancestors would no more have supped from a dog's bowl than share a plate with one of their *bruinmense*.

Soon afterwards, Pearlie resigned from the Black Sash and chose not to think about apartheid. She was never haunted by the family. Not even when winter rains fell and a paraffin stove would be of little use to warm a damp shack.

The only area of life to which Thespian did not give his usual careful attention was his and Pearlie's future. Neither of them ever spoke about it. They simply took it for granted. They were living happily ever after and never entertained the possibility that events might force them apart. As far as they were concerned, inside their magic world, time stood still and would not age them, heeding Shakespeare's instruction: 'Time! I forbid thee one most heinous crime: O carve not with thy hours my love's fair brow, nor mine. Draw no lines upon our faces with thine antique pen. Take not our nimble step nor humour. Leave us fresh and dancing through the meadows.'

All that Thespian had done was to draw up an addendum to his last will and testament. In that document, he bequeathed the whole of Maynard Court to Pearlie, all ten apartments. In the event of his death, she could continue to live in their magical, theatrical world and earn rent from the other tenants.

This addendum was witnessed by the chef and head waitress at the Lotus Tavern. It was sealed in a brown envelope, addressed to Miss Pearlie Theron and kept in the safe there. Thespian should have lodged it with an attorney but was reluctant to do so, lest somehow news of it leak to the broader legal fraternity, among whom he and Mrs Winter had many acquaintances. Thespian's instruction to Pearlie was that, should he die, she was to retrieve the envelope. He also told the chef: 'If Miss Pearlie comes here alone, without me, and you learn that I am dead, please be so kind as to give her this envelope.'

Even so, he had no pressing plan to die, and they both were certain that fate would be kind and allow them to depart together, in bed, after a hearty meal.

There was another oversight. They never photographed themselves. So after he was gone, Pearlie had not a single picture of their lives together.

Part Three

If Chester April, through his long years of working at the mortuary, knew about violent death, then Duke Ellerman knew a thing or two about loneliness.

He'd seen a T-shirt somewhere which read *Life is a journey, are you packed?* At Brabazan Bar & Lodge he saw many journeys. What he noticed was that the journey often went nowhere past this bar, beyond all the bottles. What he saw was that the baggage most often packed was loneliness. Whether or not a person was married with family, the real loneliness, the one deep inside, which joviality failed to cover, the loneliness of the long-distance traveller, or the failed traveller, all came through here, through this drinking house.

Some of these drinkers knew that the movement from birth to death was nothing but a trek. They knew that you're born squalling and cold and you end up squalling and cold. Maybe you're squalling and cold in the middle too. Maybe you get some comfort on the way. Maybe you're lucky and land in the money and on the right side of the tracks. Maybe somebody loves you and you have some warmth for a while. But at the end of the day, you're just alone. Doing that track. That route from beginning to end, without any truthful answers about why, or where you're from and where you're headed.

As a barman, Duke had met many men and women rendered in a dark palette: the alcoholic, the betrayed, the unfaithful, the terminally ill, the mentally confused, the insecure. He'd been in the retail booze business long enough to tell a person's state of heart simply from the way they entered Brabazan, from their posture, from the way they glanced around and from whether they paused at the door or came straight in.

He could read their narrative from whether they put their bodies down at the bar or chose a corner table; from the way they handled a bottle or glass; whether they downed the first goddamned drink of the night or nursed it slowly; whether they drank just that one or many. He knew their story from the way they touched each other in drunken or emotional weariness; from how they intruded into the space of others; from the demands they made on him, Duke; from whether their cellphones rang or not and whether they answered them; and, finally, from the hour in which they walked or stumbled out. If the piano or saxophone was playing – live music, not the jukebox – then he learnt a lot too. Because music teased out from the heart so much of what was hidden.

People expected, simply because they'd washed up to the edge of his life, that he should pick up their pieces, however broken or uninteresting they might be. They wanted to be touched and held and told they were worth living for. They wanted to put their soul right there, plonk, on the counter, and say: 'Pick me up. Hold me. Heal me. Believe me.' But he couldn't do this. Often enough they'd forfeited everything, abandoned their children, deserted their wives for an ideal. They'd gone after a promise, or a better-looking piece of thigh, or a pulsing, volatile vulva not contracted to them through marriage.

He'd had murderers sit in front of him and felt the confession bubbling up their oesophagus like bile, but being swallowed back again with a double brandy or cane. There had been those who'd taken a last drink and then gone out to end their own life.

Often, an anxious wife would phone, giving a

description, asking whether her man was there, pretending she had a message, but really just trying to establish whether he was alive or dead or in a brawl or crashed on the highway or over the border and far away from her and the responsibility of his children. Perhaps he was at the bar with another woman, a pretty woman, one whose body had not been stretched by childbirth, who let him believe he was wonderful, in the way a wife no longer did.

The late ones, the ones who sat deep into the night until Brabazan closed, might be on, say, their last drink, and now pretty self-pitying with it, staring into the glass. Perhaps they made pathetic attempts at small talk. Duke knew how to turn off the listening when the night was old and nothing made sense. He knew that, at that hour, when the soul was peeled down to its very core, you just saw a mess. He knew not to hang in with those late boozers, but to leave them on their own rickety, lonely rafts. They would hit the rocky coastline, sooner or later.

He'd listen to the stories, sure, with half an ear at least, and he would grunt a reply or nod. But he had long ago learnt not to take other people's shit on board. He didn't have magic tape to fix things, so he couldn't help beyond giving a place to drink. He couldn't give existential answers or advice. There were no solutions here any more than there were solutions anywhere else.

Of course, not everyone was an alcoholic or big-time boozer. There were those who came in for a quick shot after work. There were discreet drinkers, content with a single-malt whisky or glass of Sauvignon. Some people came in just to eat, not necessarily to drink. Mostly his clients were regulars but, being on Long Street, Brabazan pulled in lots of tourists and visitors. Even in these customers, whom one might judge at first glance to be pretty in touch with themselves, he could read the lie of their stressed land.

He allowed an itinerant photographer called Fairy Patterson to come in each evening with a Polaroid camera to take photos of patrons for thirty rand. In these digital days, Fairy's customers were thin on the ground. Usually, they were tourists who liked the quaintness of having their picture taken by a pimped-out man whose trousers were held up by braces, and who wore a tartan jacket and bow tie. Very often they turned their own cameras on Fairy, taking a photo of him taking theirs.

Duke allowed in another regular. This was Primo Verona, who arrived now and then with a bunch of paper roses that he'd folded himself and lightly perfumed with rose oil. These he handed out to patrons, free, and without saying anything. He lived up in Kloof Street, just beyond the intersection, in a house that was full of clocks that had belonged to his watchmaker father. Primo kept them wound up and oiled, so they ticked and tocked and chimed and cuckooed without rest.

He was a clairvoyant and had once practised as a soothsayer, but now lived in seclusion, folding flowers. His wife, Beatrice, rented one of Duke's apartments in Overbeek because Primo was impossible to live with. Each lunchtime she called on him with a meal carried in a wicker basket. They ate together, either under the mulberry tree of his overgrown back garden, or in the kitchen, which was full of potted violets that, strangely, were always in full bloom. She'd tidy up and then watch him wind and clean clocks or obsessively fold roses, which he kept in his bedroom, letting them pile up around the bed, hundreds of them.

Each evening, Beatrice called on her one-time lover, Pasquale Benvenuto. She took him his dinner too, to the room above his boarded-up restaurant, and ate with him, saying very little. Then she would go into Brabazan for a sherry, on her own.

Yes, Duke Ellerman had seen it all come and go and come round again, like a sad, paint-peeling, rust-spotted, squeaking merry-go-round. He could write a book if he put his mind to it, he knew this. But what the hell? Who would read it?

Behind him, at the bar, the mirrored shelves of bottles reflected light and colour. On the wall opposite, what he looked onto as he worked, were six reproductions of paintings by Edward Hopper, the American realist.

Duke had had them printed onto canvas and framed so that, at a quick glance, they looked like originals. They were *Automat*, *Chop Suey*, *New York Restaurant, Soir Bleu, Nighthawks* and the haunting *Night Shadows*. He had another three hanging in his room upstairs and one in the passage outside the room occupied by Not The Midnight Mass.

For him, Hopper's pictures confirmed the solitude of life, particularly in a city that couldn't give a damn about whether you were alive or dead. They described alienation and the disquieting aloneness of the human condition. Each captured a moment within a story, tantalising the viewer with the unexpressed before and after events in an unfolding narrative. Within each work rested a strange and deep grace, but no joy.

In Brabazan, the prints performed as mirrors. That which was within them, captured for all time by Hopper's sonorous brushstrokes, was enacted outside, here at the tables and along the bar counter. Each might well have been a rehearsal for the other, the representation and the reality. There was gravity inside each framed work and gravity outside of it. Why Duke chose to hang art that illustrated the very real lives of many of his customers is hard to say. You'd think he had enough of all this, here in the flesh, at Brabazan.

He owned a number of volumes on Hopper, so he knew every work that had been reproduced in books and catalogues. He'd never seen an original Hopper but, even so, he had a deep understanding of the eloquent play of light that identified the artist's genius.

If by chance he'd got himself to the Metropolitan Museum of Art in New York, where *The Lighthouse at Two Lights* hangs in its full dimensions, not reduced to fit on a book page, he would have stood before it all day, oblivious of the crowds of viewers. He would have been mesmerised by the stoic, solemn and beautiful composition of the lighthouse, set on a rocky promontory and bathed in afternoon sunlight, standing like an isolated individual. This was not his favourite work, but it summarised loneliness, for it portrayed not a single figure, nor even the sea over which the lighthouse beam would have moved.

The Hopper prints hanging in his bedroom were *Summer Interior, Morning Sun* and *Hotel Room.* These were of lone women in whose postures or scant clothing could be read abuse, abandonment, betrayal and pain. In the way that the downstairs prints resonated with the lives of his patrons, so those in his room portrayed Duke's mother's path.

As the daughter of an unwed waitress, she'd grown up at St Michael's Children's Home in Plumstead. She married the first man who showed her any interest, only to find herself in his milieu of addiction and violence. She ran away from him and entered a life of prostitution.

Duke was her only child, seeded by a passing stranger and named because of her love of jazz and because of a particular song that sounded like somewhere sweet. She managed to keep Duke out of institutions and reasonably innocent of the men she pleasured in her locked bedroom.

He hated school and left young, joining the army and doing his turn in Angola, marking his soul indelibly with it. He was largely self-taught and read broadly in history, classics and art. But he was ultimately skilled for nothing except running his bar and lodge, and in reading faces and postures.

Duke had not had sex for some years. The Russian girls were there, and he could have called one to his room any time. But he'd never done that. Using them seemed wrong. 'Don't screw the crew,' he'd say, if you commented. He'd been married once, to a coloured girl, way back in the days when to have sex across the colour bar earned you a charge under the Immorality Act. So theirs was not a legal marriage, but consensual.

His common-law wife had worked as a nurse-aid at Somerset Hospital. There she'd met a sailor, a French boy, who'd come ashore with a broken leg and had to wait at the Seaman's Institute to be fetched on his vessel's return. She had befriended him and invited him for supper one night.

Duke had recently returned from Angola, from the Battle of Cuito Cuanavale, filled inside with emotional shrapnel, and just barely holding steady. He hadn't touched his wife since coming home, afraid that if he did, if he let his guard down, he might rage and hurt her, he might enact in their bed some residual horror of war.

At their table, over *bobotie* and rice, in the kitchen of their house in Harfield Village, which had not yet been purged by the Group Areas Act, Duke watched his wife decide to go with the Frenchman. He saw his marriage unravel right there, as she resolved to make a break for it and leave South Africa. It was all so simple. No argument. No animosity. No sex outside of the relationship. No betrayal. No bitterness. No lies. No need for a divorce because the marriage was by agreement. She just wanted more than the meagre portion apartheid allotted her and he respected that. He didn't hold her back, instead giving her money and blessing her in a non-religious way as she left for France to begin a life far away from racial segregation.

He, in turn, set off for Long Street, to buy a bar and also begin again, because he couldn't bear to live in his house alone, with the things he and his wife had bought together, with the clothes she'd left behind. He walked out the place, leaving it as it was, and for the next tenant to dismantle the furnishings of his love.

The year was 1989 and the government, led by PW Botha, continued with its ferocious management of the country. The owners of Brabazan decided it was finally time to leave and booked passage for New Zealand, selling the business to Duke, who settled his mortgage within the first five years of business.

Long Street then was home to a number of brothels, restaurants, bars and some roughish drinking holes. Competition was stiff, but he gradually built up a regular clientele by offering free snacks with early evening drinks and by serving real beef hamburgers (without soya and flour fillers) with good chips. These were billed as being 'like mother made them' – crisp on the outside and soft on the inside.

He set up a jukebox loaded with fifties, sixties and seventies singles, a pinball machine and a pool table. Upstairs, he introduced pleasures of the flesh. His first two girls were sisters, bottle-blondes from Goodwood, who used the professional names of Roxi and Ruby. In a nearby junkshop, he came across photos taken by Billy Monk: evocative black-and-white shots of Long Street girls and their clients, some now on display at the National Art Gallery. They reminded him of his mother and he smarted inside of himself, because he was repeating patterns, doing the same, making money from girls' bodies, but accepting that this was what life was all about, at the end of the day.

After Duke's wife had left him, he'd had a few lovers but never trusted himself, could never be sure he wouldn't hurt them, could not risk those bits of shrapnel cutting into them. His wife sent him Christmas cards for a few years, then stopped. Recently, he realised that he'd wedded himself to Brabazan. There had been no focus on love and healing. He'd closed off to all such possibilities.

Now, he was tired. After years at the helm, he ached all over, not just in his body, but deep inside. He wondered whether there was some illness cooking away, biding its ugly time. This letter from Billy-Jean Jones, his one-night stand from so long ago, announcing that she had borne his son, *that he had a son*, added a new fatigue. Why hadn't she told him? Why had she denied him any relationship with their child? Should he, Duke, have sensed that, in all these years, running alongside his own life, was that of a boy growing up who belonged to him? A boy who might have been told that his father didn't want him? Duke realised that he'd done what his own father had – seeded a life and then walked on. Except that he, Duke, would not have walked on, had he but known. He would have cradled his child and loved it.

Yes, of course he would accept the boy, without question, but what was he supposed to do when he arrived? What life could he offer in this environment of so many silted-up lives? What good could he be as a father?

Surprisingly, given his tough exterior, Duke Ellerman had a penchant for gardens and was a member of the Botanical Society. Every now and then he drove out, early in the morning, to Kirstenbosch to wander among the fragrances for an hour or two. He also had deep compassion for mistreated horses and belonged to the Carthorse Association. Whenever he went to the wholesalers in Wetton to buy monthly bulk provisions, he would look with sorrow at the carthorses dragging, under whip and curse, makeshift wagons full of scrap metal, on their way to dealers and recyclers.

One scorching midsummer day, he saw a cart loaded with a burnt-out minibus and drawn by a single horse. The animal was all but bursting its heart as it pulled the demonic weight, while young boys whipped it with a passion.

Duke had wanted to stop them, to strangle those ignorant little bastards with their own *sjambok*, to free the horse, mop its brow, heal the bridle sores, press a gentle hand against the protruding, work-weary bones, look into the terrified bloodshot eyes and still them with his own gaze of compassion. But he did nothing, so the image of that struggle entered a place where the guilt of undone good deeds was stored.

Somehow, all these thoughts about defenceless things crystallised into a concern for water, and he found himself reflecting on the rivers that had been channelled underground, through the city. They began their lives on Table Mountain, in the pouring rain, dancing down like bridal veils, joyful and speculative of the sea they were intuitively driven to reach. But they were deceived by drains and forced down into the dark, confining chambers of the city's underground systems, denied light and frivolity.

Sometimes, at night, he thought he heard water thundering underground, beating at the sides of the storm drains, wanting to be released from that sunless place, as though knowing it was being cheated. Like Anastasia's parrot yearning for the colour green, the water had a sense about coursing across open land and fanning into reed- and bird-filled estuaries.

Duke would stand at the front door of Brabazan and look up at the clouds, thinking of the ocean floor, reflecting that the content of every bottle and can consumed at his bar, since the day he'd opened, had been effectively pissed into the sea.

In winter he enjoyed going up into Van Riebeeck Park, at the foot of the mountain, and looking at the swollen streams before they entered the drains. He would encounter people wearing the silver star of Zion on their lapels, filling bottles with what they considered to be holy water. Once, he filled a small bottle himself and kept it near his bed.

Now and then, he'd ride his motorbike out to Milnerton or Blouberg early in the morning and walk along the beaches, where feelings of despair at the plastic trash would mingle with his sense of awe at the sea's wild beauty. Once, he saw a stranded dolphin and he sat near to it. Long ago, at each full moon, before the nuclear power station was built, he used to ride to Koeberg and then walk the stretch of white dunes, where fossilised whale bones could still be found.

He always had in mind to make some sort of pilgrimage to the site of the Salt River estuary, a place now buried beneath the reclaimed land of the Foreshore. His thoughts also dwelt on the fate of Woodstock beach, now buried under pavement and forgotten. 'We have created a mass grave,' he would have answered, if you'd asked him. 'The edge here, which was once a living interchange between land and rivers and sea, is now a massive tombstone of highway, concrete and cement. Don't talk to me about the mass graves we make for our genocides. Don't reflect only on those. There are bones here too. Of whale and turtle and perlemoen. Please, drop the subject now. It crushes me.'

Very occasionally, he walked out to the breakwater at the start of a day, to look across impasto waves. He'd hear haunting reverberations twisting through storm and wind and calm, like a sort of sighing, or like the rhythmic knocking of sticks and drums, or like the plucking of a single-string calabash harp.

The breakwater had been built by captured Bushmen in the nineteenth century. An *igqirha* now listening would recognise the sighs as coming out from the hand-hewn stone and belonging to those doomed men. He would hear their lamentation for lost freedom and their longing for the plains of the Karoo, where they once roamed free. He would understand their longing for the water of their spring at Bitterpits. He would hear their mourning song for the eland, their sacred animals, whose limbs clicked when they walked across the terrain.

It remains a forgotten thing, that the eland bestowed their clicking sounds upon the Bushmen dialects. These were later taken up by the amaXhosa, the first conquerors and assimilators of the southern San bands.

One by one the Bushman dialects died, as their speakers were near-exterminated by colonists. No one would remember, nor would a single modern linguist document, that the palatal and lingual clicking, now so prevalent in Xhosa speech, had belonged to the majestic sacred eland, and been given as a gift to the Bushmen, only to be immortalised by others.

Standing there on the breakwater, amidst the haunting sounds that he couldn't fathom but which entered and moved him, so that he recognised them as having a profound and mysterious significance, Duke would find himself clicking his fingers and thinking about the end of his own days.

How would it be? Would a baying jackal or the cry of an owl warn him – creatures that no longer roamed these parts? Would these enter his dreams to prophesy his end? Would it be violent, outside in the street, or would it be at the cash till, shot by armed robbers? He was not a religious man. The self-righteousness that went with dogma turned his stomach. Religious leaders and politicians were, to his mind, cut from the same cloth. They were all liars, cheats, power brokers and opportunists who stole from poor and rich alike, misleading the innocent and those seeking explanation of mystery. This didn't mean that he had no thoughts of the Divine. He did. But he didn't believe any single religion properly served it. As far as he was concerned, religions, with their false doctrines, condemned it.

Buddhism was attractive. But, in Buddhist terms, he was altogether in the wrong profession. His dealing in drink and prostitution was far from Right Livelihood. So what could he do? He couldn't simply run a lodge, couldn't just rent out rooms. People don't only eat and sleep. People drink and smoke and want sex. People do all the things that Buddhist Right Livelihood does not approve.

Of late, though, Duke had felt himself softening even more and was angered by this. To grow up, to get out of that childhood, he'd had to harden everything about himself, not only his heart and mind, but also his fists and kicking boots. He'd learnt early on that submission got you nowhere in life.

But now, in his mature years, this new softening, where was it coming from? What was it all about? Why did he find himself waking at night with a murmur in his chest and the sense of tears? Why was he remembering scenes from childhood that he had blocked out? Why was all that shit from his army days, all that killing, why was that getting dragged up now? Surely it was all over? Childhood and apartheid were done, for God's sake. Let all those ghosts be damned.

Wasn't it enough that he felt for flowers and water and those wretched carthorses? Why should it be that, ever since a bull had escaped from the abattoir some months before, he should now have to hesitate a moment before cutting into steak? Why did the pink of that rare-cooked piece have to look like blood? Must his inner fabric start breaking apart? Must he end up a soft man just because a domestic animal had raged against its fate?

That bull. It had stormed out from the slaughterhouse, throwing men off their feet, knocking aside butchers with their electric prodders and stun guns, sending them flying. It had thundered into the traffic, steam snorting from its nostrils and hooves striking the tar, challenging cars and trucks. 'Kill me properly!' it seemed to say. 'Kill me face to face, in an equal battle. Kill me here under the sun. Give me a chance to defend myself and, if I am the victor, then let all of us go! Let us all go! Don't kill us on tiles, in those narrow holding cages, in that holocaustian chamber of horror!'

That bull. It had taken a number of bullets to bring it down. But down it came, out there, with people screaming and running in panic, in front of the few houses still left standing opposite the abattoir. And then it was forgotten. An unknown, once majestic beast, brought all the way in from a farm in Adelaide, a two-day journey on a crowded two-tiered truck, without food or water, with his fellow beasts, all of them standing in their own turds.

That bull. 'I saw you,' whispered Duke. 'I was there, on that road, driving through Maitland. I saw your enraged eyes and your rippling skin. And I saw myself seeing you. I heard my mouth say: "Let my people go", like Moses. Why did I say that? But now I'm growing soft. Because of you, I'm growing feeble.'

This was why Duke was reading Kapuściński again – to remind himself about the true nature of humankind and to toughen up with it; to remind himself that a soft man is a kicked man and that war was the true human story – war against everything and everyone. He was into his fourth study of the book. It was becoming like a rosary, a mantra, to be read over and over.

The army had nearly killed him. Up there in Angola, at Cuito Cuanavale, where three armies clashed in the largest land battle in Africa since the Desert War of the North African Campaign. Back then, fifteen thousand British and Axis fatalities had been recorded. At Cuito Cuanavale, twenty thousand soldiers are said to have been killed. But what are figures, at the end of the day? When battle is done, who assembles the cartilage and tendon, the delicate bones of hand and foot, to ensure a body is properly reconstructed and accounted for? There will always be dispute of more or less. There will always be remains forgotten and lost in the sand. There will always be debate about this war being greater than that.

At that last battle, he'd teamed up with two Jewish

guys, not for any reason except that you always bond with someone when death breathes down your neck and you stand at the edge of hell. He found their prayer – *Baruch ata Adonai* – creeping in and soothing his fear, and wondered whether his own childhood Catholic prayers were calming them. Perhaps all the prayers were merging: 'Hail Mary. *Baruch.* Mother of God. *Adonai.* Pray for us now at the hour of our death. Pray for us now. *Adonai. Adonai.*'

Sometimes the simple psalm, the most used psalm, the one worn down by overuse, swirled within them: 'The Lord is my shepherd. Though I walk through the valley of the shadow of death, I will not fear evil. I will not fear. I will not fear. *Hashem ro'iy. Gam ki elech begei tsalmavet, lo ira. Lo ira. Lo ira.*'

Those prayers, whoever they belonged to in the first instance, now belonged to all of them, but it was only their mothers who heard them. Only their mothers, not their diverse gods, picked up their terror, like radar, for gods are never present in times of carnage. War is the devil's country. It is devils we should pray to on battlefields.

Duke had seen guys falling to the left and to the right. Those who came home had all manner of madness to deal with. He didn't come back mad, not really, though there is always some madness after battle. You can't witness friends being blown to nothing and not be a bit crazy. But he had dealt with it by compartmentalising everything: That was the army. That was Angola. That was the killing. That was the mass grave. Those were the limbs hanging in the tree after the *troepie* accidentally set off the grenade box. That was the pink vapour that was once a body. That was the burnt-beyond-recognition twenty-year-old, an only child from Pretoria. That was the Ratel, burning, with all the bodies inside. That was all then. But now, this here, right now, was Brabazan. This here was regular life. This here was Cape Town. This was not Angola. This was Long Street. The war was in little boxes, all put away.

Duke now calculated, as he sat behind his bar holding the letter from Billy-Jean Jones telling him he had a son, that the Long Street party, during which his child was conceived, had indeed taken place thirteen years ago. It had started off quite innocently, as a masked fancy-dress event. Traffic was closed from dusk till dawn between Bloem Street and the Buitensingel intersection.

Crowds poured in, wearing their masks and fancy dress. There was plenty of delicious food and dancing and live music and fairy lights draped from pillar to pole. Cape Town had never seen an event peopled by so many movie and storybook characters. The ambience was wonderful and gave a taste of the cosmopolitan and the absurd.

But, somewhere along the line of that night, heavy drugs and drink had turned the atmosphere bad. A double murder had been committed, though only one body was accounted for, at Maginty's, that of a prominent plastic surgeon, killed, it was said, by his lover's black paramour. The second corpse somehow disappeared. A pool of blood in Orphan Lane spoke of a violent stabbing. An added mystery was that the blood failed to clot or dry and remained there on the tar until its arterial-scarlet was hosed down the drain and out to sea by municipal cleaners.

There was definitely something mystifying about that night, as though the very gates of hell had opened and the devil himself brazenly walked the street in a tuxedo, making out to be just a regular Joe Citizen. Yet it also seemed that the under-rigging of heaven had come adrift, tossing angels, with all their glitter, into the throng and shenanigans of the night.

All sorts of stories circulated for years afterwards and people were never sure about what was true and what was not. The high consumption of drugs and drink ensured kaleidoscopic, multidimensional and diverse memories, earning the party the status of an urban legend.

Duke never usually bothered with what went on in the streets, but he had decided to go to this gig. Midway through the party, when it was already tightly packed and in full gear, but before the drug dealers had begun their serious work, he'd smoked a joint of Malawi gold and filled a hip flask. He locked up Brabazan and told Alfonso, his guard, to keep the fire-escape door open for residents who might wish to come in and out. His staff had the night off and most went out to party and do some wild things.

Wearing a thin black mask, he set off into the crowd. Every breath around him was hot and laden with the smell of garlic or chilli or tobacco mixed with a beastly concoction of vice and vomit. People were sweating and their bodies pulsing to the loud music.

He'd found Billy-Jean leaning up against a pillar, seemingly waiting for him, dressed in a poplin retro frock with a stiff, frilly petticoat that held the skirt up full and buoyant. She wore black Louis heels and white ankle socks. A silver mask covered half her face, which was framed by a wig of blonde curls. Somewhere, early on, she'd discarded her underwear. Sipping brandy and Coke from a bottle through a straw, her perfumed loveliness was untouched by the frenzy.

They had sex right there, up against the pillar, with the throbbing crowd pressing against them, adding rhythm.

Unknown to him at the time, though she knew – oh, she knew – because she felt the flutter inside, her baby was conceived in a whoosh of the brandy and Coke that laced her veins. It was a little boy soul and he would grow up thinking his father had ridden into town on a horse and ridden out again.

Later, in his room at Brabazan, where he and Billy-Jean had stumbled when the party pitch got really bad and the energy rocketed out of control, Duke made love to her. This was not just sex. It was different from their encounter outside. This was soft. This was, if painted, a Nabistic expression of flesh and white moonlight splashed with vermilion. It was an encounter of breath and the realisation of deep touch, so very different from Hopper's moody, lonely tonalism that hung on the walls.

Something had come loose inside of Duke, some mooring rope, maybe because of the drink and the joint he'd smoked. So when he held Billy-Jean, he had in his arms not only her body, but that other part of her, the part that someone looking for labels might have called spirit, but which Duke simply equated to water – wild, beautiful, unpolluted, gay, free water. It reminded him of loving his wife, of his own tenderness which had been burnt by war.

He waited for this new person, this stranger he had picked up outside. He waited for her in that place before orgasm and they swirled there together. The bits of emotional shrapnel inside of him seemed to turn to stars and he remembered the red flares of night battle, thinking them so beautiful at the time, so surreal, so out of place there among the tanks and death, and how that old Beatles' song had come into his head: *Lucy in the sky with diamonds*. It had been so incongruous, so ludicrous. But now, it was just right. Stars and night and this woman in his arms.

Afterwards, for no reason they could discern, both began to cry. Perhaps she cried because now there was this little soul inside of her, and it transmitted to her heart some fear, some apprehension, at having been conceived into a debauched, drug-fuelled, terrifying world. Perhaps Duke cried because he had hardened himself for such a long time, not wanting to love or be loved. And now here was love, asking something of him, beckoning him to fall. But he wasn't going to, because if he fell, then he would be soft and wouldn't manage his life.

They slept tightly together, both waking with a start when they heard gunshots, then falling asleep again, before the wail of a police siren signalled the end of the party. A veil of silence fell over Long Street.

In the morning, Billy-Jean didn't want tea or breakfast. She just wanted to go home. It had been a one-night stand for her and the night was now over. In her flat, she took a shower, letting the hot water run over her for an age. Duke was sorry to see her go, but then he closed off to her. The stars and diamonds had gone out. After that night, he never drank alcohol or rolled joints, not daring to risk anything coming loose inside of him again.

Billy-Jean Jones (who'd changed her name from Beth-Joanna when she'd left school) had been married for a number of years to a political journalist and satirist called Jerry Jones, who worked at various times for the *Argus* and *Rand Daily Mail* before settling for freelance work.

Jerry detested apartheid and all its machinations. In 1976, after the Soweto uprising, there was an escalation of violence throughout the country, with spirals of revolution and repression. A State of Emergency allowed for awful police brutality and detentions without trial. One morning, driving in to town, he saw a *Cape Times* banner declaring 'Vorster rules out change'.

He pulled over and took down the poster, later sticking it up on their lounge wall, furiously shouting: 'What the fuck! The country's on fire and he rules out change! Who the fuck does he think he is?'

Later that night, having drunk a few glasses of wine, he threw the empty bottle over the balcony and, as it shattered below, said: 'That's it! We're out of here. We're leaving. Sooner or later someone's going to put a gun in my hand and I'm going to have to use it. Sooner or later this *swart gevaar* will get into my head space and make me want to kill blacks. I don't want to kill blacks.'

He had, quite by chance, avoided the army. In the year he left school, the military still gathered its fighting forces through a ballot system. In his year, 1964, they had over-balloted and he received a pink card advising him he was exempt. It was simply a stroke of luck. Four years later, the ballot system was changed to full compulsory military service. From then on, it was mandatory for all white males to serve in one or other of the armed forces. They were drafted as they left school, still young and fresh with boyhood. Those who could tried to get into the air force or navy, believing these to be safer, or at least more comfortable, options. The others joined the infantry, where they would see bloody action in Angola, Namibia, Mozambique and in South Africa's black townships.

Jerry decided on Hong Kong, securing a job as a night sub-editor on the *Hong Kong Standard*. Billy-Jean was reluctant to leave South Africa and not sure they'd be able to make a life in the East. But he convinced her that they'd do fine – they were still young, after all. They sold up everything in their apartment. After a farewell braai with her family on her brother Kleinboet's farm in Robertson, and a final Sunday lunch with Jerry's widowed mother in Sea Point, they set off for a new world, leaving Prime Minister Vorster's comment in the flat for the next tenant to mull over.

After they'd left, each October, Jerry's mother baked a traditional Christmas cake and posted it by surface mail to them. Jerry was her only child. Her heart broke when he and Billy-Jean left. She knew she'd never see them again. Baking the cake allowed her to concentrate love into it, in a way that sending a shop-bought gift would not. The cake lasted them a whole year. Each morning they ate a small square of it with their coffee. They thought of her and she thought of them.

It was not unlike the wedding cake baked by Carol Bosch for Pearlie's wedding. Perhaps the two recipes had the same source, it's impossible to say. Carol had been using hers since 1972, when it was given to her by her sister's ex-husband's aunt Shirley, who, by now herself in her seventies, had used it for years.

By 2004, ten years after apartheid's end, Mrs Jones lived in a room at the William Booth Memorial Hospital in Oranjezicht, having forgotten both her son and daughter-in-law, as well as the Christmas cake recipe, though every now and then she would reflect on her Kenwood Chef and tell the matron that one of the nurses had stolen it. By then, Billy-Jean was back in Cape Town. She'd gone once to visit Mrs Jones, but the old lady got into a bit of a panic at having this strange woman in her room, so Billy-Jean never went back.

When Mrs Jones lived in Sea Point, she'd watched the

Atlantic over many years, in all its moods and colours, from her windows. Now, up against the mountain, her senile mind wondered where the sea had gone, for all she could see was rock. She couldn't properly formulate a question about this. There was just the apprehension that something was missing.

Although Jerry had no problem adjusting to the East, Billy-Jean found Hong Kong, with its heavily trafficked streets and massive high-rise buildings, a difficult place. New constructions seemed to race each other to reach the sky, wrapped in bamboo scaffolding across which workers scurried like ants. There were just too many people and the space was too tight. Families of six or eight might live in the tiniest apartment. Windows were festooned with laundry flapping from poles.

They had to learn to accommodate space economically, not to bump into people, to sit neatly in restaurants. The first time they ate out, they took a table and presumed they'd be the only ones to sit there. Billy-Jean was sprawled across, leaning to one side, reading the menu. A waitress gently tucked in her elbows, making her sit upright in her chair, as one might do to a child. Four more diners were added to the table.

Yet, despite the crush and crowds, people were courteous, patient and genteel. There was no jostling and bumping. They were never harassed or accosted and, because there was none of South Africa's violent crime, they could stroll through parks and walk safely at night without fear. Traffic was controlled and law-abiding. Buses were on schedule, traffic lights and stop signs were obeyed. If you walked over a zebra crossing, you weren't dicing with death.

When they first arrived, they lived high up in a small flat. Below, life rumbled and tumbled along, 24/7. In the nearby street market, vendors sold fruit and vegetables, tofu and sprouts. Live chickens, turtles, frogs, snakes, fowls and even dogs were held in cages and containers awaiting purchase and slaughter. Fish moved lethargically in too-small barrels and basins, with just enough water to keep them alive. If a fish were purchased, it would be cleaved in two, down the middle, and opened out to show the customer a still-beating heart, before being gutted and wrapped. Tanks held lustreless eels and giant shrimps that wiggled and squirmed as they awaited their fate alongside crabs whose claws were bound with string. Slabs of whale meat, tuna and dolphin were sliced into delicate pieces that gave no hint of the majestic creatures they'd once been. Squares of desiccated perlemoen were on sale, and Billy-Jean knew they could only have been poached from the coastal waters around Hermanus. Medicinal stalls sold powdered or ground-down antlers and horns, including rhino, purported to treat illness and impotence. There was also bear bile – cruelly harvested from caged bears – and musk on offer.

Billy-Jean stopped eating meat. Jerry discovered that fish caught in the heavily polluted South China Sea was not safe to eat, so they cut that from their diet. They learnt to say in Mandarin: 'Is this dog? I don't eat dog. I don't eat turtle. I don't eat cat. I don't want flesh. I want tofu. I want vegetable only. *Vegetable only!*'

Jerry worked night shift. During the day, he eased the two of them into their new lives, strolling through the Jade Market and the aviary and frequently visiting the Flagstaff House Museum of Tea Ware. They explored Chinese culture and history and found themselves in awe of so much.

At the ornate temple in Temple Street, exquisitely decorated in red and gold, Billy-Jean and Jerry watched people make offerings of fruit before statues and consult soothsayers at open tables. The air was thick with incense. A man threw oracle sticks. Two women were engrossed with a Feng Shui master. What did they want to know? Billy-Jean wondered. Was this about love? Or debt? Were they dealing with illness?

After a few months, Jerry found accommodation on Lantau Island and, once they moved there, Billy-Jean's tensions eased. Each weekend, they went exploring, travelling by bus as far as Li Po, visiting temples and monasteries, absorbing the chanted prayers that emanated from them and enjoying the tranquillity of the surrounding forest.

She wrote features for British magazines and newspapers, becoming fascinated by the ancient practice of foot binding and the fate of Chinese women whose feet had been crushed into tiny embroidered silk shoes. Mao Tse-tung had outlawed this mutilation. He burnt books and musical instruments, denigrating all forms of intellectualism and art, but he released the feet of women, allowing them to walk and work after centuries of being forcibly crippled.

Their accommodation on Lantau was the old Beach House canteen in Pui O village and was situated right at the water's edge, looking onto a gently curving bay. It was somewhat run-down and had the appearance of a garage. Though its wide front veranda was a landing point for smugglers who moved goods between mainland China and Hong Kong, the place was safe and quiet. Jerry learnt that the smuggling had been going on for years, but sensed it best not to enquire about the practice.

Early each Thursday morning, a boat anchored in the bay and a smaller motorboat made a number of trips back and forth, offloading goods. Skinny, barefoot men, wearing ragged shorts, would wade ashore carrying baskets of live chickens, eggs, fresh produce, pickled garlic, jars of preserved ginger, bottles of rice wine and barrels of petrol. These goods, most of which had been ordered the week before, would be sold in less than a quarter-hour. Mostly it was old ladies who bought from the smugglers. They seemed to arrive from out of nowhere, wearing straw hats and pulling small shopping trolleys, their bent backs showing signs of advanced osteoporosis. With the Hong Kong dollars they earned, the smugglers bought Western goods and medicines not available in communist China.

Close by, behind Beach House, was a small temple dedicated to a sea goddess and full of ancient urns and statues, open day and night. In Cape Town, these treasures would have been stolen and their metals melted down and sold. Billy-Jean learned that, in China, only a fool with no understanding of supernatural implications would steal from a holy site. Also nearby was a bonsai garden, and she and Jerry would stroll through, towering above hundred-year-old dwarfed trees that grew in ceramic pots and which bore the tiniest leaves and pods.

Life settled into a comfortable pattern. Jerry started a garden. He cultivated earthworms and made compost to enrich the soil, and grew a variety of vegetables. He made his own soya milk and bought chickens and eggs from a nearby smallholding. So they ate healthily and well.

Inspired by the Flagstaff Museum, he set up a tea corner in the lounge. There they drank from porcelain bowls, sitting on cushions, unwinding, relaxing and reading poetry aloud. They ate their meals on the veranda, watching the tide rise and fall in its variety of moods and colours. Docile water buffaloes roamed freely along the beach and in nearby fields. The moon rising over the bay became one of their cherished icons of tranquillity.

Jerry commuted to work by Star Ferry between Lantau and Hong Kong. Billy-Jean often went with him and would write her articles in his office. They loved that short journey to and fro, especially at night, with its panorama of city lights.

But then, when they were well accustomed to oriental living, Billy-Jean had a panic attack at the station. It seemed to her that a million black-haired, white-shirted, black-skirted, black-shoed, slant-eyed people of the same small stature were coming towards her, marching in step to a military beat, like automatons. Fearing she might fall over, she clung to a railing, then made her way to a kiosk from where she called Jerry. After that, it was all over. She decided to return to Cape Town. They parted amicably and didn't divorce. He sent her money each month. She began to drink a bit much.

The year was 1994. Apartheid had been consigned to history and an elected democracy was newly in place. It was not the country they'd left behind. Her brother, Kleinboet, owned an apartment in Green Point and she lived there Mondays to Fridays, going out to the farm each weekend. She got a job as a research assistant at the university and befriended a coloured woman called Connie April, whose husband worked at the Salt River mortuary.

Billy-Jean bought a glass-fronted corner cupboard for virtually nothing at Katzen's closing-down sale in the Werdmuller Centre, putting on display two tea bowls she'd brought back with her.

She heard, on the radio, the announcement of a party to be held in Long Street. The whole road was to be closed off and there would be food and crowds. Maybe she'd bump into a friend from the past and start up old circles again.

It was a wild party with outdoor bands playing to a pulsing crowd. She had sex with a man that night, a perfect stranger called Duke who ran a bar and lodge. She'd just turned forty and fell pregnant with her first and only child.

Deciding not to complicate things, she registered Jerry as the baby's father and used Duke's surname as a middle name. Jerry accepted the responsibility, upping the money he sent each month. If it was Billy-Jean's baby, then it was his too.

After the birth, Billy-Jean met a girl, a film-maker, while having coffee at Giovanni's. There was an instant warmth between them, and it was not long before they moved in together, sharing the baby. Billy-Jean discovered how sweet and delicate sex was with another woman. She took on the stronger role, changing her style of dress to Doc Martens, leather jackets and low-cut Levis. She had a running wolf tattooed on her back.

Lonely without his wife, Jerry began to use opium. It wouldn't be long before the dream space it gave asked of him all that he could give, so he floated there, eventually sacrificing his job and Beach House, until he became but a bag of bones in an opium house somewhere.

When Billy-Jean's boy reached puberty, her lover suddenly reversed sexual orientation and looked up her old partner, a banker with the Board of Executors, the one for whom she'd left Billy-Jean.

Billy-Jean, now alone with a son entering adolescence, found herself beginning to resent him. She wanted her little boy back, with his soft skin and chubby cheeks. She wanted her girl-lover and life as it had been over the last thirteen happy years. But there was no going back.

Irrational and angry, she decided to take a break from maternal duties, to send the boy to his biological father and to go travelling. She would set off via Hong Kong to find Jerry, who had simply disappeared. His phone was disconnected, post to the Beach House address was returned undelivered and he no longer worked at the *Hong Kong Standard*.

Duke was easy enough to find because he'd never left Long Street. She wrote him a letter, telling him she wanted him to care for the boy for a while. Duke, with that letter in hand, now looked around his room, which was a bachelor's place, not a family home. The boy couldn't share with him. Upstairs was the brothel. He had this Oberon fellow in the corner room who'd booked in for ten days but might extend, and would be welcome to. The short- and long-let rooms on the third floor were not really suitable, just one level down and too close to his sex workers.

Dr Smith had been lying ill in bed for some days. Amèlia reported him whimpering, unable to get up and go to work. He'd witnessed something awful in the township and wouldn't speak about it. His room would be perfect, but this was not the time to ask him to move upstairs. The boy would just have to share with his father for the time being. With some skilful rearrangement, they'd easily fit in a futon. He asked one of his cleaners to clear cupboard space and sent Amèlia to buy teenager-appropriate linen.

Later that day, an odd sensation entered his heart, a feeling of anticipation, as though he'd stood at a railway siding for years and become numbed with waiting. Now the waiting was over. He took down his helmet and rode his motorcycle to the Gardens Centre. There he had his hair cut and bought new clothes.

Part Four

The scaffolding of Pearlie Theron's life collapsed on the first night of Rosh Hashana, eight months before the May morning of her contemplative gaze out the window of her flat.

On that night, Thespian Winter had sat at the head of his festive table, surrounded by family and friends and all the good energies they evoked. Not a thought strayed to his mistress, as it never did when he was at home, lest he inadvertently mention her name. He had felt himself basking, a little self-righteously, in the tradition of the night.

Neither the table settings nor the menu had changed throughout all the Rosh Hashana celebrations of his marriage. His wife had reserved, for use only on this night, the embroidered tablecloth and its serviettes, the Royal Doulton dinner service, crystal glasses, silver serving platters and cutlery that she'd bought when they first married.

Her guests dipped pieces of apple into honey to signify a sweet new year and ate slices cut from a round challah, symbolic of the cycle of the coming twelve months and their wholeness. Traditionally keeping to her mother's menu, Mrs Winter served clear chicken broth, tzimmes – a rich and flavoursome dish of silverside, prunes and carrots – together with roast potatoes, lightly steamed green beans and a shredded cabbage salad flavoured with caraway seeds.

The Winters were not religious, but both of them respected Passover, Rosh Hashana and Yom Kippur. Now,

Thespian reflected on the long line of ancestry behind him, stretching all the way back to Abraham, surviving pogroms, ghettos and camps. As his thoughts moved towards the forthcoming Day of Atonement, he felt content with his identity and with everything that being a Jew embraced. Though he routinely fasted and went to shul on that auspicious day, he decided that this time he would commit to a proper examination of self, thinking of Polonius's words: 'This above all – to thine own self be true, and it must follow, as the night the day, thou canst not then be false to any man.'

Beyond his quiet deliberation continued the chatter and laughter of the evening. His eldest daughter, Judith, was pregnant with her first child and he noticed how like her mother she looked. The beautiful bloom of her face reminded him of the early days of his own marriage. The second girl, Rebecca, had just been promoted in her job with a firm of chartered accountants. The third, his youngest, his dear Rachel, the feisty, independent, argumentative one whom he called Raychi, would graduate in psychology at the end of the year.

He had done good for his daughters and denied them nothing, leaving the disciplining to his wife. Thankfully, they'd spared Mrs Winter any complication by not falling in love with non-Jews, people of colour or lesbians. Though they'd had rather tempestuous teen years, they were composed now. Well, his Raychi still had some wildness and enjoyed a long, late party and drinking, but she would grow out of it, he knew.

Others seated at the table were his son-in-law, Gerald (a somewhat pompous, overweight, self-opinionated fellow, but otherwise fairly affable), and the two boyfriends, Rael and Shaun, whom he liked and hoped one day to welcome into his family. Also positioned around the white cloth were the Jacobsons and the Alhadeffs (husbands and wives), long-time family friends.

As he watched Mrs Winter put down a bowl of *taiglach* and proceed to slice a spiced apple torte, lightly dusted with icing sugar and cinnamon, the words of his youngest daughter broke his reverie, so his gaze moved from the cake to her, beckoned by her vivacious voice to a place far removed from festivity.

'So, my Dada, what's it with you and Miss Theron? Is there something between you? Do you sleep with her? I mean, are you lovers? Do you really only go to eat Chinese and watch Shakespeare? You must tell us now. No secrets, Dada, before Yom Kippur.'

She had been teasing, of course, and had drunk a little too much kosher wine and perhaps taken more than that single tot of whisky he'd poured her. Actually, if he thought about it, he'd been waiting for this question for a long time. But why had fate positioned his favourite child, and not his wife, to unlock the box of all things hidden?

A number of conversations had been under way and there was the lovely postprandial hubbub of content and happy voices. But all came to an abrupt halt as Rachel's question hung in the air, as though at the edge of a torrent that had no bridge. His wife said nothing.

He had sucked at a tooth, acutely aware of everything unfolding in slow motion, as he leant with one arm on the table, his sleeve rolled up, the wedding ring belonging to this marriage glinting under candlelight. Looking into his glass, at the red of its liquid, he thought: 'The wine-cup is the little silver well, where truth, if truth there be, doth dwell.' Then he took a deep breath and admitted: 'Well, yes, Miss Pearlie has been my …' and here he paused and wondered whether he should use the biblical *concubine*. Would this be more acceptable than *whore* or *mistress* or *strumpet* or *wench* or *lover*, which all worked well at number four Maynard Court, but which at this table would point to something not clean, to something sinful, and which last implied a young and frivolous relationship?

The word which hovered at his tongue was *puttana*, for it was round and rippled and good and playful. All the things that happened at Maynard Court were *puttanesque*, if one could coin such a word, so wonderfully *puttanesque*, all rolling in wine and debauchery and corpulence. He cleared his throat and said: 'Miss Pearlie Theron is my mistress. We've been having an affair for many years.'

Shock and disbelief took hold of each person at the table. They stared at Thespian, whose confession was totally out of character with the personae of the husband, father, friend and host that they knew.

'Please God, don't let this be. Please,' whispered Mrs Winter, thinking he was playing an ugly, tasteless joke. It crossed her mind that the new medication he was taking for his angina must be mixing badly with the wines of the night.

But, now that the doors of truth-telling had opened, Thespian continued: 'I'm living a dual existence. I am two people. I have two marriages, two wedding bands, two wives, two worlds. I have ...'

'Stop!' exclaimed Rachel, smacking the table.

Mrs Winter bit her lip, leaned across and squeezed her daughter's arm. Rachel, pulling away from her mother's grasp, shouted: 'Miss Theron! Oh my God! Oh my God! I don't believe this! You're having sex with your secretary! How can you even touch her? How can you touch her and then come home to Moma? How can you touch Moma?' With this she burst into tears.

'Raychi ...,' he began, but she cut him short with: 'Don't speak to me! I hate you! Speak to Moma! Say sorry to Moma! Say sorry!'

'Hush. Hush now,' said Mrs Winter, embarrassed in front of her guests and the servants, who were surely pressing their ears at the kitchen door. She wanted to kill him, to stab him, to kick him in that disgusting crotch. But she did nothing, merely held in, wishing the visitors would leave right now. She never wanted to see them again.

Mr Jacobson cleared his throat and Mr Alhadeff tapped his glass with a dessert spoon. Everyone wanted someone else to say something, but left it to Thespian, who merely drew a hand across his lips, pushed back his chair and walked out onto the veranda. There he lit a cigarette and smoked it slowly, realising that certain wardrobes would never again be opened and certain costumes never again worn. It was the end for Camilla and Frida and all their bucking-bronco love games. He felt sorry about this.

He should have walked back into the dining room and said: 'Truth is truth, to the end of reckoning. My life in this house is so limited. I'm only the provider. Mr Moneybags. Nothing else. At Maynard Court I'm somebody. My true person. A comedian. A lover. I play my violin. Do you know that? I play gypsy music. I laugh. Oh, how I laugh. You've never seen me laugh like that. I love Miss Pearlie Theron. I love her, deeply. She's my friend. My Sun. My Moon. My Star. My everything. And yes, I love you too. My family. My girls. But nothing like that love. Nothing like my love for her. Doubt truth to be a liar, but never doubt I love.'

But nowhere inside of himself could he find the courage to deliver this. He had neither sword nor pistol at his side to take on a proper dramatic role. There was no banjo strumming in the background, no balladeer in the wings and no thumping drums to serenade further pronouncements. If anything, there were trumpeting angels announcing the start of the Last Judgment.

He threw the stub out over the clivias, which were in flaming orange bloom, then walked back inside and past the table, now in disarray on so many levels, saying not a word but making his way upstairs and to bed. The Jacobsons and Alhadeffs took up jackets and handbags and said their goodbyes, *sotto voce*, as though at a funeral, and already lined up in battle formation, behind the trenches, on his wife's side, with him cast out forever in no-man's-land. From this night, he would have not one single friend in the Jewish community.

Mrs Jacobson and Mrs Alhadeff would spend the next day on the phone, enlivening the chat lines as they hadn't done since old Mr Prener was found naked and dead of a heart attack in his maid's bed.

When he woke next day, Thespian Winter remembered nothing. Not his name. Not his daughters' faces. Not his wife coming into the room and locking the door and saying awful things in a vile, bitter voice. Not her opening his wardrobe and chest of drawers and flinging everything onto the floor, with all his shoes and even his toothbrush. Not her pulling their *ketubah* out and shredding it into a hundred pieces. Not her final hysterical shouting and the daughters banging on the door to be let in. Not his son-in-law, Gerald, breaking it down, pushing him out the way and leading Mrs Winter downstairs. Not watching from the banister, looking down at his family as a servant brought out cups of Milo. Not Mrs Winter throwing hers against the ivory curtains so that the stain of chocolate might have been blood. Not her piercing scream rising up as if from hell, tearing his eardrums. And, sadly, he didn't hear his beautiful daughter Judith start crying, clutching at her swollen belly, as it began heaving into premature labour. All of this was erased along with every detail of his business life. And, of course, he never made it to the Day of Atonement.

Worse still, he never got to say goodbye to Pearlie. His farewell, in keeping with the decor and style of the diorama in which their love affair existed, should have involved a crescent moon, stars, goblets of wine, the voice of a tenor, the lapping of water, textures of velvet, colours with depth to them and a book of love poems. At the very least, one should have seen, near the Bridge of Sighs, a curtained gondola ready to carry away a cloaked mistress. But there was none of that.

The next morning, his habitual memory kicked in and took him through various movements. He showered and dressed, not at all puzzled by the contents of his wardrobes strewn across the floor. He put on his hat for work, lit a cigarette and sat on the bed, looking forlorn, until he was hauled by his son-in-law to his new abode at Deerpark Retirement Home. There he was dumped without ceremony, compassion or much luggage.

So this is how, eight months later, Pearlie came to be doing something she'd never done before. She headed off down to Long Street to have a midday alcoholic drink. She wasn't one who enjoyed walking, but she felt she needed finally to break the spell that had bound her indoors for so long. It was an easy enough stroll, even in high heels, first through the quiet Vredehoek streets, where no one ever promenaded, and where children didn't play in these days of escalating crime. She headed all the way down Buitenkant Street, crossed the heavy traffic of the M3 and kept going along Orange Street until she reached

Long. She had the air of one intent on getting somewhere. But that may have been because of the moderate wind that was blowing in the same direction, seeming to prompt her, ensuring she wouldn't change her mind and go back home.

She should, of course, have gone to the Lotus Tavern and sat there under the curatorship of that beautiful poem, in an atmosphere redolent of stir-fries and sweet-and-sour, where so many happy meals had been eaten. The cook would have welcomed her and listened with compassion as she told of her broken heart. He would have recited, over his steaming pans, various poems about the true, terrible nature of love and life and the absolute certainty of death. The waitrons would have fussed around her. Little Dove, with her dear, black eyes, she who had helped on the wedding day, would have poured a glass of house wine and watched Pearlie down it.

But Pearlie simply couldn't take herself there without Thespian. The docks, with their cranes and moored vessels and the smell of the sea, the creaking of chains, the thud of small boats against the rubber buffers, would never know her step again. Going there would have been like walking into a mausoleum.

Long Street was as much as she could muster. She had put on one of her more beautiful dresses, cut from foliage-green linen, with a deep, laced back. Around her neck she wound a string of jade beads, Thespian's most recent gift. Into her hair she clipped a velvet tulip-with-leaves.

Later, she would reflect on providence. She hadn't chosen to enter Brabazan. She'd just gone in because the sense of something theatrical had reached out, like a sprite's hand, twirling around and drawing her in. As she crossed the threshold, she thought she saw, sitting in a corner and alone, an angel, winged and beautiful. A waiter had just served him a Coke float and a plate of hot chips, trickled over with tomato sauce.

She paused for a moment and then went to the bar.

'You want a drink, Madam?' asked Duke, and she replied with a slight gasp, for her eyes hadn't properly adjusted to the subdued lighting. She hadn't seen Duke at the till, with the backdrop of bottle-laden shelves and gamut of luminous colours. Anastasia's parrot happened to be downstairs, perched on the far end of the bar. It strutted towards Pearlie, tilted its head quizzically, then fluttered down to her feet, gazing up at her green dress, flapping against her as best it could with cut wings.

'Yes. Give me a whisky,' replied Pearlie, copying a television advert, her voice husky because she'd hardly used it for so long. 'Johnnie Walker. Double. With one ice cube.'

'Don't worry about that mad bird,' said Duke. 'He won't peck at you. Just give him a swat.'

The overhead fans lapped the smoky air. Duke poured her drink and set it down in front of her. 'That's sixty rand,' he said.

Taking the glass, Pearlie looked around and walked over to Oberon, with the parrot following.

'Can I sit here?' she asked.

'Yes. Yes,' he said, standing up. 'Please, make yourself comfortable.' He patted the seat next to him and she sat heavily, sighing.

Duke was about to turn back to his book, back to Kapuściński, when Chester April walked in, wearing dark glasses. Duke remembered this new customer's preference, yesterday, for Black Label and opened a bottle.

'Well,' she began, 'I'm Pearlie.'

'I'm pleased to meet you. My name is Oberon.'

'I've such a sad story to tell. It'll break your heart. Never was a story of more woe.'

'I'm sorry about that.'

'A heavier task couldn't have been imposed, than I to speak my grief unspeakable.'

Oberon leaned down and picked up the parrot, putting it on the table and saying: 'This is such a crazy bird,' when it stood staring at the jade beads on Pearlie's bosom.

'If you have tears, prepare to shed them now,' continued Pearlie. Oberon said not another word, but listened with concern, eating his chips, offering to share them.

Duke looked across at his strangely innocent guest, who was walking around with way too much money, and the rotund, overdressed lady who hadn't drunk at Brabazan before. She had the look of someone who'd lost her mooring – the nervousness, the near-panic of being cast adrift into uncharted territory, like a paper boat. She was doing something new, drinking publicly. This was all evident and Duke rightly predicted the two would sit in their corner through the evening.

He watched them order from the waitress. Oberon asked for a toasted cheese sandwich, the woman for an omelette, but she didn't eat it. Instead she had a coffee. The omelette was taken back to the kitchen, cold, and put aside among the leftovers that the Zimbabwean staff saved.

Duke opened a second beer for Chester who, every so often, looked up with a start and wiped his face, which felt as though hands were touching it, examining its structure.

'He's in Deerpark House,' concluded Pearlie. 'In the west wing. The dementia section. He's forgotten everything. Even me.'

'How do you know he's forgotten you?'

'He hasn't phoned.'

'I think you should visit him. Maybe he won't be here much longer.'

'They won't tell me if they ship him off somewhere else,' she said, misunderstanding him. 'That's how mean they are. They could send him off to Jo'burg and I wouldn't know where to find him. That would be the most unkind cut of all. At least now I know he's at Deerpark. At least I can drive around the block and blow kisses.

'You've no idea how I want to see him. To hold him. To make sure he's all right. But I won't be allowed in. That son-in-law, he's high up in the Jewish community. He makes out that he's holier-than-the-rest, but really he's just a mean, no-good lowlife. He told me he'll burn my Thespi with a cigarette if he sees me near the home. That's why I only drive there at night.

'Can you imagine that? Burning a sick man with a cigarette? Have you ever heard anything so nasty? Can you believe such a horrible person exists? Oh, how mine eyes do loathe his visage now.'

'He won't do that. He's just talking. Anyway, no one will see you go in,' said Oberon, who knew that people seldom saw you if you didn't appear to be interesting, or if interacting with you meant you'd disturb them. If you meant nothing to anybody, you were as good as invisible. He glanced at his watch and then at Pearlie, who was on the verge of tears.

A taxi pulled up, right at the door, and hooted. Duke looked up and saw a young lad standing in the doorway, carrying one suitcase and a pack on his back. The sunlight was behind him so his posture formed a dark silhouette; his facial features weren't visible. The figure already had Duke's medium height, the same habitual pose, with one leg slightly forward as he stood there. 'How can it be?' thought Duke. 'My son. My son is standing there in the shaft of sunlight at the door. My son, Joaquin Ellerman Jones.'

Edward Hopper once said that all he wanted to do was paint sunlight as he saw it when it touched a wall. Generally, not much sunlight came into Brabazan. But this afternoon, this mild autumn afternoon, it was there – a beam, straight and yellow and strong.

'I have a son,' said Duke under his breath, and an ache ran through him as he stepped forward to welcome the boy into his new home. This was why Duke had become soft. This is why that bull had crushed the shell of his composure. So that he could embrace his child with love.

Oberon glanced up at the boy standing in the doorway, then across at Duke. If he sensed the new emotional charge in the atmosphere, he said nothing of this to Pearlie.

At nine that night, Duke was upstairs with the young man who looked just like him. He was so moved, so happy, so totally gratified by this gift that had seemingly fallen from heaven, that he was at a loss for words, so he muddled around self-consciously and seemed to be fussing. 'How shall we begin?' he rehearsed in his mind. 'What shall I call you? What do you want to know about me? What have you been doing for thirteen years? My boy. My Joaquin. My son.'

Amèlia had brought up a special supper for the two of them, and this they ate at a tastefully set, small table at the window, as though in a private restaurant above the city. She had her own fantasy going on. In her mind, the table overlooked the Indian Ocean. She had just collected fish from the boats and roasted it on coals. The *pão* was hot; the carafe of wine was a rich ambrosial syrup. The aquatic breeze coming in off the waves lapped at the curtains, lapped at her hair, lapped at her memories of times gone, times destroyed by war, times left only in dream. She had learnt that you can do anything with the components of life when you have lost everything. When all the bits are broken, you can gather them up and make a mosaic of them. Her husband and son had been sheltering inside that white-walled church with a crowd of others, while outside, soldiers stormed their mission home and then poured gasoline and set the locked church alight. Amèlia's husband and son had died in that inferno, fused together by the heat as, in a desperate embrace, her husband tried vainly to shelter their son. She had survived because on that day she'd gone off somewhere to fetch something. Where and why and what for was no longer relevant. She'd returned home to find ash and burnt bones and a fire-blackened statue of the Virgin Mary smiling benignly over the massacre that lay around her.

But now, in Amèlia's new life, a life she had escaped to, a life in the so-called new South Africa, a son had arrived. There were a father and son sitting at a window, breaking bread, eating together. They could be hers. They *were* hers, in her make-believe scenario.

Outside in Long Street, and downstairs at the bar, the tragedy and grandeur of life were being played out routinely by people at the edges of society and those comfortably within it. Duke stretched across the table and put his hand over his son's, saying simply: 'Welcome home, my boy.'

'Hey, Dad. It's fine. Take it easy,' the young man reassured him.

Duke's assistant was struggling to serve drinks on his own. At the piano sat Joe Schaffers playing 'Unforgettable'. Chester April, in his white suit, had a sense of song welling up inside of him. He wanted to let loose with his voice and sing just like Joe did. 'I'm not just a processor of dead bodies,' he wanted to tell everyone. 'Inside of me, there's a Nat King Cole and a Bing Crosby and a Harry Belafonte.'

He ordered another beer and went over to the piano, watching Joe pull music from out of those black and white keys. That must be how the Bushman on Kleinboet de Jongh's farm did it, thought Chester. That must be how he sucked lightning out of the earth.

Sipping at his beer, he realised that he had an awful lot of drinking to catch up. There was twenty years of mortuary work's worth of boozing to do. He had to get all that alcohol into him to dampen down the spooks that were hovering around the edges. At least he was safe in his new suit. None of the dead who had come his way had seen him wearing it. They only knew him in his mortuary attire, not in this slick outfit. It was appropriate for who he wanted to be, who he was deep inside, that singer, that crooner.

Fairy Patterson came in with his Polaroid and made an unsuccessful turn around all the tables, ending up beside Oberon and asking: 'Would you like a photo of you and your date, sir? Thirty rand. Special and instant.'

'Yes, that would be nice,' replied Oberon, leaning close to Pearlie as the shutter of the Polaroid came down and the magic process captured this moment of new friendship.

'Thank you, Sir,' said Fairy, taking his payment and generous tip, and handing the photograph to Pearlie, who hardly glanced at it but put it in her bag, reciting Komachi's poem: 'I long for him most, during these long moonless nights. I lie awake, hot, the growing fires of passion bursting, blazing in my heart.'

Not knowing quite how to respond, Oberon offered: 'Would you like to see something wonderful upstairs?'

Pearlie followed Oberon to the second floor. He opened the door to the room of Not The Midnight Mass and switched on the light. The chandeliers burst into brightness. Pearlie's heart almost stopped. Here was fake opulence, black and blue-black, purple-black, gold, alizarin and glitter. Surely, Verrocchio cherubs must soon emerge from behind the drapery, to blow celestial tunes on little horns and flutes.

At the far window stood the statue of the Virgin Mary, looking out over Long Street. The banquet table, laden with bowls of plastic fruit, plastic flowers and period-piece dinner plates, seemed waiting only for a group of revellers to sit down and call for platters of roast goose and duck.

'A choir lives here,' explained Oberon. 'They're at Theatre on the Bay, for their concert, right now. They rehearse in the afternoon, do their show and then come in late for dinner. I eat with them now, at night. They have a big meal at midnight. Sleep all morning. Practise in the afternoon. Concert at night.' He said this with elan and a turning movement of the hands, as if he was unfolding a story. 'Mr Ellerman lets them have a caterer because his kitchen can't cook the banquets they like. They don't eat hamburgers and chips.'

He looked around, then asked: 'Are you in a rush to go home?'

'No,' answered Pearlie.

'Wait with me, if you like. At quarter to midnight, the food will arrive. They bring it up the fire-escape stairs, not through the bar. The singers come back at twelve,' said Oberon, leading her to his room where he opened the French door and pulled up the two poufs.

Just after twelve, leaning over the balcony, Pearlie and Oberon watched the singers return from their concert. They might have been Victorian-era revellers, men and women stepping out of a black horse-drawn carriage, but they were modern-day singers, high and spirited after their show, stepping out of a black limousine, each with a black cloak swirling about them, each with knee-high boots that rang against the tar (though cobbles would have been more appropriate). A stretch-limo and two taxis pulled up, and a group of friends alighted and proceeded upstairs. People took off capes and coats and caps and hats and then sat to eat. The singers were hungry, for they never ate or drank before a performance and they had worked up a ravenous appetite

Oberon said: 'Excuse me. I need to change my clothes.' Behind the Indian screen, he undressed and put on his white nightshirt, adding: 'You'll see why when we get upstairs.'

He led Pearlie up to the magical room, where crystal sconces now bore lit candles and the chandeliers sparkled. When Graham Weir saw them at the door, he exclaimed: 'Angel of mine! Come, enter!'

He made a sweeping bow and kissed Pearlie's hand, saying: 'Dear Madam, join us, do. Here is good company, good wine, good welcome! And food a-plenty. You know the banqueters' maxim? Be ready for the unexpected guest! So, enjoy yourself, fair damsel. You'll find it quite heavenly in here, won't she, my Angel Oberon? Tonight we celebrate the end of a successful run of full houses and great reviews. Come. Take up your glasses! Drink and be merry! But first, Angel, fetch garments for your lady!'

This was a black-tie-plus occasion. Everyone was

dressed over the top. They wouldn't have been allowed in, had they come in everyday attire.

Oberon, who'd experienced four dinners with the singers, but none quite as crowded and gargantuan as tonight's would be, led Pearlie to a wardrobe and pulled out a set of wings made of wire, crêpe paper and feathers, which he clipped onto his shoulders so they hung from his back. Upon his head he settled a silver yarmulke. Pearlie rummaged through the many robes and outfits, among which hung fragrant pomanders, and took out a burgundy silk kaftan, which she changed into in the bathroom. Around her curls she wrapped a turban of gold cloth. From her handbag she took a cosmetic purse and touched up her face. 'Let me colour you in,' she said to Oberon and added some pronouncement to his brows and lips, with a polish of madder to his cheeks.

As this was the final banquet of the season, there were some renowned literary, theatrical and ambassadorial guests present with their partners, among them the outgoing Italian consul Dr Alberto Vecchi and the incoming Dr Emanuela Curnis; the economist David Kaplan; the famed film director of *Triomf*, Michael Raeburn; the legendary opera singer and tutor of operatic voices Sarita Stern; the owner of Theatre on the Bay, Pieter Toerien; the classical guitarist Peter Narun; the soprano Pretty Yende, wearing a figure-hugging, gun-metal-grey damask dress and accompanied by the tenor Given Nkosi; the Shakespearean actor and expert on San mythology Neil Bennun, costumed as Florizel from *The Winter's Tale*, complete with flakes of fake snow on his hat; the comedian Nik Rabinowitz; and the political columnist Donwald Pressly.

Also present was Zelda la Grange, Nelson Mandela's managerial assistant, who'd flown down especially for the last show and the banquet, for she was a great lover of everything theatrical and of Cape wines. She wore a maroon velvet gown, with a deep décolletage and Tudoresque sleeves, and a pink feather boa.

Four of the guests were heavily costumed and impossible to recognise because of their face masks, but they were obviously famous. Their armed, walkie-talkied bodyguards stood in the passage and on the pavement outside, and there was a sniper on the opposite roof. There were whispers of the princes William and Harry, and of Kate and Chelsy, but only Graham Weir and his fellow singers knew the identities of these top-of-the-social-range guests.

'I feel as though I've died already and entered heaven,' said Pearlie and Oberon squeezed her hand. 'Oh my Thespi,' she whispered, 'I wish you were here to see this blessed troupe that's invited me to feast. Their bright faces cast beams upon me like the sun.'

The caterer – interestingly enough, Lindy Levy, though she didn't recognise Pearlie in the thick of fancy dress, and Pearlie was too excited to realise it was her – had four waitrons assisting her, Bonny, Clyde, Lovemore and Dambudzo. Bonny placed Oberon and Pearlie on either side of Wilhelm Snyman, the urbane literary critic, Italian scholar, student of Dante and co-translator with Giuseppe Stellardi of Carlo Michelstaedter's *La Persuasione e La Rettorica*. He was dressed as Oscar Wilde and drinking a pre-prandial bourbon.

The banquet had a 'loaves and fishes' feel to it because of the impossible number of guests who managed to fit around the extended table, and the food and wine that just kept flowing. Streamers were thrown across the room and hot, crusty breads were broken into chunks. The air was burdened with aromas that defied description. Goblets were filled and refilled from pitchers of blood-coloured wine. Bowls of olives, dried figs, roasted garlic, parmesan shavings and toasted almonds were passed round. The first course, Hungarian peasant soup, was served, trickled with olive oil and sprinkled with finely chopped parsley.

There followed roast leg of mutton, studded with garlic and rosemary, and roast burst-chicken covered in cranberry sauce and placed on beds of steamed green and garbanzo beans. The chickens were overly stuffed with ground almonds, pine nuts, crumbs and herbs so that, as the mixture swelled with cooking, the breast broke open, offering its delicious contents.

These two main meat dishes were accompanied by grilled vegetables, couscous, steamed spinach and a salad of leaves, tomatoes and feta.

Dessert was simple – mascarpone and berries served with grated dark chocolate and quarters of fresh sanguinaria oranges. The meal was finished with coffee and a selection of liqueurs. There was no background music. Everyone's soul was still reverberating from the concert. The banquet went on until dawn, by which time there was much light-headedness and a touch of debauchery. The four masks slipped. The unknown guests were identified, but their secret didn't spill outside of Brabazan.

A West African couple had been living at Maynard Court for the past year and a half. In the two months before Thespian's removal from public life, an albino boy had moved in with them.

Their apartment was packed tight with furniture from Joshua Doore. The curtains were permanently drawn.

There was always someone coming or going, and it should have been clear to an observer that quite a number of people lodged there, not just the man and wife and new boy. But none of these additional people gave the impression of breaking the lease conditions, which allowed for only one family to live in the apartment, for they always arrived singly. Everyone behaved as though they had every right to be there. No one was furtive. No one initially gave any sense of criminal or untoward activity.

At about the time of the arrival of the albino boy at Maynard Court, Pearlie noticed that two men in suits, wearing dark glasses, would come by, mostly on Friday evenings, but sometimes on other days. One of them would wait in the car, parked in the street, while the other entered the flat.

To Pearlie, the men looked like the bodyguards of politicians, and she told Thespian about them. Initially, he was not perturbed. But, late one afternoon, when he'd brought Pearlie home from work and gone up for a quick coffee, he saw the parked car and the two men. He noticed that the windows were darkened and the vehicle bore no number plates. Feeling uneasy, he watched from the balcony as one of the men stood outside and the second entered the premises.

The next morning, he instructed the letting agent not to renew the lease when it came due. If this developed into a gang nest, then sooner or later there would be shooting, he reasoned, and he wanted his property clean of anything criminal. Nothing had happened yet, so he couldn't request a police search.

On the face of it, the couple were importers of curios. These they stored in a rented warehouse in the city centre. But they were also part of a drug cartel, and had been among the first to facilitate the importation of cocaine and heroin when South Africa's narcotic squad was inexplicably disbanded.

Their trade in artefacts was made possible by the destabilisation across large parts of the continent caused by war, dictatorship and abject poverty. These allowed for an unprecedented displacement of cultural objects and historical and archaeological treasures. South Africa was fast becoming the black-market gateway for such booty. The couple governed a network of people who sourced things across West and Central Africa, trawling villages and towns, bartering hard and buying dirt-cheap.

A peep into their warehouse would reveal more than the ubiquitous masks and carvings found at outdoor markets and curio shops. There were priceless bronzes and items spirited out of defunct or poorly managed museums, redundant libraries and colonial government offices. Many museum pieces still bore acquisition numbers.

The trajectories out were often similar. A ceremonial piece might have been the only thing saved from a razed Angolan village, for instance. A woman might have wrapped it in a blanket and carried it as far as Luanda, where all people displaced by the civil war headed. Perhaps she exchanged it for a cup of rice, and the man who bartered it from her sold it to a go-between for a bag of meal. That go-between sold it on and it eventually found its way to Cape Town, where it changed hands a number of times at an escalating price, until it was sold at an auction of antiquities.

The routes out from their countries of origin were never revealed, nor were the various networks unravelled. Perhaps items went out in overland trucks, wrapped in newspaper or sacking, or by plane or dug-out canoe, or simply borne upon the back of a man, walking.

Extraordinary pieces were trafficked, among them two

exquisitely carved Sanufu birds, fertility tokens, taller than a tall man, from the Ivory Coast; a *mukwale*, a sword made of wood and iron, symbol of a chief's authority, from Nanakandundu, in the upper Zambezi region of Angola; a rounded *mulondo*, a water jug, made in clay without the use of a potter's wheel, decorated with geometric incisions and masks.

Books and hand-drawn maps were also stored in the warehouse, waiting for collectors. One could legitimately argue that, left on the shelves of ruined or abandoned libraries, they would succumb to damp and mould and insects, or be burnt for fuel. At least in the hands of collectors they would be cherished and their existence safeguarded.

The couple were but one set of dealers stripping Africa of its cultural wealth, and not everything came from dysfunctional museums. South Africa had been targeted by professional art thieves since the end of the 'isolation years' of apartheid. Entrepreneurs were scouring the former homelands of Ciskei and Transkei for traditional beadwork, old pots and items salvaged centuries before from shipwrecks. From poor villages in the hinterland, they bought items of Victorian and Edwardian furniture that had been left behind by traders no longer living in the region, and that were simply in need of restoration.

Colonial art and furnishings were disappearing from government offices and even from Parliament itself. An oil painting of Field Marshal Jan Smuts, worth thousands, was cut from its frame and stolen from the Cape Town Club. El Greco's *The Apostle Thomas* was spirited from the Johannesburg Art Museum. A unique, solid gold tea set, comprising teapot, milk jug, sugar bowl, and tray with ivory handles, a gift to the South African government from the British royal family in 1952, was stolen from President

Thabo Mbeki's office. The historic five-carat Mendelssohn diamond was stolen (though later recovered) from its display position in the parliamentary library in mid-1999.

Pearlie found out from Seymour, the caretaker, that the albino boy was a nephew of the couple and that he had been sent to Cape Town by his mother, the man's sister, to have his albinism treated and to get an education. He had arrived from somewhere in Africa, brought down by a trucker and fetched from the station by the woman. This Seymour had learnt from the boy himself, who spoke English.

Pearlie noticed that the boy generally spent his time in the courtyard or outside Spar. His pigment-deprived marble-white skin looked sore in the sun and his light-sensitive, often crusty eyes bothered him. His lips were cracked. He seldom wore shoes. Normally, Pearlie wouldn't have given him two thoughts. It was his skin that drew her attention his way and made her feel sorry for him. She bought a broad-brimmed cricket hat and instructed Seymour to give this to the boy, together with an old pair of sunglasses.

She had suggested to Thespian that they give him a job in the garden. Perhaps he could help Seymour with weeding and also act as a lookout for criminals. The neighbourhood watch liked everyone to be the 'eyes and ears' of the precinct. But the boy was already on lookout duty – this for his 'uncle', to whom he had to report if anyone drove up and down Maynard Road, slowly and without apparent destination. He was also tasked to clean, do the laundry and run errands. He slept in the kitchen, on a foam mattress which he rolled up and tucked under the sink by day.

The man with whom he lived was overweight and rather

ugly. He had two gold teeth among his bright whites and often clenched a match between them. He dressed slick and smooth, with a gold chain around his neck and a gold bracelet. He wore expensive, highly polished shoes. His head was shaved and oiled. At the base of his neck he had two keloid scars, the result of cuts from a too-sharp razor. For these he consulted a plastic surgeon, who injected the fibrous tissue with Diprosone in an attempt to shrink it.

In truth, the boy had been taken from his village somewhere in Central Africa. These people were not his relations. They were child traffickers and they concealed this behind their other lucrative enterprises. Someone had accepted a deposit from his mother on the understanding that he would be brought to South Africa for treatment. She believed that the boy would be taken to the Red Cross Children's Hospital and healed of his dreadful affliction. Strong European medicine would restore his pigment, which had been stolen from him by witches while he grew in her womb. A good doctor would colour him black, like his brothers, like his ancestors before him.

His 'uncle' told the boy that the doctors were busy, that there would be a few months of waiting, but then the bed would be ready for him, with its sheets and nice nurses. The boy wanted to go to school, to Good Hope Primary just down the road, with a satchel on his back, a lunch box and a pencil bag.

Once or twice he'd stood at the school gate, hoping to be spotted by a kind teacher who would allow him in, even if his skin was not yet right. More than anything, he wanted a storybook, one with pictures.

One day, he'd gone past early, on his way to Spar. The bell was ringing and children were running in. A township kombi had just offloaded a group. When they saw him, they threw stones and shouted: '*Isiporo*! *Isiporo*! *Puma*!

Ghost! Ghost! Get away!' The taxi driver had laughed as the boy ran off, stumbling and crying.

On the day that Pearlie had decided to go down to Long Street, she realised, shortly before setting off, that she hadn't seen him for some days.

The boy's life had brushed past hers, a soft sweeping of white skin, paint without pigment to it. Had she knocked at the door to enquire, the woman would have said: 'I'm sorry, *Sistah*. We don't have a white-black boy living here. We are from West Africa. Our children are like us. Black.'

The fragrance of chicken simmering in peanut sauce would have wafted out from the kitchen and Pearlie would have realised that it was this woman who, months before, had kindly left the basket of food on her doorstep.

During the late afternoon of the ninth day of his stay at Brabazan, Oberon accompanied Pearlie up to Deerpark Home. They went by Rikki because Pearlie didn't want anyone taking down her car's registration number.

When they arrived at the reception desk, the security guard and concierge were deep in animated conversation and Oberon had to raise his voice: 'Excuse me. We're here to see Mr Winter.'

They hardly glanced at him or Pearlie. The security guard picked at his teeth with an unfolded paper clip and went out to the driveway, looking up and down. He would soon go off duty and was looking forward to a beer.

Because Thespian had not had a single visitor since his admission, the concierge had to check the register to confirm there was such a resident. Sure enough, Mr

Thespian Coleridge Winter was currently in room 24 on the fifth floor of the west wing.

Pearlie and Oberon were not asked to open for inspection the bags they carried, so they walked freely down a long passage with all the things they'd brought for Thespian. They came to a large open lounge. Outside the locked patio doors was a paved courtyard with a fountain. Along one side of the room was a row of recliner seats, all facing into the room, each holding a very old person. Their heads hung limp upon their chests, straining at cervical vertebrae. Only one had a pillow. The rest of the room was occupied by people sitting in firm chairs without cushions. Everyone seemed sedated. A television was blaring; a group of nurse-aids sat chatting loudly. Though there was one nurse allocated per two patients, for this was a high-cost section of the home, not one of them interacted with any gentle care and only occasionally glanced over at their charges.

'I hope Thespian isn't one of these,' said Pearlie under her breath, looking along the row but finding no familiar face among the all-but-corpses.

'Why don't they put them outside round the fountain, in the fresh air? Look, the frangipani are flowering,' she said, pointing out the window. 'Or why don't they put the chairs facing each other instead of in a line?'

'Sh,' cautioned Oberon, taking her hand and leading her to the lift. If they drew attention to themselves, their mission would be scuppered.

The six residents on the fifth level had already been served their late-afternoon supper by the outgoing day nurse. The night nurse who supervised them, Thandi Koliti, quite by providence, had not come to work. The matron, frantically busy preparing for the upcoming annual general meeting and open day, had failed to check for messages on her cellphone. She hadn't read Thandi's SMS advising that she wouldn't be at work. This meant that no staff member would enter Thespian's room between five o'clock that evening and seven the next morning.

Thespian's was the last room at the end of the corridor. Stored outside were three folded wheelchairs, some buckets and a flip-top medical-waste bin. Pearlie tapped on the door and opened it. Her heart sank.

Thin and pale, he was asleep on a chair. A trolley held his uneaten supper of a soft-boiled egg, two slices of buttered white bread, a bowl of custard with a tinned pear and a cup of lukewarm milky tea. This had been brought in by the day nurse, who should have fed him but hadn't, because he was asleep and she was in a hurry to get home.

The room was standard issue with nothing to soften its hospital look or alter the institutional smell of medicine and antiseptic. Pearlie leant down and took Thespian's face in her hands, saying: 'Thespi, darling. Thespi, it's me, Pearlie. Wake up, sweetheart.'

His tired eyes lifted from his sunken face and he stared at her in wonder. His mouth, drooped from a mild stroke, trembled and he let out a gasp as she continued, chattering breathlessly so as not to start crying: 'Thespi, this is our new friend, Oberon. We're going to make this horrid room pretty. We're going to make a little Maynard for you and have some fun. What do you think about that?'

They got to work right away. First, Pearlie shoved the tray of food into the waste bin outside. Oberon locked the door and she opened the window that faced the mountain. A puff of wind entered to join them in this clandestine visit. Then she unpacked the various bags, taking out a bunch of paper flowers. 'Aren't these pretty, Thespi? A man was handing them out this morning. He had baskets full of them outside 7-Eleven. He gave us this whole bunch. They smell like roses.'

She pinned a length of mulberry chiffon at the window, spread a cloth over the trolley and threw a silk quilt across the bed. Oberon suspended wind chimes from the light fitting and they began to tinkle. On the dresser, he placed a bowl of plastic cherries and then opened lunch boxes and a bottle of wine.

All the while, Pearlie chatted away, threading her words with Shakespearean lines in the hope that they would stir Thespian's memory. Her voice meandered like a silver stream into the sad crevices of his mind: 'Look, we brought you yummy things to eat. Some Jack's Red. Ciabatta. Pastrami. Pickles. Peppadews. I've even got capers and some smoked trout.'

With Oberon's help, she led Thespian into the bathroom where they took off his pyjamas. 'When last did anyone do anything nice for you, Thespi?' she asked, checking his body for cigarette burns and needle marks.

They sponged him down, rubbed him all over with baby oil and dressed him in his favourite frilly frock, the peach and yellow one. 'Now, my honey love,' Pearlie recited, 'We'll return unto our house with silken coats and cape and golden rings, with ruffs and cuffs and fardingales and things.'

Oberon gently guided Thespian's feet into socks and slip-ons. Pearlie rubbed moisturiser onto his dry cheeks, rouged them and put gloss on his lips. To finish off, she draped a necklace round his neck and clipped on earrings. Then she stepped back as though examining a work of art and said: 'To me, fair friend, you never can be old, for as you were when first I saw you, such seems your beauty still.

'What do you say, Oberon? Is my husband gorgeous or what? Now, it's my turn to get ready.'

She undressed and, from her holdall, pulled out her

wedding dress. Oberon did up the buttons. She positioned her tiara and slipped on her Gallardo flamenco shoes and with these did a little tap-tap on the floor. A small zigzag gave life to Thespian's drooping lip as he watched.

'There, that's altogether much better, don't you think?' she said. 'Now, let's eat.

'I wish we could be out there in the park, having a wedding anniversary picnic. I know it's not our anniversary, but I still wish.

'Under the greenwood tree, who loves to lie with me, come hither, come hither, come hither.

'I wish we could be out there, in the wood, where often you and I, upon faint primrose beds were wont to lie, with a jazz band and the piano rocking the whole mountain. But we'll still do it one of these days.

'I know a bank where the wild thyme blows; where oxslips and the nodding violet grows, quite over-canopied with luscious woodbine. That's where we'll set up some fun, my darling.' Pearlie fed Thespian pieces of asparagus, roasted brinjal, falafels and baby tomatoes. Whereas in the past months his appetite had completely evaporated, it now returned in full measure and he ate heartily. She de-pipped olives and put them onto his tongue. She held a wine glass to his lips and a serviette beneath it to catch any trickle. The feast ended with Portuguese custard cakes, which she fed him in dollops from a fingertip, gently pushing the sweetness into his mouth, saying: 'I must fatten you up, my darling, you've lost too much weight.' Finally, she and Oberon ate their portions and he poured three cups of black coffee from a flask, to which was added a dash of grappa.

She lit a cigarette and gave Thespian a few puffs, before finishing it herself. Looking out at the stars, she said: 'The skies are painted with unnumbered sparks. They're all fire and every one doth shine.'

Then, quite miraculously, Thespian spoke – in a slightly staccato and hesitant manner – through the good side of his mouth, the first words he'd uttered since that terrible Rosh Hashana: 'Pearlie. My God. Pearlie Theron. Who would have guessed. That a man already. In the grave. Could have such a wife. As you? Then happy I. That love. And am beloved.'

At this point the zigzag turned into a smile and tears ran down his face. 'You look. So beautiful. My Pearlie. My bride. My lovely.'

'Don't cry,' she said, wiping his cheeks with her palms. 'Don't cry. Otherwise I will too. And you'll mess your make-up. Now listen, we've found a place of eternal heavenly banquets. Every night there's a monumental fancy-dress feast. Oberon's been to lots of them. He dresses as an angel. Look, we brought his wings to show you,' and she pointed to Oberon, who had clipped the crêpe paper and feather wings to his shoulders and now turned around twice to give Thespian a good view of them on his back.

Pearlie continued: 'Tomorrow night, we're going to take you there. So we're going to come out, out of the affair closet and into the moonlight, me and you, dressed up, me on your arm and you proud. Why must only gays come out the closet? What about lovers? We're going to let everyone see us. There'll be a newspaper man there, Wilhelm. He's a good friend already. I sat next to him last night. He'll splash our story right across the *Cape Times* and *Die Burger* and even papers in Italy.'

'What place. Is it?' he asked.

'Brabazan. In Long Street. It has a magical room upstairs. Dark and bright together. I can't explain. Full of beautiful things and frankincense and a gorgeous midnight singing group. Oh, you've no idea how marvellous they are.

'They sing like heaven and can recite and quote Shakespeare just like we do. And every night, after their show, they have this banquet. Everyone is dressed up. It's all costume and make-believe. But so real.'

'A banquet. At Brabazan. Fancy that,' said Thespian. 'That sounds nice. But I can't walk. Easily. You'll have. To wheel me in. And I have. This gammy arm. To match the gammy. Leg. And look. At this face now. I look half dead. Already. I am a corpse. Almost. They don't want a corpse. At the party.'

'I'll wheel you in,' she said, 'and your face is fine. And you know what? A lot of people have got gammy arms and legs and whatnots that don't work any more. It's nothing new. But now you must rest, my darling.'

Oberon helped Thespian onto the bed and Pearlie lay next to her man, closely, for the bed was narrow and the lace of her wedding dress took up space. To give them privacy, Oberon carried the chair through to the shower cubicle and made himself comfortable enough to fall asleep.

The two lay quietly for awhile, enjoying each other's presence, listening to the wind chimes. Pearlie whispered Hitomaro's poem, softly so that Thespian wouldn't hear and be saddened: 'I sit at home, in our room, by our bed, gazing at your pillow,' continuing louder with Juliet's lines: 'Good night, sweet prince, and flights of angels sing thee to thy rest. Kind is my love today, tomorrow kind, still constant in a wondrous excellence.'

He held her hand and she listened to his breathing change as he fell asleep. Their dreams intertwined and became a tangle of images. A few moths flew in, attracted by the sweet smells and the insuperable glow of love.

Just before daylight, before the sun had touched anything, Pearlie woke with a start and shook him gently: 'Thespi, my sweet. Thespi. The day begins to break and night is fled. It's time to get up. I have to go before anyone comes in.'

'What angel wakes me. From my flowery bed?' he replied. 'Wilt thou be gone? It is not yet. Near day. It was the nightingale. And not the lark. That pierced. The fearful hollow. Of thine ear. Nightly she sings. On yond pomegranate tree. Believe me. Love. It was the nightingale.'

'Night's candles are burnt out,' replied Pearlie, 'and jocund day stands tiptoe on the misty mountain top. I must be gone.'

In the background could be heard the dull clank of bedpans, trolleys and medicine boxes and the piercing voices of the nursing crew, announcing that Deerpark Home was now astir.

'I'm going to go out in my wedding dress. I'm going to wear it from now until I have you home again. And Oberon must keep his wings on. Just for good luck. It feels like magic will happen,' said Pearlie, calling Oberon from the bathroom.

They lifted Thespian off the bed and seated him on the chair, being careful with him, for his limbs were sore.

'Yes. Stay like that. And leave me too. As I am,' whispered Thespian. 'Throw those terrible pyjamas. Away. I wish. You could burn them. Leave my frock on. Leave me. In my frock.'

'Are you sure? Won't there be trouble?'

'Let there be trouble. Throw everything out. Out the window. I hate them. Throw the bedpan. Throw the pills. Throw the blankets. Everything.'

Which she did, one by one, so the bedding landed softly outside and draped over the hydrangeas. She then brushed his hair, touched up his cheeks and lips, and smudged blue over his eyelids.

'Give me. One of those paper flowers. You brought,' he said, and then: 'Pearlie. Remember that actor? That Jamie Bartlett. From *Rhythm City*? Remember that time. We saw him. Outside Lotus Tavern? When he shouted out. To his wife: "I love you. Like the driven wind." Remember that. Pearlie? Well that is how. I love you. Like the driven wind.

'You'd better go. Don't let them. Catch you. Pearlie. Don't let them. Get hold of you. Because then. There will be retribution. That's for sure. Go now. Go my sweetie.'

'We'll fetch you tomorrow evening, my darling. Same time,' said Pearlie, deepening her voice so as not to let it break. 'We'll be back. Remember that, all day and tomorrow. For the banquet.'

'For the banquet,' he repeated.

'Tomorrow night. A joy past joy calls out on me.'

'Tomorrow night. And then you won't bring me. Back here. You'll take me home. My Pearlie. Take me back. To Paradise.'

'I'll take you home, dearest. To our own bed. Back to Verdi and Paganini.'

Oberon pulled Pearlie by the arm, afraid that they'd be arrested for trespassing, as she whispered: 'Oh for a horse with wings, that I might take my Thespian with me now.'

He closed the door without a sound, not noticing Thespian raise a hand to call them back, to tell Pearlie to fetch the brown envelope from the Lotus Tavern and to take its contents, the addendum to his will, to a lawyer, to make known that Maynard Court was to belong to her, now that he was as good as dead. Now that he saw the Grim Reaper stepping out from the shadows and reaching towards him.

Pearlie and Oberon took the lift down and walked

through the recliner-chair room, where the breakfast trolleys, rattling in cacophony over the tiled floor, destroyed all tranquillity.

In the way that no one had paid them much attention when they'd arrived the previous day, so now no one saw them leave. Or perhaps one of the cleaners did notice. Perhaps, from the corner of an eye, she noticed what she presumed to be ghosts, and thus dismissed them. There were many ghosts in this place that housed so many unwanted folk, as they stood at the threshold of death, longing for a little shove. Perhaps she might later tell, in the staff tea room, that she had seen a phantom bride hurry past with a winged man who might have been an angel. Some of the staff would have laughed, but others, the older ones, the ones who knew a thing or two, would have nodded reassuringly and placed their hands on whatever talisman they wore on their bodies.

Out they went, through the front door into the morning light, with Oberon holding Pearlie's hand, walking off the premises and a little way down Gorge Road, where they hailed a Rikki. They were both emotionally exhausted. Oberon had dark rings under his eyes.

'I tell you what,' said Pearlie, putting on a brave face. 'Let me stop off at my flat. I'll have a sleep and come down later. You go back and eat something and also have a rest. How does that sound? Tonight we'll work out how to move Thespian from that place. Maybe we'll just wheel him out. Sweet and simple.'

'Yes,' he said, leaning against her, loving the lace of the wedding dress, as she put her arm around him.

The taxi pulled up at Maynard Court. She gently kissed Oberon on each cheek and said: 'Here we are. Okay, I'll join you later.'

'Is you all going to a fancy-dress?' the driver asked as

he drove off and Oberon, hearing the question as 'Isn't she fancy in that dress?' replied: 'Yes, she is.'

At Brabazan, feeling hungry, he sat at his corner table. He drank a hot chocolate with a slice of carrot cake and watched the morning unfold and get busier. At midday, the usual lunchtime crowd started arriving and a tour bus dropped off a group of Canadians. Brabazan was listed on their itinerary as a 'quintessential fifties joint'. Duke and his bar assistant hardly had a break and the waitrons were back and forth from the kitchen. Two young women were playing pinball. The jukebox had been set to play a whole run of blues and soul numbers.

Oberon, revived and refreshed and now caught up in the vibe, ordered beer-batter fried fish of the day with potato pie and salad, to be followed by a banana split. No one questioned his wings, for they seemed so utterly a part of him.

Meanwhile Thespian, in his room, holding the paper rose, aware that his blood pressure needed some management, recited softly: 'Thy love is better. Than high birth. To me. Richer than wealth. Prouder than garments' cost. My dear one. My beloved.'

A good two hours after Pearlie and Oberon had left him, when the day-duty nurse-aid assigned to the fifth floor came round, she found Mr Winter dressed in his frock, the paper rose clenched between his pink, femme-fatal lips, his slippered feet crossed demurely, one over the other.

The bed stripped of its linen and the medicine tray cleaned of its bottles gave the impression that robbers had come up the gutters and in through the window. The room smelt of cigarette smoke, perfume, alcohol and rich food.

There was no sign of Thandi, who should by now already have bathed Mr Winter and prepared him for breakfast, before going off duty.

In her strong Cape Flats accent the nurse-aid exclaimed: '*Jislaaik*! Mr Winter, you old *skelm*. What you been up to, hey? You always pretending you can't dress yourself. Now look at this *moffie* nonsense.' But then, noticing his bloodshot eyes, with one pupil dilated and the other not, she said: 'Now there's going to be *skiet en donder*!'

She rushed down to the office and announced with authority: 'Mr Winter is dead! He gave hiself a heart attack! You must just look at him!'

Dr Adam Baldinger happened to be in the complex. He was doing a fortnight's locum for Deerpark's resident doctor and had just arrived for an early round, only to have to certify Mr Winter's demise.

He'd grown fond of this lonely man, whose file showed that he'd suffered a stroke during his second day in residence. He was permitted visits only from family members. When Dr Baldinger queried this, the matron told him that not a single person had called on Mr Winter since his admission. So the good doctor had made a point of visiting him each day and staying a little longer than required, chatting to the poor fellow in the bleak room, even though the only response given was the glint in an eye.

He was startled now to see Thespian attired in a brightly coloured frock and slippers. But then he chuckled, realising that the man had had another life and a friend or two, and that someone had finally come to visit, making his last hours comic and happy.

Though he was sad to have to certify the death, he felt strangely pleased to see Thespian released. He tapped the corpse on the shoulder and said: 'Goodbye, old chap.'

It was left to Rabbi Steinberg, who oversaw the spiritual affairs of Deerpark Home, to notify the Winter family of Thespian's death. He tried to phone the son-in-law, Gerald Radison, who was the person the matron liaised with, only to be informed by a recorded message that the man was away on business.

He then dialled Mrs Winter, who happened to have her manicurist at the house. It wasn't appropriate to advise her of the death telephonically, so he asked her to come to the home as a matter of urgency.

Urgent was not a word Mrs Winter cared to use in relation to her husband. She could have postponed her hand treatment, but chose to continue with it, thinking that she was needed to sign some or other hospital papers. Damn it! Couldn't it be done when Gerald got back from Australia?

While he waited for her, the rabbi reflected on death. In his experience, those on the outside of the home, those still vitally alive, tended to wish away the days of these their aged relatives, who were variously senile, decrepit, incontinent, deaf, blind, crumbled by osteoporosis and generally as good as dead.

There was an old lady called Dora Grossman, who, this very morning, had taken his hand in hers and looked up at him with rheumy eyes, asking from a dry-lipped mouth that had not a single tooth in it: 'Have you come to fetch me? Have you got the key?'

Struggling to undo her tight, cold, bony grip, he'd replied: 'No, dear, I have no key,' to which she sadly closed her eyes and tightened her brow.

However awful these old husks looked, he respected them. When they were finally freed from their earthly travails, he announced their deaths with sensitivity, though he knew that, in most cases, the scramble for money and property would begin immediately.

As greed often overtook mourning, he saw a dark side of human nature. It was then that he wanted to caution the heirs that they too were mortal, that all the inheritance in the world wouldn't buy immortality, that a shroud has no pockets, that not even small change can be transported from this life and that they should take it easy when dividing the spoils.

Mr Winter belonged to one such greedy family. Despite his wealth, he'd been booked in as a basket case through the clever work of his wife's lawyer and accountant. They had managed to declare him insolvent at death, reserving all his wealth for his wife. He'd been assigned to the most basic care the home gave, the one allotted to the indigent, those in the lean palm of charity for whom funding was sought. These were the ones who were generally heavily sedated because it was the easiest, most cost-effective way to manage them.

The rabbi, having waited for as long as he could, was about to leave Deerpark Home when Mrs Winter arrived wearing a loose, ankle-length linen dress and Roman sandals. A gold chain was wrapped around her neck. She made it clear that she couldn't stay long, that she had other, important things to do. It was immediately obvious that he was dealing with a spoilt woman. In the matron's office, he broke the news gently, concluding with: 'He hasn't been moved, because the circumstances of his death are somewhat suspicious. The police had to be called. I'll take you up to him. But please prepare yourself. The sight of the dead isn't an easy one. Even under normal conditions.'

Mrs Winter followed him up to the fifth floor, feeling irritated.

They met Dr Baldinger, who had just finished his rounds, and was on his way to his own practice in town. The doctor was surprised at how young and lovely Mrs Winter looked, but how angry and miserable too, and how the loveliness was marred by the mood.

Outside, walking to his car, he reflected on how, in May, the days were like a capricious dresser. They started off draped in a cape of fog, only to let this fall away and reveal a crisp, autumnal hue, as it did on this very morning. Yellow lilies bloomed in the beds along the driveway and he glanced at them appreciatively

The door to Mr Winter's room was locked and police tape marked the area as a crime scene. A constable stood guard, but facilitated the rabbi and Mrs Winter's entrance.

When she saw her husband's body, sitting in his chair, in his dress, the paper rose held undisturbed between his lips, his red eyes like those of the devil himself, Mrs Winter let out a single expletive: 'Jesus!' She immediately left the room, marching to the lift where the rabbi caught up with her.

Now all the complexities of the double life that her husband had admitted to at their fateful Rosh Hashana table fell into place. The cruel reality, as she discerned it, was that he was a gay transvestite. His obsession with his own perfume should have alerted her to this dirty secret, she now realised. And as for that repulsive Pearlie Theron! She was not an ugly spinster at all, but a man. A homosexual. How stupid of her not to notice – the shadow on the upper lip! Those athletic thighs! That camp overkill of her dress sense!

It was all clear – her husband had been having an affair

with a man for all these years. His senility had not erased this ugly side of his life and he had somehow managed to smuggle a set of women's clothes into his room. Perhaps he'd sensed he was near death. Or perhaps he'd hoarded pills and then taken them all in one go. Whatever the truth, he'd decided to put on this monstrous show. This diabolical circus.

As she stood in an igneous rage at the lift door, everything she had learnt from Jane Osborne during her one year at drama school – the studied speech and eloquent use of colonial English – fell away, along with her demeanour.

'Oh shit, what a fool I've been,' she seethed. 'What a fool. He was fucking *gay*. A cross-dresser. He was covering it all up with that fat son of a bitch.'

'What am I going to tell my daughters?' she flamed at the rabbi. 'How am I going to tell them? My eldest nearly lost her baby because of him. Now this! This will kill one of us.'

But she needn't have worried about how to tell her daughters. That evening, a cellphone photo taken by Deerpark Home's caterer was posted onto Facebook and it hurtled round the Jewish community, needing no embellishment from the more skilled gossips.

Mrs Winter now understood Maynard Court to be the place where her husband had practised his debauchery. It was a Sodom and Gomorrah. In an act of spite and retribution, she arranged for the building to be demolished immediately.

She phoned the letting agent and advised that all tenants were to vacate the building by the end of the week. They were to be housed, at her expense, at the Holiday Inn for the next few months. She would pay for the removal and storage of furniture and added a cash incentive. None of this was to apply to 'Miss' Theron of number four, who was simply to be evicted.

When the letting agent cautioned her as to the legality of what she planned, she shut him up with the assurance of a high payment. Nothing, absolutely nothing, was going to stand in her way. Having made all her phone calls, she got into her 4x4 and raced crazily fast on the M3 highway, all the way to the Tokai turn-off and then back again to town, where all she could think to do was drink. She sped up Long Street and parked outside the first bar she saw. It seemed like an old-fashioned dive with a jukebox and pool table and smoky interior light.

Thandi had no idea of what had transpired at Deerpark Home in her absence, nor what terrible repercussions had rippled out from her taking compassionate leave without getting clearance. Such a huge consequence from such a small deed, she would later reflect.

Arriving at work an hour or so late, she braced herself for a lecture and possible deduction from her wages. She was surprised to find the staff entrance locked. An unknown person, from an external security company, sent her round to the front. There too she didn't recognise the guard or the concierge and, once again, was refused entry, even though she was in uniform and showed her identity and staff cards.

She had to wait while the concierge phoned through to the office to get clearance. Only then could she enter, escorted by a volunteer who didn't speak to her. Every staff member she passed turned away without greeting. There was a pall in the corridors. She imagined there must have been an armed robbery. It was bound to happen one day – gangsters coming in for Jewish jewels and money.

Her meeting with the matron and deputy matron was short and to the point. She was fired on the spot and given a letter of dismissal signed by the chairman. Three months' severance pay would be deposited into her bank account at month-end, together with a portion of her annual bonus. She was not owed leave pay. On the contrary, the matron told her, if one conducted a proper audit, it was she who owed Deerpark Home money, for the way she had abused the sick leave allocated to staff.

She was given a brisk dressing down. Each sentence was strung to the next and left no space for Thandi to offer a word.

'It's entirely on your account,' began the matron, 'that strangers – it hasn't been ascertained how many there were – spent an entire night, undetected, in Mr Winter's room.

'These strangers precipitated his death, feeding him rich food and alcohol. That it was not kosher food, I also mention.

'The smoke detector was disabled and, judging by the packets left behind, everyone, including Mr Winter, smoked. Never mind that this was harmful to him, but there could have been a fire. The whole place could have burnt down.

'Cigarette ends, bottles, bedding and medicine were thrown out the window.

'Before leaving, his visitors dressed Mr Winter in most unbecoming, shameful, indecorous and inappropriate clothes, making an utter fool of him. They then propped him up and left him *unattended*.

'He was left *unattended* for hours. That was how he died. *Alone*. On the chair. Unable to reach his emergency bell. Unable to call for help. Mercifully, the other residents on your floor were spared any violation by the intruders, but they too spent the whole night unattended. I could be dealing with more than one death today. All of them messed themselves. Mrs Blacher smeared herself. Are you listening to what I'm saying? Are you following the severity of this? The indignity? The humiliation? The shame of it all?

'Now get out of my office. Go to the staff room and wait there. The police are questioning everyone. When they finish with you, kindly leave the premises. I never want to see you again.'

Later that day, at an emergency committee meeting, the impact of Mr Winter's death was reviewed.

The chairman announced that a homicide docket had been opened. Mysteriously, the CCTV, though in perfect working order, had twice captured only a flash of light – once at early evening and the other the next morning. Throughout the day, the images of all persons entering and leaving had been recorded. These had since been identified as bona fide visitors or staff.

'The damage,' he said, 'that Mr Winter's death will do to our good name is incalculable. Already the phone hasn't stopped ringing.

'There's no doubt that Mr Winter's family will sue for a fortune and the finance committee must brace itself. God knows what will happen to our donations drive. We'll discuss this at next week's AGM, but I think it best to cancel our open day.

'We're going to have to put expensive security measures in place. I want nurses to log in on the hour and we'd better employ some temps as a catch net for absentees. Rabbi Steinberg suggested we set up a walk-and-watch programme, monitoring the corridors and regularly looking in on each resident.'

The matron came away from the meeting with a headache. She personally believed that Mrs Winter had hired someone to dispatch her husband. But the autopsy revealed massive intra-cerebral bleeding brought on by malignant hypertension. There had been no foul play.

Normally, the staff bus drove Thandi to and from the taxi rank at the station. Now, at eleven-thirty in the morning, there was no bus, so she walked all the way down Buitenkant Street, along Orange Street and into Long, dragging her feet, the weight of her predicament sitting heavy on her mind.

As she went past Brabazan, she heard Aretha Franklin's 'Amazing Grace' and, thinking this might be a gospel venue, entered, only to realise it was a pub with a jukebox. She looked around at all the patrons and then at Oberon, meeting his eyes. It seemed that his expression beckoned, so she walked towards him. He imagined she was going to sit with him, as Pearlie had done, but she took the opposite table, which had just been vacated, and ordered a coffee.

Glancing at Oberon now and then, she considered her options. Without her job, she would be dependent on her mother's meagre pension. Though they lived in a shack that was little more than a pig's shed, they paid rent to a self-proclaimed landlord, who said he owned the square of council property upon which over a hundred makeshift dwellings were crowded.

Thandi had an uncle living in Gugulethu, next door to the clinic, who always said they were welcome to stay with him. He was immensely generous, living up to his name,

ThankyouGod, even though he had no money. She had not taken up his offer, because his daughter and her three children shared his one-roomed house.

But now there was no choice. Tomorrow, she would dismantle her zinc walls and hire a cart to transport them to Gugulethu. Somehow, she'd have to squeeze her *hok* next to those of his pigeons in the small yard.

Maybe she could set up a *spaza* outside the clinic and sell bread and cigarettes. But then she'd be competing with the Somali traders, who drove prices too low for competition. Anyway, with this new xenophobic violence, it was probably better to stay away from informal selling, in case you got mistaken for a foreigner. Maybe it would not be only foreigners who got targeted next time. There was no telling who was behind it, maybe it was a criminal thing, and she'd just be putting herself at risk with stock and a cash box.

She watched Oberon finish his lunch and go through the yellow curtain, only then noticing his wings, feeling overcome with awe, even though they were obviously paper. She moved across to his seat, where she stayed for the rest of the day and all night, soothed by the atmosphere she sensed he'd left behind.

Upstairs, Oberon took off the wings and lay down. As he hovered on that quiet plateau which is neither sleep nor waking, he suddenly remembered Gerrit and the Salvation Army Home. He opened his eyes and gazed up at the patterns on the pressed-tin ceiling, breathing deeply, holding on to this bit of memory, which had surfaced apparently from nowhere. Then he got up, steadying himself against a whoosh of light-headedness.

The sunflowers in the vase had not withered over the days of his stay and their yellow was still exuberant. He packed his few belongings, straightened the bedding, looked around the room with a certain melancholy and made his way up to the second floor.

He quietly opened the door to the Not The Midnight Mass room and stepped in, switching on the chandeliers that cast their light on furnishings covered with white dust sheets. The shutters were closed, the blinds down and the heavy curtains drawn. The statue of the Virgin Mary had been taken back to Pasquale, to stand at his window, for the group had flown to Johannesburg that morning. Their season was over. They would leave the next month for shows in New York and London and would not perform again in Cape Town for another year. The room would remain still and quiet until their return.

Walking round the table, Oberon reflected on the last banquet and all the goodbyes at the end of it, with the guests wrapped in their capes and coats, shaking hands, embracing, some tearful, most tipsy. Graham, with Zelda la Grange's feather boa wrapped around his neck, had leapt onto the table, gingerly stepping between empty platters and goblets, for a closing performance, magniloquently proclaiming: 'Friends, Romans, countrymen! Lend me your ears! Don't be deceived – all the world's but a drama, a mere conte. We everyday souls are simply set to play upon a tabula rasa, then scripted into each other's lives with tragedy, comedy, history, pastoral and poem unlimited. It's all just a piece of spectacular theatre.

'See how we touch each other. Some lightly, like mere petals. Some with abuse. Some embrace and dance till the night is done. There is love and hate and goodness, fidelity and betrayal, light and darkness, memory and loss, all of it together, creating credible lives, only for the curtain to fall and the show to be over. Only for a wind to hiss across the vacant stage and for us to ask what the point was of it all. There is no point, but to seek beauty and pleasure and music and to create our own heavens.'

He dropped a wine glass onto the floor and it shattered. 'So, good night, dear friends. Let the copper shades of evening fall. 'Tis time for bed!'

Oberon put the wings back into Graham Weir's costume cupboard, switched off the light and closed the door. He noticed for the first time, hanging in the passage, Duke's tenth Hopper print, *Two Comedians*. It was of two clowns, Pierrot and Pierrette, stepping forward from a darkened stage to give a final bow, taken from audience angle, with a glimpse of scenery in the wings. These were not smiling characters. Their firm lips and sad, maquillage faces suggested not just the end of a show, but the end of lives as well, which indeed it was, for this was Hopper's last work before his and his wife Josephine's death.

Oberon stood for a moment looking at the picture and then made his way downstairs and out again through the yellow curtain. The lunchtime crowd and Canadian tourists had left and only a few tables were occupied. The midweek repertoire of afternoon drinkers was trickling in and the bar was already resonating with braggadocio talk. Thandi watched Oberon walk towards Duke and put down his case. From the jukebox Elvis Presley sang the haunting 'Dark Moon'.

Duke looked up at his guest and felt a pang of sadness. In another world, in another time, he'd have come out from behind the bar, taken the man by the shoulders and looked into his eyes, saying: 'Don't go. Stay here. I've never before had an angel live alongside me. I think I need you here. Everyone needs you here. Didn't you sense that? Didn't you see how you touched people? You won't have to pay me. You can stay for free, like the Archbishop's own angel in residence. He has one, I've read that somewhere. Tutu has his own angel who prays with him and for him and for all of us wretched of the earth. And shall I tell you something? That young man, that beautiful young man, the one the taxi brought, the one who stood in a beam of afternoon light, he's my son. I have a son now.'

But in this world, the real world that holds back on emotional truth, seldom daring to be honest with itself, Duke took the room key and merely said: 'So. Your days are up already. Well, they went fast. Was everything to your liking?'

Oberon smiled and said: 'Yes, the days are up. It was all to my liking. Thank you.' He put a pile of money on the counter and said: 'Please, take what I owe you. And keep the rest for the staff.'

'No, it's not necessary,' said Duke, pushing the money back. 'Let's call it quits. You don't owe me. And my staff do fine here. Keep your money. I'll give them something extra from the till.'

'There are some flowers in my room. Will you give them to my friend, the lady? Will you tell her I said goodbye?'

'I'll do that.'

'Goodbye,' said Oberon, putting the money back into his pocket.

'Cheers,' Duke replied and lit a cigarette, feeling his throat squeeze and his eyes moisten. He looked across at the nurse, discerning that she wouldn't buy another coffee. Thandi had watched the interaction between the bartender and the man, and then the bartender's eyes had met hers, in the same way that Oberon's had. Perhaps she should come back in a few days and ask for a job, even if it was just washing dishes, even if, as she'd observed, there were mostly Zimbabweans working here.

As Oberon walked out, Mrs Winter strode in, brushing against him and almost knocking him over, but not noticing. At the bar, she calmed herself with a gin and tonic.

She paid with a single hundred-rand note, not waiting for change, and then went out to her vehicle, leaving behind a wake of turned heads. Her wheels were being clamped by two traffic officers. She pulled out her purse and paid the required bribe, then accelerated off towards home. She had a Nora Jones CD on loud. The windows were open. Her hair blew and suddenly she felt exquisitely free again, like before marriage and entrapment, like before that bastard husband had bought her. She felt more real than she had felt in years – Ava Katzen herself, a pretty, happy woman.

Outside, choppy and Impressionistic clouds unravelled across the sky, giving a fleeting sense of going somewhere in a hurry, riding the wind. Oberon wanted to remember these days forever, filled as they were with such nice people.

At the next-door mosque, there was some altercation going on between an old African man and the imam's sister, who was scattering crumbs to a flock of pigeons on the pavement. The old man was leaning heavily on a cane and holding on to the shoulder of a small boy. Mr Pigeons had come to town to find out what had happened to his friend Dr Smith, who had vanished from the clinic without a word after that child's dismembered corpse had been found in the river.

There was no doctor now at the clinic, just a humourless nurse who couldn't cope and who shooed him off when he went for lozenges. Some days before, he'd witnessed her turn away a labouring mother on the point of delivery, only to have the baby emerge into its harsh world on the clinic doorstep.

Mr Pigeons had Dr Smith's address and, with his grandchild's help, had caught a *kwela-kwela* to town. He hadn't come to the city centre for many years, and the child had never been there. Their transport brought them to the terminal on the station roof, and they walked from there, in the tight midst of commuters, among criminals and opportunists.

Mr Pigeons remembered Long Street. They had just to walk along Strand Street and then turn left and head up, facing Table Mountain. They stopped often to catch their breath and to rest, but eventually they arrived at the mosque, just before Brabazan Bar & Lodge, where Mr Pigeons immediately recognised his birds feasting on the pavement.

He swung his cane back and forth, feeling betrayed, disturbing the flock, which flew up and settled on Brabazan's roof, cooing down at him. The imam's sister shouted and he told her: 'These pigeons are my pigeons,' to which she responded: 'Who feeds them? Me or you?'

Alfonso didn't allow the child to enter Brabazan, and Mr Pigeons was unwilling to go in alone. Too old to have washed apartheid from his system, he couldn't enter a place previously reserved for whites. Alfonso called Duke to the pavement.

Mr Pigeons removed his hat and said: 'I am looking for the doctor. The English doctor. Doctor Smith,' to which Duke replied dryly: 'He's gone back to England.' He didn't elaborate by telling the old man that, earlier in the week, Frederick had come downstairs, dressed only in long johns, sweating profusely, his hair dishevelled and his wild eyes darting all over the place. He had given Duke his mother's number and asked for him to phone her, then lent on the counter and began to cry. Duke had called Dr Adam Baldinger, who sedated Smith. His mother had immediately arranged for a paid companion to fly him back to London.

Mr Pigeons stood there awhile, not knowing how to respond. In an *ubuntu* set-up, Duke would have urged him to come in and let the child sit in the kitchen, recognising that the two had made a long journey. They would have discussed what had happened at the river and the real possibility that the phantom of the corpse had spooked the doctor. In such a scenario, Duke would have offered some advice, together with the forwarding address, and called for sweet tea and bread to be served. But he said nothing, immediately. Thandi, sitting inside, leaning back in her seat with her eyes closed, did not see her uncle at the door.

Mr Pigeons squeezed the child's shoulder and the child looked up at the white man, a little afraid. Duke was about to turn back inside, but then his new softness came into play. 'What the fuck,' he thought. 'I'm going so belly up here.' He called Amèlia, saying: 'Wrap all the leftovers from last night. Give them to this old guy. Throw in a loaf of bread and a bottle of milk, for fuck's sake.'

So Mr Pigeons and his grandchild set off back to the township, with Doctor Smith's address and a packet full of good food, stopping now and then for the old man to catch his simoomian breath. He waved his stick up at the birds on the roof and they chuckled back. In the packed *kwela-kwela*, the boy sat on his grandfather's lap and the old man stroked his head, saying: 'Do you know why I am called *EnkosiThixo*, boy? Do you know why my mother gave me this name of ThankyouGod?'

'No, Grandfather. Why did she call you by this name?'

'Because she was without child for many years. Until my father said it was time to take a new wife. If they had no child, there would be no one to care for them in old age.

'So she walked from our village. From Qumbu to Port St Johns. To the Catholics. To the church there. It was a long journey. By foot. Longer than our journey today. She took her beaded skirt. Her marriage skirt. She gave it to the white god. The god of the Catholics. She put it on the table at the front of the church. Under the cross. And that white god was pleased with the skirt. The white god liked the beads. They were threaded so well into the cotton of the skirt. That white god liked the pearl buttons and the stitching. So he sent a wind, a holy wind, *uMoya*. And the holy wind filled her with child.

'I am that child. I am called *EnkosiThixo* for that reason. ThankyouGod.

'Thank you, God,' he said, patting the packet of food and the child copied the old man: '*Enkosi, Thixo*.'

They were both tired when they reached home, but the family ate well that night from pieces of steak, burger and chips that had been left on plates by Brabazan customers. They saved the bread and milk for morning.

The flock of pigeons arrived back just before sunset and settled down in their *hoks*. 'Now I know where you go,' said Mr Pigeons, closing the doors. 'It is fine. *Kulungile*. You can go there. I am pleased that you eat well. I am pleased that you come back to me.'

A month or so later, Mr Pigeons went to his neighbour, a schoolteacher, and dictated a letter to Dr Smith. This letter told the doctor that he shouldn't have left the clinic; that the queue now moved very, very slowly; and that those at the back of the line were not attended to. The letter instructed the young doctor to consider coming back immediately to Gugulethu. Mr Pigeons signed it with a careful, trembling hand.

He now slept in the backyard with his birds. Not long after his trip to town, his niece had arrived with her zinc sheeting and possessions all piled onto a horse-drawn wagon. The yard was too small to accommodate the new structure as well as his pigeon *hoks*, so only one small room was rigged up against the back wall of his house. This made for very cramped space, so he instructed Thandi, her mother and children to move in to the main house with the others, and he took the shack. He dismissed their concerns by saying he had always wanted to sleep near the birds. This way, he explained, he could listen for cats and *tsotsis*, but everyone knew it was really because he had a kind heart. 'Just thank God,' he had told Thandi. 'Just thank God every day.'

In London, Frederick Smith's mother withheld all post that came addressed to him from Africa. Africa had done him no good at all. It must leave him alone now. Under her careful watch, he began to keep homing pigeons and tend an allotment of cabbages.

Back at the Salvation Army Home, Richard Bland, one of the residents, was at the duty desk. He greeted Oberon with: 'Where've you been, Pete? We were getting worried.'

'I just had a few days off. With some new friends,' said Peter, reminded of his real name and now prompted to return it.

He went upstairs to his room, where Gerrit was sitting hunched over on the bed, staring desolately at the floor. When he saw Peter, sobs came from his chest as he tried to say but couldn't: 'I thought you were dead. I thought you were never coming back. Thank God you're back.'

Peter soothed Gerrit and helped him undress and bathe and put on clean pyjamas. The mattress was damp, so Peter turned it over and went to fetch new linen from the storeroom at the end of the passage. He covered his friend carefully, pulling the blanket up and tucking it around his face to make him feel secure, as one might do with a child. He retrieved, from under the bed, a pile of blood-soaked hankies and went to wash them. He placed a fresh one on Gerrit's pillow. Then he unpacked his own clothes and put them away neatly. He went back downstairs and handed the case to Richard, saying: 'Rick, I found this money. Will you give it to Major Martin? I don't know what to do with it.'

Rick opened it and ran his hand across the tightly packed bundles saying: 'Holy shit!'

'There's more,' said Peter, emptying his pockets and money pouch of their notes.

Back upstairs, he took off his shoes and lay down, too tired to undress, sapped of his last bit of energy, and with his temple now throbbing.

Next morning when he woke up, he saw that Gerrit lay dead, with eyes open and a smudge of blood against his mouth. With a shudder of sorrow, Peter got back into bed. He felt terribly cold and pulled his mother's knitted blanket tightly over himself, longing for those hands which had knitted the blanket to stroke his face, to sooth him with a lullaby. As he fell asleep, he had the same sensation he'd had some days before, after he'd been attacked, of his soul gently dislodging, like a butterfly shedding its cocoon. He was aware of himself drifting away from earthly existence, as though borne on a light wind and, this time, he went with the flow.

Pearlie, back in her flat after visiting Thespian, lay on his side of the bed, completely overcome, and started to cry. Tomorrow she would ask Oberon to help her get him out of that terrible place. But how would they do it? Surely security wouldn't let them leave the building with Thespian. And if they managed to get him out and into a taxi, could they safely bring him back to Maynard? Wouldn't there be a hunt for him? Wouldn't his family just come and grab him back?

Unable to work it all out and not knowing what to do, she cried until she fell asleep, only to be woken by the doorbell ringing. It was the letting agent delivering her eviction notice, assisted by a young intern from Weinberg, Sonenburg & Sisulu. The intern had been sent along because the manner in which Maynard Court was to be emptied of its residents was not entirely legal.

Tenants were to be told that there was some exaggerated structural failure caused by spalling concrete, and that this rendered the building immediately unsafe. The munificent terms surrounding the end of their tenure were to be properly explained, accepted and signed for. So far, everything had gone smoothly and there had been no resistance from the other tenants. With the help of Pickfords, whom the letting agent had contracted, they would spend the coming days packing their belongings and seeing them off for temporary storage until they all found new accommodation.

The West African couple would normally have put up resistance because living in Maynard Court suited them. But, just two weeks before, one of their compatriots had got caught up in a bad drug deal. Someone had to be executed and dumped. A suitcase of cash had gone missing. The couple suspected that the hit men had taken the money. They didn't want to draw attention to themselves right now by making a fuss around what was clearly a blatantly illegal but cleverly orchestrated eviction.

Pearlie's was the last apartment to be dealt with. When

she answered the door, she was still wearing her wedding dress, her hair was wild and tangled and her eyes puffy. The young men were taken aback and there was a moment in which no one said anything, until the agent handed her the envelope and the intern began with the explanation.

Behind them, the roaring of two bulldozers firing up filled the air as they knocked down a portion of Maynard's perimeter wall and were driven into the grounds. There they were parked, ready to begin their work as soon as the complex was cleared of its inhabitants.

Without saying a word, Pearlie took the envelope and closed her door. She went out to the balcony and looked in horror at the heavy vehicles and the bit of wall they had crushed like so many pieces of Lego.

How was Pearlie supposed to pack up her belongings, which had now been reduced to the mere components of a still-life painting, a *natura morta*, and then transport them away? How was she to put a whole magical life into a tin trunk? One could compare the task to closing a circus or Luna Park – to putting away the big tent, the trapeze ropes, the costumes, the dancing dwarves, the clowns, the merry-go-round, the big dipper. How could these possibly be packed for travel, except in a whole line of colourfully painted horse-drawn wagons? Without that method of portage, which implied a joyful destination, everything was as good as dead, echoing the decrepit, rusty, abandoned machinery in some deserted diamond-mining town.

Where was she to go? Back to Port Nolloth? To that place of childhood, prodigally, to Madge, to work in the gun shop, selling ammunition and fishing tackle, weighing out pellets and birdshot?

And how would she ever dare open her meagre luggage and let spill out those memories of pleasure she'd managed to pack? Would they not simply break her heart, spread there like fragments of a broken Ming vase upon a single bed, with its mended, faded patchwork cover that her grandmother had made, in a small-windowed bedroom, from which one could hear the wind blow off the ocean across the flat, quartzite-glittered landscape?

As Pearlie stood on her balcony, a heavy mist covered the sea and the lower part of the city. The sombre voice of the foghorn spoke to seamen and melancholic persons like her. In her kitchen, painted on the wall, was the trompe l'œil of an ancient towered town, with an aqueduct and domed church. Into this painting Pearlie now wished she could tumble. Was this possible? To commit suicide by falling into a painting, as if into a deep well?

She began to pack on the fourth morning after her eviction notice had been delivered, by which time the rest of Maynard Court had become an empty, echoing place. She filled two cases with her favourite outfits, two hats, some of Thespian's dresses and a single volume of *Shakespeare's Complete Works*. To these she added her folio of share certificates and endowment policy, jewellery, the porcelain bridal couple, the Mogul dagger and the Situational Bowl. She slipped Thespian's wedding ring above her own, then called out from her balcony to Seymour, who was standing, smoking, near the bulldozers. He had been tasked by the agent to phone through when the last tenant had vacated and was just waiting for Miss Theron.

Confused and undecided, but presuming that she'd eventually take a flight back to Port Nolloth and thus have no need for her car, she handed the keys and registration papers to Seymour, saying simply: 'You can have my car, Seymour,' putting up her hand to stop him saying anything, for she did not want to hear how grateful he was. 'I'll leave here tonight,' she told him.

She prepared herself a meal of baked trout, asparagus, steamed baby potatoes and Waldorf salad and set the dining table for two, lighting candles. From the freezer, she took two portions of halva ice cream and trickled them with Cointreau. She ate slowly and drank a bottle of Jack's Red. When she was done, she called a Rikki and put Sparkey and his blankets into his wickerwork travelling box. She switched *Carmen* on at full blast, on repeat, on a battery-driven player, took one last look at her world, locked its door, tucked the key between her breasts and made her way downstairs.

The demolishers tore down Maynard Court and cleared the ground over a week. Pearlie's CD of *Carmen* played on and on until the claws of monstrous machinery seized and silenced it. The contents of number four were crushed and taken away to Vissershoek with all the broken bricks and mortar that had once been an elegant edifice. There, sparkling among the tons of plastic and filth generated by the city, little chips of mirror, glass, porcelain and fabric told of a once well-lived and artistic love story.

Within two years, Maynard Court was replaced by a tastelessly designed, face-brick and steel high-rise block of lifestyle apartments, aimed at professional gays, the Thinkies (Two-High-Incomes-No-Kids) as they were commonly known. It had a gym and sauna, laundry, designer bakery and restaurants on the lower floors in which tenants and visitors could strut their stuff. It obscured the good views that the neighbours had always enjoyed and which they believed they owned, but now realised they did not, for bribes had been paid and building-plan files lost, allowing height and zoning restrictions to be ignored.

Hurriedly put up and named The Maynarderie, the apartment block earned a lot of money for the usual crop of ruthless investors and banks, but incurred ongoing costs for all future tenants, as they battled the results of bad workmanship, lack of on-site supervision and poor project management – leaks, rising damp, ill-fitting doors and windows, and shoddily installed second-grade fixtures.

Back at Brabazan, everything seemed the same, with the usual sizeable cast of players assembled in the smoky, diffused atmosphere, all drawn there like moths, thinking thoughts coloured or cross-hatched by the crayons of alcohol.

In one of the toilets, a man in leather biker pants and studded jackboots snorted cocaine. In the side ally, smelling of fries and cheap perfume, a too-thin girl slumped, overdosed and comatose, a line of blood running from a nostril.

Upstairs, the Russian girls were in various states of undress, having worked a hard night. Anastasia wore a petticoat, Tatiana a gymslip, Olga her nightgown and Marie was naked, stitching a tapestry. They smelt of armpit, sex and cologne, so the odour in the room was stale but aphrodisiacal. It could have done with an open window, but that would have brought in a draft.

None of them noticed the dead Tsarevich, now a crumpled pile of green feathers with an awful red claw-mark cutting him near in two. Nor did they see the cat, Stalin, staring with nasty eyes at the pile.

A client lay on the floor, knocked out by excessive drink and drugs and an earlier, short sexual encounter. He was too heavy for them to haul out, so they left him. Later they would call Alfonso, the guard, to take him out to the alley, where the sharp air would wake him, and where he'd look at the thin girl lying next to him, half dead, and start to cry, thinking of his own teenage daughter, hoping she was at home.

In the rubberdoll room, unrecognisable in his black wig, latex suit and mask, enjoying the last of the night, while his wife thought he was working late, Gerald Radison, Thespian's son-in-law, lay back on cushions. He sucked a deep, orgasmic breath while a buxom rubberdoll leaned hard against him, fondling a rubberbreast and squeezing his rubberlabia.

The as-yet-undiscovered saxophonist Simon van der Linden was playing in the bar. He generally came in very late at night, an hour or so before closing, and continued playing after the last customers left, serenading the waitrons while they cleared away glasses and bottles and stacked the chairs on top of tables to make things easier for the cleaners next morning. His saxophone's lone sound gathered up all the raw, sore emotions left lying around Brabazan, like the cottons in an untidy embroidery basket, and brought them to order. It drew them together into a plait and swirled them through the smoky air, saving them from the indignity of being swept out with cigarette stubs and ash, lifting them high, healing them.

Pearlie arrived just as the last drinkers were finishing up. The taxi driver placed her cases at the bar. She glanced across at the corner table, then turned to Duke, who replied to her deeply sad, questioning eyes with: 'He asked me to say goodbye.'

'Do you know where he went?'

'He didn't say.'

'Did he leave a note for me? A number?'

'No, I'm sorry,' said Duke, sensing himself slip down into her emotional space and promptly hauling himself out with: 'Can I pour you a drink?'

'No. But I need a room. Can I take his room? Is it available?'

'You can.'

'From tonight? Now?'

'Sure. I need one grand up front and your ID number.'

'I'm Pearlie Theron.'

'Call me Duke. Oh, the flowers up there. He left them for you.'

A waiter picked up Pearlie's luggage and she followed him, carrying Sparkey's basket herself, through the yellow curtain and up the yellow stairwell to the room where the vase of brilliant sunflowers welcomed her. Lingering in the air, there was still a touch of the perfume of the tenant before Oberon, but of him was left not a trace.

She stood in the centre of the room, in the little pool of light dropped from the ceiling lamp, and wiped the tears from her face.

'Farewell, dear friend!' she said aloud. 'A long farewell to all your greatness. As many farewells as be the stars in heaven. As many stars to shine you on your way. Forever and forever, farewell. If we do meet again, how we shall smile.'

She settled Sparkey on his velvet blanket at the foot of the bed and then sat on a pouf at the lover's balcony, her whole being stabbed by pain and grief. With the Indian screen behind her, through the dark hours between midnight and dawn, while the wind played against the curtain and the lace of her dress, she tried to figure how best to get Thespian out of Deerpark Retirement Home.

Just before daybreak, the street was strangely quiet, with not a single car or passer-by disturbing it. The wind picked up a pile of paper flowers that Primo Verona had left outside 7-Eleven, carrying them to beneath Pearlie's balcony. There they swirled, round and round. A soft rain began to fall, a *guti*, so soft that, illuminated by the street and neon lights, it looked like glitter.

This is how she knew that Thespian had died. This was how she sensed him saying goodbye. She stood up, a Juliet figure, and recited into the neon night Li Hsun's poem, adapting it to suit her own bereavement: 'Rain falls on fallen flowers, perfuming the pavement, where I grieve. When the night's song closes, I will close this silver screen. Night and day, sailboats will leave this shore, searching the waves for you. In my pain, I will tune a lute. The melody will carry my grief. My words will vibrate its strings. I cannot bear to sing.'

By next morning, when the traffic was up and hectic, the paper flowers had blown all the way down the road and the *guti* had lifted.

Pearlie took up residence at Brabazan, living fairly modestly despite the generous portfolio of shares Thespian had given her to celebrate their marriage. She changed nothing in the room, instead coming to enjoy the pared-back, simple decor that Oberon had briefly lived in, and never venturing up to the second floor, leaving her memory of that banqueting room intact.

Duke's staff took her on as royalty, calling her Pearlie Ma'am, and sympathising over her duel mourning of Thespian and Oberon, drawn to her by a charisma that grief did not shield.

Breakfasts, lunches and teas were brought up to her, but she took evening meals downstairs, at Oberon's corner table, which was always reserved, and upon which Amèlia kept a vase of fresh flowers. A waiter would uncork a Merlot as she took her seat, and this she would drink in its entirety.

She wore her wedding dress each day. It felt like an additional aura, an aura of love and happiness, and it gave the sense that Thespian was as close as her own breath. Within weeks of her arrival, she became a feature of Long Street, for she took a slow daily walk after breakfast, in that gorgeous volume of lace and her flamenco shoes, from Brabazan to the Baths and back again, occasionally giving out cards with hand-calligraphed verses and quotes. These she wrote out herself with a real fountain pen.

Each afternoon, between lunch and four-o'clock tea, which was served in a Susie Cooper set that the Russian girls had bought her from Atkinson's, she sat on the balcony, from where she recited love poems to the passing crowds and traffic. Sparkey lay at her feet, watching a cataract-hazed Long Street, but never venturing out the room and therefore not encountering the nasty Stalin, who, sensing an intruder in the building, had taken to stalking the passages.

At night, after dinner, Pearlie sat at the bar drinking Johnnie, as she called it. While the evenings wore on and the Johnnie Walker went down, she'd talk to Duke about the intricacies of the *Othello* or *Macbeth* plots; or introduce him to this or that analysis of *King Lear*; or speculate on how Not The Midnight Mass were doing on their overseas tour. Duke would half listen, for his mind was always on his son, upstairs, sleeping after a day of school, where he was gingerly engineering a way through his new social milieu. Father and son were still expressing wonder at having found each other, and were not yet focusing on the complicated transition in both their lives. The time for sore questions would soon come. But right now, the boy was here and diamonds seemed to be lighting up again inside of Duke.

Sometimes Pearlie chatted to Chester. Each evening he sat at the far end of the bar, trying to ignore a spirit standing in his peripheral vision and holding a palette of colours, seeming about to paint. Chester would listen to the piano, trying his damnedest to release his song, that song deep inside of him, drinking until the last order, when his wife, Connie, would arrive to walk him home. Connie, in her turn, could not fathom why he was slipping so fast towards alcoholism, nor why he had bundled up all his clothes and given them to the *bergies* who slept in the alley alongside their home. All he wore these days was his new white suit and red hat.

When anyone struck up conversation with her, Pearlie would tell them that an angel had once lived at Brabazan. She would take from her handbag Fairy Patterson's Polaroid photograph and show it, saying: 'You see, there we are sitting at the corner table. That's me. And next to me, that flash of light, that's the angel. Oberon. You know, angels look like real people. But they're really made of light. So when you take a picture of them, you just get this flash. Like a bursting star. Like a supernova.'

If Fairy Patterson happened to be in Brabazan, Pearlie would call him over and he would assure sceptics with: 'Yes, indeedy. Yes, Sir. The lady is absolutely quite correct. My camera has never glitched. This never happened to me before or after and I've been using this same camera for twenty years. That fella was an angel alright. That flash in the picture is an angel. Just like the lady says.'

Pearlie was having a coffee at the bar one Friday morning, just after Duke had come down, when two men in black suits moved in on him. On her recommendation, he had recently put away Kapuściński and turned to

Shakespeare's *The Tempest*, focusing, as she told him to, on Ferdinand, the good son of Alonso.

She watched, aghast, as one of the men took out a pistol and swung it round on his middle finger, while Duke opened the safe under the bar and took out a pile of cash. These were not the men who had hung out at Brabazan for a while. They just wore that moniker costume of all rogues, Mafiosi, politicians and bodyguards – black suits with *idimas*, gold teeth and, of course, Prada shoes. Their Hummer was parked brazenly outside. From now on they would call each Friday to collect protection money. Duke's boy, his Jojo as he lovingly called him, was at school, so he didn't witness his father's acquiescence.

Pearlie, in her bridal gown, was not the only special feature of Long Street. Pasquale Benvenuto's statue of the Virgin Mary also earned a legendary name as she stood at the upstairs window of either his room or that of Not The Midnight Mass, depending on where she was in residence. From there, looking down over Long Street, she bestowed blessings upon revellers, ravers, alcoholics and youngsters doing drugs.

There was talk about a young girl who had overdosed in the alley, and then been woken from her drug-induced coma by a Madonna leaning over her, placing holy water upon her lips. The apparition apparently took the girl by the hand, hailed a taxi, paid the fare and sent her home to her parents in Tamboerskloof.

The story of the girl's miraculous return from death spread like wildfire and the statue became known as the Madonna of Long Street. Quite by chance, a light, steady seepage of water came up through a side wall of Brabazan, the one facing the alley. Duke recognised it as mountain water escaping from the drains. He had a ceramic trough cemented there and the water filled it, trickling like a perennial spring. The pavement beneath the Madonna's window was soon established as a site of night pilgrimage. Believers would stand there looking up, receiving her electric benediction with each pulse of Brabazan's neon light. People would come with small bottles and collect what came to be considered holy water. And then legend took over, as the Madonna and Pearlie merged into one after a dramatic shoot-out nearby.

On the very afternoon that Sparkey concluded his eighteen-year life by simply not waking up from his post-cibum nap, Pearlie was caught by a single bullet in the crossfire between police, security guards and cash-in-transit armed robbers outside the 7-Eleven. Under the new shoot-from-the-hip approach to crime management, police were instructed to aim to kill and sometimes the hapless just got in the way.

She lay until the shoot-out was over, spreadeagled across the pavement, her bridal gown stained scarlet exactly over her heart, her eyes open like those of a broken doll, a handful of her poetry cards scattered around.

From the verandas of Overbeek, tenants, like theatre patrons seated in a gallery, looked down at her and each cried out in anguish, as though at the loss of Desdemona or Cleopatra, so a sort of mourners' song rose into the air and then came down gracefully like a piece of silk upon the wind, to cover her on the closing pages of her life's libretto.

Later, among the addicts outside Brabazan, there would be talk of the spectre of a matador striding towards her body, his *traje de luces* glittering in the sun as he lifted his beloved and placed her across the back of a blindfolded, quilt-covered picador's horse and led her away, up Kloof Street and beyond. Another story said that it had been a film shoot, not a shoot-out, and that Charlize Theron was playing Bess, the landlord's daughter in Alfred Noyes's 'The Highwayman'. A Federico Fellini lookalike had banged his clapperboard and the beautiful bride just stood up and walked over to her dressing-room wagon. According to that dry version of events, it was not blood but mercurochrome on her breast.

But this is what actually happened. On one of those days when the clouds tumble and heap languidly in a blue Cape sky, Duke strolled up to the intersection, where he stood on the traffic island in the middle of the road to get a better view of them. Gunshots drew his attention away from the extravagance of cirrus castellatus and cumulonimbus towards Pearlie, spinning in slow motion, in the way that all ghastly scenes unfold, as a bullet struck her and brought her down onto the hard pavement. He rushed across the road, narrowly missing a run of cars jumping the red light. Cupping his hands about her face, he bellowed like a bull at the instantly lifeless eyes, then cradled the dead bride to his chest, weeping hoarsely and bitterly.

Some months after Maynard Court's demolition, as he tossed mushrooms into an oil-smoking, garlic-infused wok, the chef at the Lotus Tavern wondered why Thespian and Pearlie had not partaken of his food for so long. There had been such regularity to their dining pattern and now months had gone by without their charming presence. Later, when he took a cigarette break, he asked the others what they thought could possibly have happened. Had there been a problem with their last meal? Had anyone upset them?

No, there had been no incident, nothing that anyone could remember. The customary generous tip was left, Thespian had expressed courteous thanks and Pearlie had said her usual, cheery 'See you soon!'

Though Little Dove had not breathed a word of Pearlie and Thespian's marriage, everyone knew that she had once been waitress for them on a special occasion, years before, and that secrets laced the lives of these two rather favourite patrons. The chef now turned to her, with the instruction to take money from the till and catch a taxi to their apartment.

She arrived at a wasteland. The entire edifice was down and all building rubble cleared away. Nothing remained of the oleander bushes and agapanthus beds that Seymour had tended. The southeaster happened to be blowing at near-gale force and this added to the desolation that greeted Little Dove. Barely able to stand in the wind, she was about to get back into the taxi when the glint of something caught her eye and she bent to pick it up. It was the little ballerina of Pearlie's musical box.

Back at the Lotus Tavern, she showed the chef the dancer and tearfully related that only a bomb could have so shattered the landscape. As the only outside acquaintance who had ever seen the magical interior of the apartment, she found it impossible to express the measure of its ruination. The chef put a hand on her shoulder to still her crying, and heard the poem of a secret life in the three single expletives that came from her mouth: 'Love. Love. Love.'

From his pocket he took out one of his poetry books and read aloud lines he had written on the back flyleaf: 'Believe not in permanence. Even the mountain is erased, finally, by wind, by time. Even the glacier melts and runs. Believe not that all will be as it is. Nothing material lasts. Know this – that only love abides.'

He went back to his wok, wondering whether Thespian's brown envelope would ever be collected.

Now, we look back at Peter Brightstone, as we did when Oberon Yoruba first booked in at Brabazan Bar & Lodge.

We move to his room at the Salvation Army Home, to where he had returned after his ten-day sojourn, and we see him lifted, for the second time in his life, by what feel like butterfly wings. We watch him look down at his body and that of Gerrit, as morning sun pours into their room. The two men lie as though asleep, with faces that seem to be masks.

The view from their window across Table Bay to Blouberg is as beautiful as ever. Container ships lie at anchor. Shipping cranes stand to attention like giant, skeletal giraffes, and a tug can be seen leading a vessel into the dock. Robben Island lies flat upon the sea, looking as though it will one day float away on the outgoing tide.

With a gentle, tumbling movement, Peter finds himself away from there and delivered back to the extraordinary dream space he had entered when sleeping in the care of the Zimbabwean dwarf and his wife, under the curatorship of their magical fetish. The setting is the same, with its Dantesque components and elaborate interplay between angels and mythic figures, all rendered by masterful brushstrokes in a full spectrum of absolute colour ranging from the pastel to the bold, from massicot to purpure.

This time, Peter finds himself at the centre of it all, upon its vast stage, for curtain call. His earthly garments transform into a magenta robe and angelic radiance gives the touch of a halo. His shy stoop is gone. Stage lights illuminate him. The theatre sets are so structured that they give multidimensional depth when viewed from the audience perspective.

High above, as though painted on a domed ceiling, reminiscent of Goya's cupola fresco in the chapel of San Antonio de la Florida, stands a large group of people, wearing medieval courtly costumes and leaning against a circular balustrade. Some look down at the stage and others up towards a mountainous, cloud-tumbled landscape. A green parrot flies towards a lush, fruit-filled Fauvian grove of trees, while a strikingly beautiful, firm-limbed albino boy flings his arms in joyous abandonment.

Peter Brightstone glances up at the balcony crowd and then towards the seated audience. Recognising that his earthly performance is over, he smiles broadly and heroically and steps forward to take a bow, mimicking Pierrot and Pierrette in the Hopper painting back at Brabazan. There is rapturous applause. Confetti and petals shower down. From the orchestra pit, someone throws paper roses and fresh sunflowers and these fall all around the wonderful man on the stage. Heavy crimson curtains drag across the playhouse stage and the lamps of a fantastic ten-day piece of installation theatre are blown out.

The End

Addendum: Self-portraits

It is not uncommon for an artist or writer to find the world they have created to be so authentic, so tangible, that they are unable to remain detached or distant from it. While creating the piece, they invariably have to enter it and they might find, when the work is done, that they are unsure which world is real – the absolute one upon the canvas or in the text, or the one in which they supposedly reside.

In certain works, the artist makes so bold as to paint himself into the world of his canvas, leaving no doubt that he is not only the fabricator of that milieu, but also a participant within it.

Piero della Francesca shows himself as a sleeping soldier in his fresco *The Resurrection*. Sandro Botticelli looks out from his *Adoration of the Magi*. Michelangelo Buonarroti's *The Last Judgement* portrays an anguished self-portrait in the limp folds of the flesh of the martyred St Bartholomew. Diego Velázquez, in his depiction of day-to-day Spanish court life, *Las Meninas*, upstages the little princess, Infanta Margarita Teresa, by placing himself provocatively close to centre canvas.

Similarly, at Brabazan Bar & Lodge, we find the practitioner of its fiction. She is the estranged sister of Peter Brightstone, and the one who anonymously pays for his keep at the Salvation Army Home.

This author enters the scene on the pretext of giving final touches; of ensuring that the props and costumes, the lighting and sound system are ready for a final rehearsal. But she is really there because the fine line between truth and fiction in her personal narrative has lost definition.

In the first-floor room at the end of the passage, she

positions a vase of sunflowers – Van Gogh's sunflowers – and sprays a gloss of her perfume on the bed linen. As an adjustment to the decor, she takes down the cheap print of Tretchikoff's *Lost Orchid* and replaces it with the unrecognised original, bought for very little at the closing-down sale of Katzen's Second-Hand.

In an interplay between her two realities, the pool of light cast by the overhead tubular shade grows dimmer and dimmer, until there is almost darkness. At this point, the pulsing gun-metal-silver and fire-orange neon lights of Long Street take over the task of illumination. She lies on the bed and closes her eyes, not noticing a figure concealed in the shadows as she falls asleep. The ghost of Brabazan, wearing an embroidered, red-braided Spanish *majo* jacket, tight breeches and stockings, steps forward, intruding into the privacy she has erroneously believed to be hers.

The candles stuck on the brim of his hat throw a glow onto her supine form. He props his easel and begins to paint, copying her surrendered pose, positioning her at the front of the composition, against a nocturnal-black background, with arms against her sides and face turned slightly away towards the darkness. He bestows a classic visage with a maquillage of pale cheeks and kohl-defined eyes and brows. The fine, transparent cloth with which he lightly covers her naked body has the flow to it of a clear, shallow stream, coloured by gold and tannin.

With the dawn, he steps back into umbra, taking his work. When his unwitting model wakes, the curtain at the open balcony door ripples, but there is no wind. She senses intrusion and shivers, but interprets this as the agitation of the Brabazan characters wanting to enact their story. It is time for her to exit and for them to animate, to begin their performance in the wide chromatic range she has set up in this playhouse.

Just before going, she places a marker, a positioning point, in case this side, this Brabazan, is indeed her reality, and not the other, everyday life she conducts with supposedly real people.

The marker is a black and white photograph of herself and her brother, taken on a Kodak camera sometime in the 1950s. This she puts in Peter Brightstone's jacket pocket; therefore it is not visible to the reader. The photograph is of the two of them as children, sitting with a younger friend. She is wearing a hat, leaning forward, her chin propped on a hand, in a thoughtful posture.

Peter and their little friend squint slightly in the African sun. Behind them is the dense arboretum of unspoilt savanna, with all its tangled branches and holding the abundant certainty of spiders, insects, butterfly eggs and snakes. Its virgin self is untouched as yet by slash-and-burn or agricultural poison.

There the children sit, in the African heat, long before their adulthood and the quenching of innocence; long before the Chimurenga War and all its sad, brutal, unnecessary death and repercussions. The image holds them before they grow up and apart, thrown out with so much flotsam when Rhodesia and later Zimbabwe implode, creating a diaspora in white and black to pepper the world, under the plaintive notes of *mbiras* and tin guitars.

Glossary

baas (Afrikaans) Master or boss.

bakkie (Afrikaans) a small container.

bandiera (Italian) A flag; banner; colours; ensign.

Baruch ata Adonai (Hebrew) Blessed art Thou, Lord our God.

bergie (South African slang) A homeless person, usually living on the slopes of Table Mountain.

Black Sash An organisation of white women who opposed apartheid.

blerrie (South African English slang) Bloody.

blommetjies (Afrikaans) Little flowers.

bobotie (Afrikaans) A traditional Cape Malay dish of curried minced meat covered with a savoury custard preparation.

bok (Afrikaans) Wild buck.

bont (Afrikaans) Variegated, pied, multicoloured, sometimes gaudy.

borrie (Afrikaans from Cape Malay) Turmeric.

Boschjesman (Dutch) Bushman.

Bruinmense (Afrikaans) Brown people.

cesto di frutta (Italian) Basket of fruit.

chakalaka A spicy African vegetable relish.

Chevrah Kadisha (Hebrew) Lit. 'Holy Brotherhood'. Organisation that carries out the holy rites appertaining to burial according to Jewish lore and tradition.

Chimurenga War (Shona) Zimbabwean guerilla war of 1966–1980 fought against the minority regime of Rhodesia. Correctly known as the Second Chimurenga, the First Chimurenga being the insurrection against British colonial rule (1896–1897).

Churrigueresque Lavishly ornamented late-Spanish baroque style. Named after the Spanish architect José de Churriguera (d. 1725).

dominee (Afrikaans) A minister of the Dutch Reformed Church.

gaan (Afrikaans) Go.

geelrys (Afrikaans from Dutch) Rice flavoured with saffron and coloured with turmeric.

guti (Shona) Very soft, light rain.

Haai! Julle kinders! Staan onder daardie boom! (Afrikaans) 'Hey! You children! Stand under that tree!'

hok (Afrikaans) A cage or enclosure for animals or birds.

idimas (Xhosa) Sunglasses. From the English 'dimmers'.

igqirha (Plural *amagqirha*) (Xhosa) A traditional healer; a diviner.

isiporo (Xhosa from the Dutch) The ghost of a dead person condemned to wander about without a resting place. Can also mean spectre or fairy.

jelaba (Arabic) A long loose garment with full sleeves, traditionally with a hood.

jislaaik (Afrikaans) An exclamation of surprise or shock.

jongedochter (Dutch) A young farm girl or spinster.

jonkmanskas (Afrikaans) Also *jongmanskas*. A fairly small clothes cupboard with two drawers side by side above and the cupboard space below, frequently in yellowwood and stinkwood.

kakelaar (Afrikaans) The red-billed hoopoe, *Phoeniculus purpureus*, which gets its name from its loud and strident call. '*Ek is n kakelaar*': I am a kakelaar.

ketubah (Hebrew) Jewish marriage document, stating the obligations of husband and wife and recording the circumstances of the marriage.

klap (Afrikaans) A smack or a clout.

korrel and ***waatlemoen konfyt*** (Afrikaans) Grape and watermelon preserves.

kwela-kwela (Xhosa) An informal minibus taxi.

laatlammetjie (Afrikaans) Lit. 'late lamb'. The last-born child, born long after the other children.
langarm (Afrikaans) 'Pump-handle' style of dancing with both partners' arms horizontally extended.
majo (Spanish) (Fem. *maja*) An exaggerated style of traditional dress worn by the upper classes of late-eighteenth to early-nineteenth-century Spanish society.
malva poeding (Afrikaans) A traditional baked pudding soaked in sweet sauce.
mbira (Shona) A musical instrument played with the thumbs, sometimes over or inside a calabash.
melanzane sott' olio (Italian) Brinjals preserved in oil.
melktert (Afrikaans) A traditional Cape Dutch/Malay custard tart, dusted with cinnamon.
mezuzah (Hebrew) Parchment inscribed with biblical passages.
milchig and ***fleishig*** (Yiddish) In kosher terminology, dairy and meat products.
mitzvah (Hebrew) A good deed.
moffie (South African slang) A homosexual. Sometimes a transvestite.
muti (Zulu) African medicines, spells and herbs, parts of animal or occasionally human bodies, used in traditional therapy or in witchcraft or magic.
Nabis (Hebrew) Group of artists who straddled the gap between post-impressionism and modernism.
pão (Portuguese) Bread.
poffertjie (Afrikaans) A traditional Cape Dutch sweet, light fritter.
potjiekos (Afrikaans) Food of many sorts – usually meat, fish or shellfish with vegetables – cooked as a stew in a three-legged pot over a fire.
puttana (Italian) A prostitute.
Ratel (Afrikaans) Armoured combat vehicle, designed by

Armscor. Named after the honeybadger.

Recces Operatives of the reconnaissance or Special Forces battalions of the old South African Defence Force (SADF).

roosterkoek (Afrikaans) Bread dough cooked over hot coals.

sadza (Shona) Maize meal porridge.

salottino (Italian) Sitting room; boudoir.

sjambok (Afrikaans) A rhinoceros- or hippopotamus-hide whip.

skelm (Afrikaans) A rascal.

skiet en donder (Afrikaans) Lit. 'shoot and thrash'. Equivalent to 'blood and thunder'.

skollie (Afrikaans) A criminal or potential criminal, or a member of a gang.

skottel braai (Afrikaans) A wok-like cooking dish used with hot coals.

smous (Afrikaans from Dutch) Formerly, an itinerant pedlar, often Jewish, who made a living hawking various goods from farm to farm.

soetkoekies (Afrikaans) Traditional spiced, sweet biscuits.

sousboontjies (Afrikaans) Dried haricot beans cooked in a sweet-sour sauce.

Soweto Uprising On 16 June 1976, the black youth of Soweto marched in protest against being taught in the medium of Afrikaans. Police fired on them, precipitating a massive flood of violence that overwhelmed the country.

spaza A retail outlet run by an entrepreneur trading at home, usually in the townships and informal settlements, and selling various goods, especially foodstuffs.

spekboom (Afrikaans) A small-leaved succulent shrub with pink or lilac flowers (*Portulacaria afra*).

stompies (Afrikaans) Cigarette butts.
stywe pap (Afrikaans) Stiff mealie porridge.
swart gevaar (Afrikaans) Lit. 'black peril'.
taiglach (Yiddish) Small pieces of fried dough dredged in honey and eaten at various festivals and celebrations.
troepie (Afrikaans) Lowest-rank national serviceman.
tsotsi Criminal, usually a gang member.
ubuntu (Xhosa) Human-heartedness.
Umbria paper Paper made from jute fibre.
Umshini wami, mshini wami! Khawuleth'umshini wami! (Zulu) My machine gun, my machine gun! Oh won't you bring me my machine gun!

Art references

Fernando Botero: *Adamo ed Eva; Ballerini; Cesto di frutta; Donna 1981; Donna 1983; Donna che piange; Donna con pappagallo; Donna con volpe; Donna di fronte alla finestra; Donna seduta; Donna in piedi; Il Bagno; I musicisti; La casa di Mariduque; La Lettera; La Strada 1988; La Strada 1990; La Toilette; Malinconia; Omaggio a Bonnard; Travestito; Una coppia; Uomo che fuma; Uomo che suona il violino*

Sandro Botticelli: *Adoration of the Magi*

Michelangelo Buonarroti: *The Last Judgement*

Piero della Francesca: *The Resurrection*

Francisco Goya: *Miracle of St Anthony of Padua; Self portrait in the studio; Sleep*

Edward Hopper: *Automat; Nighthawks; Chop Suey; New York Restaurant; Summer Interior; Morning Sun; Hotel Room; The Lighthouse at Two Lights; Two Comedians; Soir Bleu; Night Shadows*

Vincent van Gogh: *The Night Café; Sunflowers*

Diego Velázquez: *Las Meninas*

Unknown Artist: *Trek-wagon*

Unknown photographer: *The Voortrekker Monument*

Bibliography

Botero, Fernando. *Botero: Antologica 1949–1991*. Rome: Edizioni Carte Segrete, 1991

Branford, Jean and Branford, William. *A Dictionary of South African English*. Cape Town: Oxford University Press, 1991

Carr-Gomm, Sarah. *Goya*. London: Parkstone Press, 2000

Dickson, Andrew. *The Rough Guide to Shakespeare*. Second edition. London: Rough Guides, 2009

Hamill, Sam. *The Erotic Spirit: An Anthology of Poems of Sensuality, Love and Longing*. Boston and London: Shambhala, 2003

Hamill, Sam. *Love Poems from the Japanese*. Translated by Kenneth Rexroth. Boston and London: Shambhala, 2003

Hughes, Robert. *Goya*. London: Vintage, 2004

Irving, Mark. *1001 Buildings You Must See Before You Die*. New York: Quintessence Books, 2007

Kerrigan, Michael (editor). *Shakespeare on Love*. London: Penguin Books, 2003

Lamb, GF (editor). *The Wordsworth Dictionary of Shakepeare Quotations*. Edinburgh: Wordsworth Reference, 1992

Shakespeare, William. *The Complete Works*. London and Glasgow: Collins, 1970

Souter, Gerry. *Edward Hopper: Light and Dark*. London: Parkstone Press, 2007

Vaizey, Marina and Russell, John (editors). *Art: The Critics' Choice*. New York: Watson-Guptill, 1999

Poems

Izumi Shikibu, 'My black hair tangled', from *The Erotic Spirit*, page 62

Kakinomoto no Hitomaro, 'I sit at home', from *Love Poems from the Japanese*, page 18

Li Hsun, 'Rain falls on fallen flowers', from *The Erotic Spirit*, page 58

Ono no Komachi, 'I long for him most', from *The Erotic Spirit*, page 61

Webography

Cristina de Prada HATS: http://kuki.deprada.net; www.deprada.net

Lorenzo Nassimbeni wallpapers: www.lorenzonassimbeni.com

Metropolitan Museum of Art: http://www.metmuseum.org/home.asp

Rubberdollism: http://en.wikipedia.org/wiki/Rubberdoll

South African history: www.Southafrica.info

Theft of cultural heritage: http://museum-security.org

Theft of gold tea set from Tuynhuys and five-carat Mendelssohn diamond ring: http://www.museum-security.org/02/047.html

Theft of historic five-carat Mendelssohn diamond from parliamentary library in 1999: http://www.museum-security.org/99/036.html#4

Werdmuller Centre in Cape Town, information: www.werdmullercentre.blogspot.com

Werdmuller Centre photographs by Gaelen Pinnock: www.werdmullercentre.blogspot.com/2007/12/

Other sources

Closure of Khayalami hospital: *Mail & Guardian* 31 July 2009

Crumbling road network – Minister of Transport S'bu Ndebele's admission that South Africa's road maintenance had so fallen behind that it faced a backlog in excess of R38.3 billion: *Cape Times* 20 October 2009

Minister in the Presidency Trevor Manuel's purchase of BMW 750i series for R1.2 million: *Cape Times* 13 October 2009; 29 October 2009; 2 November 2009

Muti-harvesting of albino body parts: *Cape Times* 6 May 2009, and *eTV: Third Degree* documentary, May 2009

Purchase details of Tretchikoff's *Lost Orchid*: Craig Jacobs and Gwen Gill, *Social Scene Sunday Times* 10 May 2009

Rubberdollism: 'I dress this way every day at home by myself – heaven!' Judy Elliot. *Sunday Times* 4 October 2009

Tretchikoff's *Lost Orchid: South African Art Times* June 2009 'Lost Orchid original – for now.' First published by *SAPA* and *News24*

Acknowledgements

I am grateful to my agent, Stephanie Cabot; editors Lisa Compton and Sean Fraser; and to all those who played a part in the construction of this fiction, some of whom had walk-on parts and others who gave generously of their knowledge or who inspired me: Keith Addison, Jessica Aronson, Julie Atkinson, Dr Adam Baldinger, Neil Bennun, Dr Ruth Bloch, Carol Bosch, Emily Botes, Dr James Cavanagh, Denis Collis, Vernon Collis, Henrietta Dax, Cristina de Prada, José de Prada-Samper, Margaret Evans, Esther Falconer, Marinella Garuti, Hugh Hodge, Laura Hutchinson, David Kaplan, Vincent Kolbe, Dr Bruce Lakie, Lindy Levy, Emma Lincoln, Francesca Liversidge, Jackie Loos, Tino Mogentale, Peter Narun, Lorenzo Nassimbeni, Given Nkosi, Tiara Odendaal, Leone Oram, Michael Raeburn, Avi Ragaven, Brenda Scarratt, Joe Schaffers, Julia Shapiro, Johan Simon, Diana Simson, Wilhelm Snyman, Roland Stanbridge, Gilad Stern, Sarita Stern, Pieter Toerien, Simon van der Linden, Vicky van Kets, Chris Wildman and Pretty Yende, as well as the staff and residents of the Salvation Army Home in Cape Town.

I especially thank the Italian consuls in Cape Town, Dr Alberto Vecchi and Dr Emanuela Curnis; Graham Weir and the other members of Not The Midnight Mass; and Zelda la Grange.

This tribute is made complete by mention of Don, Gaelen and Romaney Pinnock for their invaluable inspiration, encouragement and assistance in all my work.

Quotations: William Shakespeare (1564–1616)

Shall I abide in this dull world, which in thy absence is no better than a sty?
Anthony and Cleopatra IV, 15

There is no living, none, if Bertram be away.
All's Well That Ends Well I, 1

This was the most unkindest cut of all.
Julius Caesar III, 2

The croaking raven does bellow for revenge.
Hamlet III, 2

By Jupiter, an angel! Or if not, then an earthly paragon!
Cymbeline III, 6

This above all: to thine own self be true, and it must follow, as the night the day, thou canst not then be false to any man.
Hamlet I, 3

O carve not with thy hours my love's fair brow,
Nor draw no lines there with thine antique pen;
Sonnet 19

Truth is truth, to the end of reckoning.
Measure for Measure V, 1

Doubt truth to be a liar, but never doubt I love.
Hamlet II, 2

Never was a story of more woe.
Romeo and Juliet V, 3

A heavier task could not have been imposed, than I to speak my grief unspeakable.
The Comedy of Errors I, 1

If you have tears, prepare to shed them now.
Julius Caesar III, 2

O, how mine eyes do loathe his visage now.
A Midsummer Night's Dream IV, 1

Sit down and feed, and welcome to our table.
As You Like It II, 7

I can express no kinder sign of love than this kind kiss.
2 Henry VI I, 1

Shall I compare thee to a summer's day?
Thou art more lovely and more temperate.
Sonnet 18

So smile the heavens upon this holy act.
Romeo and Juliet II, 6

Come now, what masques, what dances shall we have?
A Midsummer Night's Dream V, 1

Sound music! Come, my Queen, take hands with me!
A Midsummer Night's Dream IV, 1

Now, my honey love. We will return unto thy father's house with silken coats and cape and golden rings, with ruffs and cuffs and fardingales and things.
The Taming of the Shrew IV, 3

To me, fair friend, you never can be old, for as you were when first your eye I eyed, such seems your beauty still.
Sonnet 104

Under the greenwood tree, who loves to lie with me, come hither, come hither, come hither.
As You Like It II, 5

In the wood, where often you and I, upon faint primrose beds were wont to lie
A Midsummer Night's Dream I, 1

I know a bank where the wild thyme blows; where oxslips and the nodding violet grows, quite over-canopied with luscious woodbine.
A Midsummer Night's Dream II, 1

The skies are painted with unnumber'd sparks; they are all fire and every one doth shine.
Julius Caesar III, 1

Then happy I that love and am beloved
Sonnet 25

Saw you not even now a blessed troup, invite me to a banquet, whose bright faces cast beams upon me like the sun?
Henry VIII IV, 2

Good night, sweet prince, and flights of angels sing thee to thy rest.
Hamlet V, 2

Kind is my love today, tomorrow kind, still constant in a wondrous excellence.
Sonnet 105

The day begins to break, and night is fled.
I Henry VI II, 2

What angel wakes me from my flowery bed?
A Midsummer Night's Dream III, 1

Wilt thou be gone? It is not yet near day. It was the nightingale and not the Lark that pierced the fearful hollow of thine ear. Nightly she sings on yond pomegranate tree. Believe me, love. It was the nightingale.
Romeo and Juliet III, 1–5

Night's candles are burnt out and jocund day stands tiptoe on the misty mountain tops. I must be gone.
Romeo and Juliet III, 5

A joy past joy calls out on me.
Romeo and Juliet III, 3

O for a horse with wings.
Cymbeline III, 2

Good company, good wine, good welcome.
Henry VIII 1, 4

Friends, Romans, countrymen, lend me your ears!
Julius Caesar III, 2

Farewell! A long farewell to all your greatness!
Henry VIII III, 2

As many farewells as be the stars in heaven.
Troilus and Cressida IV, 4

Forever and forever, farewell, Cassius!
If we do meet again, why, we shall smile.
Julius Caesar V, I

Quotations: Other

Drink to me only with thine eyes,
   And I will pledge with mine;
   Or leave a kiss but in the cup,
   And I'll not look for wine.
Ben Jonson (1573–1637), 'To Celia'

The wine-cup is the little silver well,
   Where truth, if truth there be, doth dwell.
Rubáiyát of Omar Khayyám: A Paraphrase from Several Literal Translations, by Richard Le Gallienne (1901 edition)

Acclaim for Patricia Schonstein

Skyline
A magnificent book about human spirit
Cape Times

A great epic. The characters live like lighted candles
Expressen Sweden

A Time of Angels
Tender, witty and engaging
JM Coetzee

A marvellous novel, written with style, gusto and immense charm
Joanne Harris, author of *Chocolat*

The Apothecary's Daughter
A richly romantic tale of sexual awakening, love and betrayal
JM Coetzee

A wondrous narrative, a poignant complex drama, stitched through with rich imagery and tenderness
Sunday Independent

A Quilt of Dreams

An enthralling story, consummately told

Cape Times

Opulent, textured and full of magic

O, the Oprah Magazine

The Master's Ruse

Mesmerizing, poetic and beautifully written

Ute Ben Yosef, Librarian: Jacob Gitlin Library, Cape Town

Colourful, lyrical, filmic, beautifully woven and beautifully visual

Nancy Richards, South African Broadcasting Corporation

Banquet at Brabazan
Patricia Schonstein

In *Banquet at Brabazan*, Patricia Schonstein takes us to the heart of Cape Town's violent inner city, creating a cornucopia of events featuring an angel, drug money, a *muti* murder, superb food, romance, a cappella singing, reflections on South Africa's war in Angola, visions of the afterlife, poetry, Shakespearean drama and various works of fine art, with flashbacks to her wondrous *A Time of Angels*.

This is a heavily furnished and costumed, opulent, theatrical, mildly erotic, tantalising, masterful feat of baroque magic-realism with a large cast and improbable encounters.

Patricia Schonstein grew up in Rhodesia and now lives in South Africa. She completed her Master's degree in creative writing under the supervision of JM Coetzee at the University of Cape Town.